SUDDEN IMPACT

A TOM ROLLINS THRILLER

PAUL HEATLEY

INKUBATOR
BOOKS

Published by Inkubator Books
www.inkubatorbooks.com

ISBN (eBook): 978-1-83756-394-4
ISBN (Paperback): 978-1-83756-395-1

For Aidan

1

Nathan Wood owns three motorcycles. His favourite is his Harley-Davidson custom Softail. His second favourite is his chopper, which he mostly uses when he's cruising around his home town back in Texas. Right now, he's on his touring Harley-Davidson. It's his third favourite of his bikes, but it's the best for long trips, and right now he's far from home. *Real* far. A few states northwest, in Utah. He's been riding for a few days, and he's tired. His touring Harley is feeling heavy, and the extra weight it's carrying is putting pressure on his joints. His arms ache. His back is stiff. His thighs are throbbing. This is why the tourer has taken third place and become his least favourite of his three bikes. When he rides it, it means he's working. He hates working. He didn't join a motorcycle club to feel like he has a job.

The way back, at least, should be a lot lighter. When the delivery is done, he knows from experience the relief on his joints will be immediate.

It's an easy run, and Nathan is riding solo. He's used to

riding in a group, with other members of the Texas chapter of the Forever Road Dogs. It can be lonely on the road on his own. It's been stressed, every time he does one of these runs, that he's not to wear his kutte. Instead, he wears a generic leather jacket so as not to stand out. Over the last couple of years, he's done this run through Utah seven times. This is his eighth. Sometimes he's sent north, and sometimes he's sent east, and sometimes he's sent further west. Every time he goes, wearing his general leather jacket, he feels more exposed than if he was wearing his denim kutte with its patch on the back of the crowned, snarling dog with eyes of fire, Forever bannered across the top, and Road Dogs bannered beneath. The kutte acts as a shield. Shows that he may look alone, but he's never out here on the road solo. He's part of something bigger. A brotherhood. When he's wearing his kutte, he knows he's invincible.

It's evening. The sun is already starting to set. Nathan still has a hundred miles to go. He's tired. He sees a sign for a roadhouse, just five miles further. As much as he aches, he can last five more miles.

By the time those miles are up, his legs are numb with the engine's vibrations, and his back is screaming. Nathan parks the bike down the side of the building, gets off and places his hands on his hips, stretching back and twisting side to side. He balls his fists and pounds them against his back and the fronts and sides of his thighs, trying to get some feeling back into them. To pump his blood. To chase away the pain.

He looks around before he goes inside. There's a long-haul truck parked up, and a few other cars. He can hear music playing dimly. A jukebox, as opposed to a live band. Outside the roadhouse is a sign for a motel just two more miles down the road. Nathan needs to rest. After he's eaten, and had a drink or two, he'll check into the motel for the night. Get back on the road early in the morning. Get this run over with. He longs for a lighter bike.

Inside the roadhouse, it's quiet. The music is only slightly louder inside. He doesn't recognise the song. It's not something he would listen to. Too light. He likes his music heavy – Slayer, Pantera, Motorhead, Machine Head. He's wearing a Pantera T-shirt. As he unzips his jacket, he reveals the Vulgar Display Of Power album cover – the man being punched in the face. It's his favourite T-shirt. It's his favourite album.

Nathan takes a seat and orders a burger and a beer. It doesn't take long to come. While he's eating, he checks out the talent. There's not much, but there's a couple of women worth looking at. One of them is thicker-set and not his type. She and a similarly heavy guy are playing pool together. The other woman catches his eye in a big way – slim little thing, with brown curls cascading down the sides of her face. She wears a white vest and a red shirt tied into a knot at the front. A pair of denim shorts – *real* short. Her legs look strong. Nathan's always been a leg man. Some men like tits, others like asses, but he's always been a fan of a good pair of thick thighs, whether muscular or soft – he doesn't have a preference. It's got him a reputation in the FRD. He's the leg man, and everyone knows it.

The woman sees him staring and she twists her body away from him, to the side, looking briefly uncomfortable. Nathan doesn't care. He keeps right on staring. No law against looking.

There's a guy with her, sitting opposite at the table, but he's no kind of threat. To Nathan's eyes, he doesn't look anything like a real man. Just a pretty boy, with a physique built from too long spent in a gym instead of out in the real world. Nathan has muscles where it counts. He has muscles where they're useful.

"Can we help you?"

Slowly, Nathan looks up. He's still chewing. He takes his time, looking into the eyes of the guy the girl is with. Her boyfriend? Probably. Nathan belches.

The boyfriend presses. "I asked if we can help you," he repeats.

Nathan shrugs. He's supposed to behave himself. He knows this. But he, and the rest of the Road Dogs, they've all been behaving themselves for a long damn time now. It's oppressive. So instead, he pokes bread and meat from between his teeth with the tip of his tongue, and says, "I dunno. Depends on what you're offering." He winks at the girl.

The boyfriend is playing tough. His brow is furrowed. He's leaning away from their table. "You wanna stop staring at my girlfriend?"

Nathan shrugs again. "I'm just admiring what she's showing."

"She's not showing you anything."

Nathan takes another bite of burger, and washes it down with a mouthful of beer. "She's right there, ain't she? And it's a free country, last I checked."

"Damn it, stop staring at her. You're making her uncomfortable."

"That's her choice."

"You're being an asshole."

The girl speaks up now, though not to Nathan. She addresses her boyfriend. "Just leave it," she says, reaching across the table and placing a hand upon his arm. "He's not worth it – just ignore him."

The boyfriend ignores *her*. Right now, he only has eyes for Nathan.

"You keep staring at me like that," Nathan says, "and soon I'm gonna ask if you're ready to follow through."

The boyfriend doesn't respond. He keeps staring.

Nathan finishes his burger. He takes his time. Slowly, he drains the beer bottle and turns his attention fully to the boyfriend. "What you gonna do, kid?" he says. "You gonna come over here and throw me out? You think you got it in you? Cos if you don't stop staring at me like that, I'm gonna come over *there* and you know what I'm gonna do?"

The boyfriend sneers. He's trying to look tougher than he is. He's refusing to back down, defending the honour of his wide-eyed girlfriend. "What?" he says.

"I'm gonna take your fucking eyes out," Nathan says. The boyfriend falters at this. He can see the look on Nathan's face. The way he grins. He can see that this is no idle threat. His eyes flicker down to Nathan's thick, gnarled hands, wondering at the damage they could do – at the damage they *have* done. Nathan grins. "And then me and your lady there, we're gonna head down the road to the motel and I'm gonna show her the time of her life. How's that sound?"

The girlfriend swallows. She's gone pale. Nathan blows her a kiss. The boyfriend doesn't do anything. He's shaken. He wasn't prepared for this. He's realising what he's done, and how deep he's got himself.

"There a problem here?"

Nathan glances to his right. The heavier guy who was playing pool has sensed what is happening and has made his way over, playing at knight in shining armour. He's still wielding the pool cue. His fat wife is close to his shoulder. She's similarly armed with the other cue.

"No problem for you, buddy," Nathan says. "You can go and finish your game. You don't need to worry about what's happening over here."

"I get the feeling maybe I *do* need to worry," the man says. "The kid here's my buddy's son. So if you're looking for trouble with him, you've got trouble with me."

"I don't want nothing from him," Nathan says. He knows the new arrival will be more of a challenge. From the bend of his nose and the scars on his eyebrows, it's clear he's been in his fair share of fights. Nathan doesn't fear him, though. He doesn't fear anyone, whether he's wearing his kutte or not. Because of this, he can't help himself. He looks to the girl. "Now, *her* on the other hand – there's a *lot* I want from her."

"Time for you to leave," the man says, taking a step too close and grabbing for the back of Nathan's collar.

Nathan grabs his empty beer bottle by the neck and spins, slamming it into the side of the man's face. It shatters, cutting him up. The man falls back, holding at his cheek, blood pouring through his fingers and dripping into the sticky carpet below.

Nathan is already to his feet. The boyfriend is coming for him. He's swinging wild fists. The punches are sloppy. He hasn't had any kind of training, and despite all his posturing he hasn't been in a real fight before. Nathan grabs a fist and slams a punch of his own into the boyfriend's chest. He falls back, gasping, holding at himself like he's having a heart attack. He stumbles over a chair and falls flat. The girl screams, rushing to him on the ground.

Next thing Nathan knows, he feels a heavy weight attach itself to his back, almost dropping him to his knees. It weighs him down, and its hands claw at his face and his eyes. He realises it's the man's fat wife. He swings side to side, trying to shake her off. He reaches back, trying to grab a handful of her hair. She bites at his hand. Nathan slaps her as well as he's able, then grabs the handful and drags her over his shoulder, slamming her down onto his table, shattering the plate he was eating from. Nathan feels a sting in his right cheek where her fingernails have caught him, and the sting pisses him off. He flips the table, dumping her to the ground.

Her husband is on the floor still, hands to his face, plugging the wounds from the bottle. Nathan picks up one of their dropped cues and swings it like a baseball bat, snapping it against the man's ribs. He laughs to himself as the man goes down.

The fight is over. The other patrons in the bar are all looking their way, wondering if they should get involved. There's enough hesitation apparent in their faces that Nathan knows they're not going to be stupid enough. One of the bartenders is waving at him, saying something.

"Stay there!" she says. "The cops are gonna be here any minute – don't you go anywhere, asshole!"

Nathan laughs again. He looks down at the girl tending to her fallen boyfriend. The boyfriend is breathing hard, but he's not clutching at his chest anymore. The panic has faded as he's realised he's not having a heart attack, that he's not dying. He's not going to be able to pull himself up off the ground for a while yet. Nathan knows this from experience. It's not the first time he's punched someone straight in the chest with all the force he could muster.

He waits until the girl looks up at him. She's hesitant to do so, and Nathan admires her bent legs while he waits. Eventually, hesitantly, she does so. Nathan gives her another wink. "Shame we didn't have more time, sweetheart," he says. "You change your mind and wanna come see a real man, you heard where I'll be."

He can hear the sirens now. The cops that the bartender threatened. Reality sets in for Nathan. The realisation of what he's done, and what he's carrying.

"Ah, *shit*," he mutters to himself, hurrying from the bar. The bartender calls after him to stop. She calls for someone to stop him, but no one steps up.

The motel will have to wait. He needs to get clear of here. *Very* clear.

Outside, already he can see the approaching cop cars. There's two of them, which he thinks is overkill for a barfight. Must be a slow night. It's not something he can dwell on. He races to his bike and starts to wheel it clear, fumbling in his pocket for the key.

One of the cruisers screeches to a halt in front of him, blocking his escape route. Nathan tries to turn the other way, cursing, regretting how long he waited just to give the girl a parting message. The other cruiser stops nearby and two cops get out, wielding guns.

"Stop right there!"

Nathan doesn't have any choice. "*Fuck*."

"Step away from the bike!"

Nathan does. He raises his arms in surrender. The cops who blocked his escape come to him. One of them tackles him to the ground. They cuff him.

"Jesus Christ, you already got me, don't ya?" Nathan says, sputtering in the dirt.

The scene begins to calm. Nathan is hauled to his feet and put in the back of a cruiser. Nathan presses his head back into the rest, cursing silently. It's not his first time being arrested. He knows what's coming. All he can hope is that they don't notice what he's carrying. He watches. One of the cops goes into the bar. To check on everyone, and to take statements.

Nathan sits up as one of the cops starts to move his bike. The cop hesitates, frowning, looking down at the bike. Nathan swallows. He wonders if the cop rides. Wonders if he's familiar with touring Harley-Davidsons. Wonders if he notices the heaviness.

The cop calls another over. They converse briefly. Nathan wishes he could hear what they're saying. The cops start searching the bike. They go into his baggage. Nathan feels his heart rate quicken. His mouth goes dry. He breathes hard. He shakes in the seat, but all that this accomplishes is a chafing where the cuffs bite into his wrists.

They find the hidden compartments in his baggage. They notice a loose cover and pull it off. It won't take them long to find all the other hollowed-out points in his bike. All the other hiding places. For now, they take out the bags of meth they've found, and they look back at Nathan, holding them up. One of them raises his eyebrows. The other grins. Nathan closes his eyes. He wishes he was free and could wipe the looks from both of their faces.

"*Fuck.*"

2

Davenport is a small town in the state of Mississippi, roughly thirty-five miles south of the city of Natchez. A fishing town, most of its income is derived from its proximity to the Mississippi River. Everyone who lives in the town makes their living from the river one way or another, whether they work on it, or are in service to those who do.

Lyle Bound owns a trawler. In his sixties, he's worked the river since he first left high school. He's hauled in thousands of pounds' worth of fish over his working life – bream, crappie, bass, catfish, and freshwater drum. He can't foresee a day when he won't take his trawler out and pull back into Davenport with a full hold. Retirement is a dirty word to him. What else would he do with his time? The river is his home, and has been for as long as he can remember. His friends tell him they expect him to die on the water. Lyle laughs, and tells them he expects the same, and for his funeral he wants them to push his coffin straight into the river. Or, if one of his employees finds him, they can feel free to roll him straight over the side.

Lyle has a small crew of four men. Tom Rollins is his most recent recruit. He's been working the boat for the last three months, since he first arrived in Davenport and decided it would be a pleasant enough – and quiet enough – place to kill a little time and make some money.

Tom found work quick enough. His first night in town, he went to the bar to get an idea of the lay of the land. He got talking to the owner, Valerie Reynolds. Her last bartender had just split town, and she was in need of an employee. Bartender/bouncer. Tom stepped up. Valerie told him for the most part there's no trouble in Davenport, but sometimes the locals can have a little too much to drink and they need to be calmed down before they can cause damage in her bar. And sometimes out-of-towners turn up. Most of the time they just want a quiet drink, but sometimes they come looking for trouble with the hicks. Tom told her he had no problem with getting his hands dirty, and he took the job. As a bonus, there was a spare room at the back of the bar. A place for Tom to stay, its rent taken out of his pay. When Tom asked Valerie if there were any jobs for during the day, she hollered across the bar to Lyle and got them to talk to each other. Tom's been saving his money since, barely spending a penny until he's ready to move on again.

The sun beats down now on the back of Tom's neck and shoulders through his oilskin jacket. He wears a baseball cap to avoid sunstroke. He wears dark green chest waders that for the most part keep him dry. The nets are out, and while they wait, Tom stands at the railing and watches the water. He sees how it ripples and undulates. He breathes deep, inhaling the coolness on the air. It's spring, and it's getting warmer, but there remains a chill in the air in the early morning and late afternoon, like now, that Tom enjoys.

Lyle joins him at the railing. "Breathing it in?" he says.

"Every day," Tom says.

Lyle chuckles.

"Peaceful out here," Tom says. The river is three miles across at Davenport, and they sit in the centre of it.

"One of the things I love best," Lyle says. "The peace." He pauses a beat, breathing deep. "And I love that smell, too. The water. The shore. Hell, even the fish as we reel them in. We're in a beautiful part of America here. Hell, a beautiful part of the world. We're very lucky."

Tom grunts. "I won't argue."

"How long you think you're gonna stick around here, Rollins?"

"Not sure," Tom says. "Through the summer, maybe. I'll see how it goes."

"I'm willing to keep you on as long as you're staying around. Whenever you do move on, it's gonna be a damn shame to see you go. You're a good worker, Rollins."

"Always have been." Tom grins.

Lyle laughs. "I don't doubt it."

"You take on many transients?"

"Maybe one a year," Lyle says. "Guess you've filled my quota." He leans on the railing, breathing deep again. He looks to the opposite side of the river, where it's no longer Mississippi, and it's instead Louisiana.

"The state line runs down the middle of the river, doesn't it?" Tom says, seeing where he's looking.

Lyle nods. "For the most part."

"We in Louisiana right now?"

Lyle shrugs. "Never can tell," he says. "I try to keep us closer to our half than theirs."

Tom looks to Louisiana, too. "A friend of mine is from there," he says. "A good friend. I haven't seen him in a while now. I always mean to keep in touch, but we all get busy and time just slips on by."

"When it's a good friend, the passage of time don't matter any."

"True," Tom says. "Still, it's regrettable."

"What's his name?"

"Zeke Greene," Tom says. "We used to work together." Tom thinks to himself, but doesn't say out loud, how it would be nice to catch up with Zeke sometime without bullets flying around them. "I think he changed career recently. Least, I think he did. Last we spoke, he was talking about it. I should ask him how that's going."

"I give you days off, don't I?" Lyle says, grinning. "I'm not a total slavedriver. Nothing stopping you from paying a visit, especially if he's so close."

"That would depend on what part of Louisiana he and his family are in these days."

"Married man?"

Tom nods.

"You ever been married, Tom?"

"No," Tom says.

"Good-looking guy like you, I suppose you wouldn't want to limit yourself."

"What're you trying to butter me up for, Lyle?"

Lyle laughs. "I'm just talking, is all. Making conversation. Getting to know you. You ever come close to it? There a heartbroken lady out there somewhere?"

Tom thinks about Hayley, back in New Mexico. His high

school sweetheart. They gave it a go for a while. They did their best, but it didn't work out. A year ago, Tom had to move on. That was around the last time he saw Zeke, too. It was safer for Hayley for Tom to leave. The way he lives, the enemies he's made, he couldn't keep putting her at risk. "I sure hope not," Tom says. Whatever Hayley is doing now, Tom hopes she's happy. He hopes she's found someone who doesn't bring constant danger into her life, and is there for her at the end of each day. Someone without restless legs, desperate to get back onto the road, to keep moving.

Since he left Hayley, Tom has thought about his movements. He's thought about the ghosts of his past. He's asked himself, is he trying to outrun them? And the trouble he finds, the trouble he's always on the lookout for, is that to compensate for what he's done? Is it to make up for past sins? Or, as he's so often feared over the years, has the danger become an addiction?

"Have I touched a nerve?" Lyle says, snapping Tom back to the present. "Whatever you were thinking about, you were deep in it."

Tom shakes his head. "It's nothing," he says. "It time to bring the nets in?"

"I reckon it is," Lyle says, straightening. He puts fingers into his mouth and whistles, drawing the rest of the crew to attention. They get to work.

It's a decent haul. They get the fish on ice then turn the boat around and head back to shore. Tom stays on deck, feeling the cool breeze on his face. Again, he breathes deep. He closes his eyes. It feels meditative. It feels peaceful. He fills his lungs, in through his nose, and exhales slowly out of his mouth. When he opens his eyes, they're not far from the shore.

Off to his left, he sees movement on the banks of the river. Two women, in waders, taking water samples. Tom recognises them. He doesn't know their names, but he's seen them before. They're often near the river. Lyle says they're ecologists. They come into the bar sometimes, but Tom has only ever exchanged pleasantries with them. They've never held a full conversation. One of them is a similar age to Tom – thirty-four – but the other looks younger. Early twenties, either not long out of college or doing some kind of post-grad out in the field. Tom raises a hand, waving. The younger woman waves back, but the older is busy with her work, focussing on what she's doing.

The boat pulls into the bay, and Tom joins the rest of the crew to unload the fish.

3

Sometimes, the shift at the bar can run late. The latest Tom has worked so far is four in the morning. That was a one-off, though. A young couple from town were celebrating their engagement, and all of their friends came out to join them. It was an easy night. There wasn't any trouble. Everyone was too happy to cause issues.

More often, it's one or two in the morning. When Tom finishes his shift on the boat, he takes a shower to wash off the smell of fish, then grabs a few hours of sleep before his second job commences. At least the commute is easy – he wakes, dresses, and walks barely two dozen steps around from the back room through to the bar.

"Good fishing?" Valerie asks him as he joins her. She always asks, and the answer is always the same.

"Good enough," Tom says.

"Quiet in here so far," Valerie says.

"It's still early."

"Sure, but you never can tell with a weeknight."

Valerie Reynolds is seventy-five and has run the bar for

the last twenty years. When she first took it on, she wasn't alone. Her husband was still alive back then. Buying the bar had been his idea. He died ten years ago, and Valerie has been on her own since. "If I didn't have the bar, I'd be completely alone," she's told Tom. "And I don't want that. I don't want to be lonely." She and her husband never had kids. Most of her friends are either dead, or live elsewhere. Too far to visit. Her sister died seven years ago. She was a spinster, childless too. Ownership of the bar brings daily and nightly company. It brings regulars. It brings conversation, and companionship. Warmth. Life and light and sound. Like Lyle, Valerie will never retire. She'll run the bar until she dies. It makes her happy, and she doesn't have anything else.

The evening rolls on, and the bar gradually fills up. It never gets loud, but it contains the life that Valerie likes to see. Tom watches the bar while Valerie mingles with a couple of people she knows, sitting at a table with them. Tom keeps an eye on the door, too. If there's trouble, or anyone who looks like they're going to be trouble, it's no effort for him to clear the counter and interject himself.

A couple of familiar faces walk in. The ecologists from down by the shores of the river. Much like Tom, they're not wearing waders anymore. Instead, the older of the two is wearing jeans and a black blouse. The younger is wearing a flower-print summer dress and Doc Marten boots. They come straight to the bar to order drinks. The younger one is smiling. She cocks her head, looking at Tom. "You were on the boat, right?" she says. "You waved."

"You waved back," Tom says.

The other woman looks between them, not understanding. "Did I miss something?"

"Looked like you were hard at work," Tom says.

"I try not to stay in the habit of waving at strangers," the younger woman says. "What's your name, Mr Bartender-slash-Mr Fisherman?"

Tom grins. He tells her.

"I'm Emma Killick," she says, then turns to her friend. "And this is –"

"Laila North," the other woman says.

"She's my boss," Emma says.

"Do I treat you so poorly that this is how you introduce me?" Laila says. She's caught up now to Tom and Emma's initial conversation. Her tone has become more playful. "Your *boss*?"

"She's a very good boss," Emma says.

Both women have dark hair, though Emma's is cut short. Laila's hair is longer, and has lighter highlights from so much time spent out in the sun. She's taller, too, and through the blouse and jeans she wears it looks like she keeps in shape. She has an athlete's build, almost like a gymnast. Tom imagines she probably spends most of her time outdoors, and not just for her job. She likely goes running, and does calisthenics in the park or her back yard. Her skin has a healthy tan, much like Tom's own currently does. Emma carries a few extra pounds, though she carries them well. Her cheeks still contain puppy fat, as opposed to Laila's, whose face is almost supermodel angular.

Tom grins. "The two of you are ecologists, right?"

"That's right," Laila says.

"Well," Emma says, "I'm an assistant."

"Don't sell yourself so short," Laila says. "You're the best damn assistant I've ever had."

"You flatter me," Emma says, fluttering her eyelashes.

"What can I get you, ladies?" Tom says.

"I'll have a rum and coke," Emma says. "And since I'm the *best* damn assistant, I think my boss – nay, my *friend* – Laila will happily pay for my drink."

Laila raises her eyebrows, but she laughs. "Make it two," she says. "And yes, I *will* pay for this round."

"You make more money than me," Emma says. Before Laila can respond, Emma twirls away, hurrying to a table.

Laila turns back to Tom. "Y'know, I don't remember being that much of a pain in the ass when I was twenty-four."

"You don't look that much older," Tom says.

"I'm thirty-two, and that's my point. Barely ten years. Do you think she'll mature so much in such a short space of time?"

"I don't know you that well," Tom says, "but I'm sure you're *very* mature, and with your influence, Emma will be just fine."

Laila grins while he makes their drinks. "Next time you wave, I'll make sure and wave back."

"I'd hate to distract you from your work," Tom says, placing the drinks on the counter. "You have an important job."

"More important than you can imagine right now," Laila says, taking the drinks.

Tom wonders what she means, but she's already turned and going to join Emma at the table she's found. Tom doesn't dwell on it. He soon has to serve someone else looking for a refill.

The evening rolls on. Outside, through the windows, Tom can see it get darker. Valerie rejoins him behind the bar. They make small-talk. Laila and Emma get a couple more drinks. Laila has the one rum and coke, and then switches to soda. "I need to drive," she says.

"Very sensible," Tom says.

The two women make conversation at their table. Mostly, they smile while they talk. They're having a good time. When Emma laughs, she throws her head back. She's uninhibited. When Laila laughs, Tom sees how she covers her mouth with her hand, the sound much more contained.

Two men enter the bar. Tom doesn't recognise them. As they make their way to the counter, one of them glances around the room. The other stands in front of Tom, blocking his view. "Couple of beers," he says. He has a handlebar moustache, and thinning hair slicked back.

"Sure," Tom says, twisting the tops off two bottles and handing them over. He takes payment as the second man comes into view. His head is shaved. His cheeks and chin are thickly stubbled, close to becoming a beard. Both men are heavyset. Tom recognises the type. They're not afraid to fight. Probably enjoy it, in fact. Right now, they don't appear to be looking for any trouble. Just two guys in search of a drink.

They pay and take the beers, retreating to a booth in the corner. A couple of heavies, sure, but Tom didn't feel much threat from them. Neither of them was sizing him up. They weren't leaning in close over the counter, trying to invade his space to see how he handled it. Tom doesn't give them much thought. Doesn't expect them to cause trouble.

Until he's turning to the harder liquor behind the bar to pour a regular a shot, and he sees the stubbled man leaning down over his drink and staring across the room. As he turns, Tom follows the trail of his gaze, and it leads him straight to Laila and Emma.

Tom pours the shot, then as he turns to put the bottle back, he double-checks what he thinks he has seen. The stubbled man isn't making it obvious, but he glances up and across the room every so often. Every time he does, he's looking at Laila and Emma. Tom checks to be sure. There's no one else sitting near the two women. There's no one else he could be staring at.

Tom doesn't like it. Sure, it could be nothing – there's no law against looking – but two young women alone in a bar, enjoying a drink? He doesn't like how it feels. It turns his stomach. Puts him on high alert.

"I'm gonna clear some tables," Tom says to Valerie, grabbing a tray and heading out from behind the bar.

He makes his way around the room, gathering up glasses and bottles. He keeps an eye on the men as he does so, and checks that Laila and Emma aren't showing any signs of leaving yet. It's getting late. The bar is clearing out. They could get ready to leave at any time. Tom takes the full tray to the bar and grabs another. He continues on his route. He doesn't want to make what he's doing obvious. He's getting closer and closer to Laila and Emma. At the booth, the moustached man sits with his back to the room. The stubbled man continues snatching glances. The two men talk.

Tom reaches Laila and Emma. He places the tray down and smiles at them while he gathers up their glasses. He squats down and keeps smiling, like they're making friendly conversation. "Don't look up," he says, "and don't be alarmed. Just listen to what I tell you."

Laila frowns. Emma looks unsure. "What is it?" Laila says.

"The two men in the booth back there," Tom says, "don't look – they've been eyeing you both since they arrived."

"Are you sure?" Laila says. Her back is to the men, and she keeps her eyes on Tom. Emma, however, is angled more toward the booth, and Tom can see her struggling not to turn and look.

"I'm sure," Tom says. "I've been watching *them*." He leans a little closer, blocking Emma from view of the booth. "Just stay calm," he says, smiling at her until she starts to imitate him. Tom nods. "Everything's okay. They're not going to do anything to you. I won't let them."

"Do you recognise them?" Laila says. She's calm. Tom's impressed.

"I've never seen them before," Tom says. "Best I can figure, they've spotted two young women here on their own, they've seen that you're drinking, and they're planning on taking advantage."

"They haven't approached us," Laila says.

"I've noticed. That concerns me. They could be waiting for you to leave."

"I haven't been drinking," Laila says. "I stopped after one. I'm practically sober still. I'm hardly an easy target."

"They're not going to know that. Your drink is the same colour as Emma's, and they have a better view of her. They've seen her start to look drunk, and they've assumed the same is happening to you."

"I was never drunk," Emma says. "I was *buzzed*. That buzz is fading *real* fast right about now." She frowns suddenly, as if something has occurred to her. She looks at Laila. "You don't suppose –"

Laila cuts her off. "It's crossed my mind," she says. To Tom, she says, "I need to see them."

"You having some trouble?" Tom wonders if it could be an ex-boyfriend. Neither of the two men look young enough, handsome enough, or good enough to have dated either Laila or Emma, but there's no accounting for taste.

Laila doesn't respond, but she and Emma exchange a look.

"I need the bathroom," Emma says. "I'll check."

"Okay," Tom says. "I'll go back behind the bar. Come see me there when you're done. Maybe you should both laugh as I walk away. We don't want them to think we've been discussing anything serious."

Laila and Emma laugh as he straightens. Tom grins. He returns the glasses to the bar. Valerie raises an eyebrow as he passes, sensing that something is up. Keeping his voice low, Tom tells her they'll talk soon. He stands behind the counter, busying himself.

Emma has got to her feet. She goes to the bathroom on slightly shaky legs. She coughs, clearing her throat. The stubbled man at the booth watches her go, then looks back at Laila to make sure she's not going anywhere. When Emma returns, she locks eyes with Tom behind the counter. She nods a little. She gets back to the table and talks with Laila. The two women stand and come to the bar.

"I don't recognise them," Emma says. "But I saw them looking."

The women aren't panicking, but Tom can see that they're both concerned. Laila is calmer than Emma. Cooler.

"I don't like it," Emma says.

"What's happening?" Tom says. "What's got you spooked?"

They don't answer. "Maybe we should call the cops," Emma says.

"It'll take them a while to get here," Tom says. "I know from experience. But they're not going to do anything.

They're not going to give those two men a slap on the wrist just for looking. They haven't hassled you. They haven't done anything yet. Right now, the law can't help you."

Emma stares at the top of the counter, digesting what Tom has said.

"What do you suggest we do?" Laila says.

"Sit tight for now," Tom says. "Give it a half-hour. I'll keep an eye on them. If they're still here, I'll drive you home."

"I have my car," Laila says.

"Then we'll use your car, and I'll walk back."

Laila and Emma confer briefly.

"We'd appreciate the ride home," Laila says when they're done.

Tom nods. "Half an hour," he says. "I'll leave the bar first. You both follow. We'll meet outside." He pours them another couple of drinks – both sodas – and hands them over. Laila and Emma return to their table.

When they're gone, Tom motions to Valerie to come into the corner with him, out of view of the men's booth. In a low voice, he tells her what he's seen, and what he's going to do.

"Jesus, okay, yeah," Valerie says. She starts to look back at the booth but Tom stops her. "Do you want me to follow along, pick you up?"

"I don't know how long I'll be," Tom says. "I want to make sure they both get back safe. I'll walk back – I don't mind it. I enjoy the air."

When the half hour is up, the two men remain in the booth. The bar is quiet, almost empty. A couple of regulars nurse drinks at the end, locked in conversation with Valerie. The rest of the tables and booths have cleared out. Tom gets Valerie's attention and they exchange nods. Tom heads outside. Laila and Emma follow.

"This one's mine," Laila says, taking out her keys. She drives a Honda Civic. She gets in and Tom takes the passenger seat. Emma gets into the back.

"I feel sick," Emma says.

"Try not to worry," Tom says, watching the entrance to the bar in the mirror. The men have not followed them out. "If we're lucky, they saw us leave at the same time and they won't try anything."

4

Laila starts the engine and pulls out of the bar's parking lot. "I would like to draw attention to the fact that I'm aware this could all be an elaborate ruse," she says. "And that there's every chance *you* could be the one we need to worry about."

Tom doesn't answer straight away, choosing his words carefully. "I get that," he says. "All I can do is promise that's not the case."

"I saw them looking," Emma says. "The two men in the booth. I saw them watching us."

"I saw them, too," Laila says.

"I didn't notice you look," Tom says.

"I was very subtle about it. And because we saw them both looking, we're inclined to believe that you really are just a good guy doing your job. And also, we have other reasons to believe those two men were watching us. But I'd just like to point this all out because I don't want you to think we're a pair of morons. I don't want you to think that if you try something, I'm *not* prepared to kick you in the balls and gouge your eyes out."

Tom chuckles. "I'm glad to hear it. And I promise it won't come to that."

"Good," Laila says.

"I'd like to think I'm a good judge of people," Emma says from the back. "And I think Tom is a good person. He waved at us from the boat."

"Don't let that fool you," Laila says. "I don't just mean for Tom. I mean in general."

"She's always trying to teach me things," Emma says to Tom, leaning forward.

Tom watches the mirrors. The road behind them is quiet. It's dark behind, and dark up ahead. "How far out are you?" he says.

"My place is about twenty minutes away," Laila says.

"Mine's a little further," Emma says.

"You should stick together tonight," Tom says.

Laila nods. "All right. We'll stay at mine."

Tom still can't see anyone following. Either he was wrong about the two men, or they weren't prepared to work so hard to follow two young women. If they saw Tom leave, too, perhaps he was deterrent enough. Tom has kept the faces of the two men in mind, though. Has filed them away for later, should they ever come back to the bar.

His phone buzzes. It's Valerie. "Tom, those two guys you were concerned about, they've just left."

"Did you see which way they went?"

"They got in a car and turned right onto the road, same direction you all did."

There are still no lights behind them. They could have

their lights off, if they're following. But also, Laila has a good head start. "Thanks, Valerie. Appreciate it."

"What is it?" Emma says.

Tom doesn't lie. "They've left the bar. They're coming this way."

"They're following us?" Emma says, her voice high.

"It doesn't mean that," Tom says, shaking his head. "We don't know which way they came from."

Laila remains focussed, staring straight ahead into the darkness. Tom sees how tendons clench in her cheek, her teeth clamped together and grinding. Her grip tightens on the steering wheel.

"Tell me about your work," Tom says. "It sounds interesting." He needs to keep them calm. He doesn't want them to panic. Emma already sounds like she's on the verge of hyperventilating.

"You know what ecologists do, right?" Laila says.

"Sure," Tom says. "Tell me anyway. What do you do in the water when I see you from the boat?"

"Taking samples, usually," Laila says. "Checking the pH levels. Making sure they're still at a healthy level for the fish, and the other animals that live nearby."

"We do soil samples sometimes, too," Emma says. "Grass, branches – all kinds. And we make lists. We keep a *lot* of lists..."

"Do you have an office?" Tom says. "Somewhere close to the river?"

Laila nods. "I'm surprised you haven't seen. It's a temporary building, about a mile back from where you would have seen us in the water today."

"Is it raised? Looks like it came out of a pack?"

"That's the one," Laila says. She laughs. "We want to leave as little imprint as we can."

"It ever get dangerous?" Tom says. "Some of the animals around here, they can be rough, right?"

"We're very careful. The main part of our job is *not* disturbing the animals. We're just trying to make sure they're safe, that their environment is safe, that there's nothing immediately threatening them."

"Sure, but there's alligators around here, right?"

"It's very rare for them to go into the river," Emma says. "They prefer marshes. They like brackish water. The Mississippi isn't as salty as they'd like."

"It was the first thing Emma asked about when she came to work with me," Laila says. "Alligators."

"It's a reasonable concern," Tom says.

"I sure thought so," Emma says. "I love nature, and I want to help preserve it, but I also love my life, and having all of my fingers and limbs."

"Listen," Tom says, "back in the bar, and just earlier, you both mentioned something, but didn't go into detail. About the men. You suggested –"

Laila is already nodding. "I know what you're talking about," she says. She takes a deep breath. "Lately – past few weeks or so – it feels like we've been watched while we're working."

Tom's eyes narrow. "Watched? Who by?"

"We don't know for sure," Laila says. "But we have our ideas."

"What happens?" Tom says. "What makes you think you're being watched?"

"Let's use today for an example. You saw us in the water, collecting samples, right?"

"Right."

"We'll be out in the field, collecting samples, completing surveys or whatever, and we'll notice a car parked close to where we are. Usually it's pointing away from us, but not always. And we'll see men inside, two of them. A couple of times they've gotten out, like they're just stretching their legs or having a cigarette, but they'll be looking right at us. They're brazen about it."

"I've seen them taking pictures," Emma says. "They try to be subtle about *that*, but I could tell what they were doing. They'd lean across the roof of their car, like they were just playing on their phone or responding to a message, but the phone was turned toward us. They were taking our pictures."

"That's if there's a road," Laila says. "If not, if we're out in the middle of nowhere, it's worse. Suddenly, we'll see someone walking along, whereas in the past we've never seen another person there before. They'll just walk right on by, like they're on a hike, like it's no big deal. Sometimes they'll even smile and nod at us, like they're just taking a stroll through a protected area and it's a completely normal thing to do."

"You ever confront them?" Tom says.

"We have, but they just play dumb, act like they've gotten all turned around and they're lost now."

"But when we're alone out there, we don't always want to confront them," Emma says. "Like, what if they're dangerous? I think they *want* us to see them. I think they want us to know that they're watching."

"Why?" Tom says. "Who are they? What's that theory you mentioned?"

"It's not so easy to explain," Laila says. "Not without giving you a little background first."

As Tom is about to respond, he spots lights in the mirror.

Laila notices his demeanour change. "What is it?" she says. She looks in her own mirrors. "Is that them?"

"I don't know," Tom says. "But someone's coming for sure, and they're coming fast." Tom looks ahead. They pass a house, but then a little further down there is only trees lining the right side of the road, and a field on the left. Tom spots an opening on the right. "Kill the lights," Tom says. "And take that turning. Don't signal."

Laila does as he says. Over his shoulder, Tom can see Emma twist in her seat, looking back. Laila turns up to the right. It's a dirt road that jostles them. Laila slows the car down to stop them bouncing so much. "How far should I go?" she says.

"Turn us round," Tom says. "Point us back toward the road."

"What if they figure out we turned up here?" Emma says. "We'll be sitting ducks."

"They were coming up fast," Tom says, "but they were too far back to see where we turned."

"But they could work it out from when the lights went out."

"The road dipped just ahead of where we turned. When they reach that, they'll figure that's where our lights went. I reckon they're going so fast they'll miss the turn. Unless they're *very* familiar with this road, they'll never know it's here."

"What if that's not what happens?" Emma says. "What if they *do* come up here?"

"I keep telling you," Tom says. "Stay calm. I'm here. You're safe. I'm never a sitting duck."

Laila has turned the car around. They can see the road again. The car has not passed yet. They sit and wait. Tom looks to his left, through the trees. He sees the headlights cutting through. The car is coming fast, as he suspected. It speeds by.

"Keep the lights off," Tom says. "Go back to the road. Do you know another route to your place?"

Laila thinks for a moment. "We'll have to go back on ourselves for a bit, but yeah, I can think of another way."

"Take it."

The alternative route adds ten minutes to the journey, but the road is quiet all the way. Tom's eyes have been glued to the mirrors. No headlights appeared. If it was the men from the bar, they gave them the slip when they pulled up the dirt road.

By the time they reach Laila's place, it's past midnight. It's a small house, one floor, in what looks to be a quiet neighbourhood. The other houses are in darkness. Laila pulls onto the driveway.

"Go inside and lock the doors," Tom says. "Check the windows. Make sure you're secure. I'm going to give you my number. If you get concerned about anything, call me."

"If anything happens, how would you get here in time?" Emma says. "Aren't you going to be walking back?"

"I'm not going far," Tom says. "I'll be close."

"What, you're going to stay outside?" Laila says.

"I've stayed outside in worse places," Tom says.

"And, what? You're going to keep watch?"

"I'll be close," Tom says again. "If they turn up, I'll see them."

Laila pauses. "What kind of bartender are you?"

"The kind that wouldn't feel comfortable heading to bed knowing that the two of you were potentially being stalked. That something bad could happen to you both."

Tom gets out of the car. He holds the back door open for Emma. She and Laila go inside the house. Tom listens until he hears the front door lock. When it is, he walks away. He circles the block. The street is as quiet as it looks. If the two from the bar were just a couple of random men looking to take advantage of a situation, they shouldn't know where Laila's home is, and there shouldn't be anything else to worry about.

However, Laila and Emma talked about having been watched. Watched while working, by people who seemed to know where they went and what they did. If the two men from the bar are connected to these watchers, then there is cause for concern. If they know where Laila and Emma go when they're working, there is the potential that they know where they live, too.

Tom needs to ask Laila and Emma more about the people watching them. Who they are, and what they want. He'll save the questions for another time. Right now, there is a different task in hand.

Tom circles back round to Laila's home. He crosses to the other side of the street and sticks to the shadows. He listens to the night. It's quiet. If he hears any vehicles at all, they're distant.

One of the houses opposite Laila's has a tree in the front yard. The lawn is lined with bushes. The house is in darkness. The window blinds are all drawn. Tom enters the lawn and takes a seat under the tree. He can see over the top of the bush. He has a clear view of Laila's house. He settles in, his side resting against the trunk of the tree, and he watches.

5

It's two thirty in the morning before anything happens.

Tom hears the car before he sees it. The engine is idling. There are no revs. It rolls slowly down the road, passing by Laila's house. Tom sits very still. The bushes and the tree conceal him. The car doesn't stop. It keeps rolling. Tom watches it go, moving only his eyes. The car reaches the end of the block. From there, it speeds up. Tom doesn't hear it go far. He strains his ears to listen. It's around the back of Laila's house now, in front of her rear neighbour's home. It's stayed close. Soon after, the car falls silent.

Tom wonders if it was a neighbour. He never got a good look at the car that was potentially following them on their way here. He didn't see what the men at the bar were driving, either, and Valerie never mentioned.

He waits. He remains very still. No other vehicles approach.

Then, there is movement. Tom looks to the right, again moving only his eyes. He sits so still, like a statue.

Two shapes approach. They walk across lawns to mask

the sound of their footsteps. Smart. However, their heads are bare, which is not so smart. Tom can see their faces. When they get close enough, passing through the shadows, caught in the radial glow of the streetlights, he can see exactly who they are.

Stubble and Moustache. The two men from the bar.

Tom continues to watch, though it's clear where they're going. It's clear they know exactly where Laila lives. If the two men are potential rapists, then they're very determined. More likely, they're involved with whoever has been watching Laila and Emma. Tom closes his fists.

The two men go up to the house. They continue to step lightly, sticking to the grass. Stubble goes to the front door. Moustache looks around, checking up and down the street. His eyes cast over where Tom is, but he doesn't see him. Stubble tries the door handle, but finds it locked. As Moustache turns and the two men begin to confer, Tom rises to his feet. His steps are naturally light – force of habit – though he makes no effort to conceal himself. He crosses the road, striding straight to them.

"This is a crazy coincidence," Tom says once he's within earshot, startling both men, causing them to spin toward him. "Because I'm *sure* I saw two guys who looked exactly like you earlier tonight."

Moustache stares, blinking, but Stubble speaks up. "It's the barman," he says.

Moustache grunts and steps back. "He left just ahead of them," he says. "Looks like maybe he left *with* them."

Stubble moves away from the door, stepping closer to Moustache. "You should get out of here," he says. "Leave now, and we'll pretend you were never here. We'll pretend like we don't know where you work, too."

Tom shrugs. "I don't care if you know where I work. Assholes like you are the reason I was hired."

Stubble chuckles. "You ain't got any idea what kind of asshole I am."

"We ain't a couple of drunk barflies you get paid to bounce," Moustache says. "You have no idea what you're trying to involve yourself in. Leave. Now."

Tom looks both men in the eye, one at a time. "I don't believe I will."

Moustache looks at Stubble. Stubble raises his eyebrows. Moustache nods, then takes a step to the left. They're fanning out. Encircling him. They both reach back. They have knives. Moustache holds a karambit, the wickedly curving blade pointing low, toward the ground. It's a serious knife. It's not for amateurs. Stubble has a finger-hole knife, and he holds it out in front of himself, the short, vicious blade pointing toward Tom. From their stances, their grips, both men look like they know how to use them.

Tom is unarmed. His Beretta and KA-BAR are in his room back at the bar, tucked into the bottom of his backpack under his spare clothes and burner phones. He glances around the street. They're speaking at regular volume, but the houses remain in darkness. No lights have come on. In Laila's house, though, he sees a twitch of curtain as Laila and Emma peer out.

"Looks like I'm the fool who brought fists to a knife fight," Tom says. He raises his hands, preparing to defend himself.

"It hasn't got to be this way," Moustache says, though he's still circling, looking for a perfect position from which to strike. "We don't have to cut you up – but if you don't walk away, that's exactly what's going to happen."

Tom grins. "You're going to try."

Stubble attacks first, jabbing the point of his knife toward Tom's chest. Tom backs up, then bats his arm away and steps to the side, pushing Stubble toward Moustache. Moustache swipes with the karambit, arcing it toward Tom's midsection. Again, Tom is backed up. Moustache follows through, swinging it upward, missing Tom's chin by mere centimetres. Out the corner of his eye, Tom sees Stubble coming around, attempting to sneak up on him while he's distracted. Both men are proficient with their knives, it's clear. If he isn't careful, and if he doesn't deal with them soon, he's liable to get cut – and *bad*.

He drops to a crouch and sweeps the ground with his right leg, knocking Moustache's own legs out from under him. Moustache lands awkwardly on his elbow, only the grass to break his fall. Tom quickly turns as Stubble jabs at his face, the knife narrowly missing his nose. Tom keeps moving, stepping through. Stubble spins toward him again. Tom captures his arm and drives an elbow back into his ribs, knocking the air out of him. Then, he uppercuts the back of his knife arm, causing his hold on it to go limp. The knife dangles from his finger in the hole. Tom doesn't take the knife from him. Instead, he grabs the handle and wrenches it back in a snapping motion, breaking the man's finger.

Stubble cries out, snatching his arm back. The knife drops to the ground, lost in the dark. Tom drives a left into Stubble's solar plexus, then uppercuts him under the chin, rattling the teeth in his head and lifting him an inch off the ground. He comes back down flat on his back.

Moustache is back to his feet. He swipes at Tom from the left, then the right. Tom ducks and weaves. He kicks at Moustache's left leg, knocking it out from under him, and as

Moustache falls forward Tom brings a knee up into his face, busting his nose. As he lands, Tom grabs a handful of the lank hair at the back of his head and drives his boot into the centre of his face, again and again, until Moustache has gone limp and the karambit falls from his hand.

As Tom gathers up the two knives and moves them away from the prone bodies, Laila's front door opens. She and Emma emerge from inside, looking over what he has done with wide eyes.

"Now we call the police," Tom says.

6

Wyatt Jefferson is at home in Texas, and he's not expecting bad news.

He's not expecting good news, either. In fact, he's not expecting to hear anything at all, and especially nothing to do with Nathan Wood. Nathan is on a run. He's doing his job. It's a run they've all done before, many times now, across many different states, and there haven't been any issues so far. They do their job, then they come home, and life for the Forever Road Dogs goes on.

But before he receives the news that will ruin his day – if not his week – Wyatt is at home. He's not alone. In the kitchen is his wife, Karen. She's drinking coffee with his father, Vic Jefferson, the founder of the Forever Road Dogs. Vic is an old man now at sixty-nine, and he doesn't ride as often as he used to – limited to maybe once a month during the summer – but he still partakes in FRD business, working mostly on the logistical side of things: he keeps track of the business happenings of the other Forever Road Dogs across

America, and makes sure they're all kicking up their dues to the founding Texas chapter in a timely manner.

He retired as president of the club seven years ago, when the arthritis in his knees and wrists first started to take hold. If he'd continued to ride, he wouldn't be able to walk now. As is, some days the arthritis is worse than others, and on those days his hands are practically useless to him, and his legs will not bend at the knees. It's been five months since he last had a flareup so bad, back when they were first learning how to sail a boat and Vic threw himself into it with too much energy, exhausted his ailing body. He spent five days in bed before he was able to move around again.

When Vic had to give up his presidency, Wyatt finally stepped into the role he was born for. He'd been serving as vice-president for ten years before that. He was ready. There had never been any plan for a Shakespearean takeover. Wyatt always knew that when the time was right, his father would pass the crown to him. Even if the arthritis had not struck, Vic would only have remained at the head of the table for a few more years. He'd told Wyatt that his time was winding down, and he was ready to take a step back.

Karen kisses Wyatt on the side of his mouth, the kiss lost in the bristles of his beard, as she pours him a coffee. "You slept in," she says.

Wyatt grunts and takes a sip. It's hot, and feels good going down. "It was a late night," he says. He'd been at the clubhouse. It was Donnie Willis's birthday, and as is the FRD way, they went all out for him. There was alcohol, and lots of it. There were drugs. There were women.

Usually, Wyatt would partake in all three vices. Last night, however, he only had a few beers. There are other things on his mind. Issues that sometimes keep him awake, such as the current business partnership that exerts more pressure than is comfortable upon the FRD. Last night, at least, the party had been a distraction. It meant that when he finally came home, he was able to crawl into bed and just *sleep*. He didn't want to let go of that feeling this morning, and happily drifted in and out of consciousness.

"Donnie have a good night?" Vic says.

"You'll have to ask when you see him," Wyatt says. "An hour in, and he disappeared."

Vic chuckles, remembering how the parties were back in his day. "Alone?"

"Not alone, no," Wyatt says, grinning.

"And how was *your* night?" Karen says, leaning in a little too close.

Wyatt laughs. "Mine was a couple of beers and then coming home to you," he says, wrapping an arm around her waist and squeezing her to his side.

"You came back awful late for just a couple of beers," she says.

"I'm the president," Wyatt says. "I have to hang around, make sure my face is seen. You know how these boys can be – I stick around all night for Dale but not for Donnie, how's that gonna look?"

"Mm," Karen says, then slips out of his arm, but not in an aggressive way. "Do you want anything to eat? Eggs?"

Wyatt sees that his father has had eggs already, and bacon, remnants of them scattered around his plate with smears of ketchup and yolk. Wyatt isn't hungry. He checks the time. It's closer to lunch now than breakfast. "No, I'm good. I need to get along to the clubhouse."

"Are the rest of them gonna be awake yet?" Karen says. "Seeing as how they probably all had more than just a couple of beers."

"They probably slept there," Wyatt says. He looks at his father. "You coming in today?"

Vic shakes his head. "Not today. I'm gonna take some painkillers and spend the day in my easy chair with a whisky. I don't feel like driving. I don't have it in me."

When Wyatt was a boy, his father was the biggest man he'd ever seen. When Wyatt was a teenager, Vic remained the biggest man he'd ever seen. It stayed so until Wyatt was thirty-seven and he started to realise his father was becoming an old man when the arthritis struck. He'd already stopped lifting weights every day at that point, and he was getting softer around the middle. After his diagnosis, he stopped lifting entirely. Over time, his muscle has withered away, replaced by fat. He remains a big man, just not the bull that Wyatt grew up with and admired. Vic has become old. He's lost his strength, his bike, even his club, remaining only as a nostalgic relic to whom the rest of the boys pay their due respects. His glory days are behind him. Without his son and his daughter-in-law, he'd have nothing. His wife, Wyatt's mother, died when Wyatt was still a boy.

Perhaps most jarring of all for Vic, he's lost his independence. He doesn't live by himself. He lives here, with Wyatt and Karen, the garage of their home converted for him with a bed, a refrigerator, a record player, and a television. When not at the clubhouse, he spends most of his days in there listening to Lynyrd Skynyrd, AC/DC, Eagles, and The Doors. Karen checks in on him, pours him a fresh drink or brings him a sandwich.

Wyatt drinks more coffee. "You said you don't feel up to driving?"

Vic nods.

"Just today, right?"

Vic rolls his eyes. "Right."

"Other days, you're fine, right?"

"Yes."

"Don't keep rolling your eyes – you know why I'm asking."

Vic nods. "I know. It's important. It's better I rest up now, and make sure I'm good for when we make our move."

This sounds sensible to Wyatt. "Okay. But if you're feeling worse, you let me know. We can't be let down at the last minute."

"I know, I know," Vic says, sounding agitated. It's hard for him to be old. To be weaker. To be *ill* and a potential liability. "I know my limits. I know what I can do. I know how to sail the goddamn boat. And more than that, I've got my pills. I've got my injections. I'll be ready. When the time comes, I'll be good to go."

Wyatt lightens the mood. "Make sure you are, old man. Because if you ain't, I'm leaving you behind."

Vic snorts, but he's smirking, too. "Then I'll come swimming after you."

"Oh, that right? You're gonna *swim* after me?"

"You don't wanna see it happen, believe me."

"Oh, no, I think I *do*. I think maybe I *will* leave you behind just so I can see it happen."

"I won't let him leave you behind, Vic," Karen says. "Even though *I* want to see you swim like that, too. Maybe you can show us when we're down south."

"If you can drag me away from the beach long enough,

I'll show you whatever you wanna see," Vic says, a gleam in his eye.

"Don't flirt with my wife right in front of me," Wyatt says. "Makes me worry what you might be saying when I'm not here."

Vic and Karen both laugh. When Karen turns her back to load the dishwasher, Vic addresses his son in a lower tone. "Logan still there when you left last night?"

Wyatt nods. "I told Glen to keep an eye on him. I ain't heard from Glen so I assume there's nothing worth passing on."

"It was just a party," Vic points out.

"Exactly. No business. I wasn't so concerned about him last night."

Wyatt drains the coffee then heads for the front door. Karen follows him. After he's pulled on his boots and his kutte, he pulls her in for a longer, deeper kiss, out of view of his father.

Wyatt first met Karen in high school. They'd dated on and off a little back then, fooled around some, but they didn't get together properly until they were both thirty. She and a group of friends were at the FRD clubhouse. They'd been invited along by Brad Smithson, Wyatt's best friend and his former sergeant-at-arms. Wyatt and Karen remembered each other very well. They got married a few years later. Karen is a loyal wife. She doesn't badger him for his various infidelities, nor does she hassle him about his timekeeping – sometimes Wyatt can disappear for up to days at a time, always for business, or on a ride with the boys. She didn't complain when his father was moved in. She understands FRD business, and sometimes she helps out with it. Unofficially, she *is* a Forever Road Dog.

Of course, under the by-laws written up by Vic himself, she could never be an *actual* Road Dog. No women.

Wyatt prefers her as his wife, as opposed to an associate and brother.

Karen has kept herself in shape. She works out daily, and looks better than women half her age. Her hair is long and dark, the occasional white hairs kept at bay with dye.

Wyatt's mind begins to wander. Instead of remembering those early days with his wife, as well as their more recent escapades, his thoughts begin to shift. It's his own fault. He remembered him. He was such a big part of Wyatt and Karen's reunion. His thoughts turn to Brad Smithson.

"What's wrong?" Karen says, looking into his face with concern. "Where've you gone?"

Brad was killed a few years ago, his body left to rot at the side of the road under the hot Texas sun. Wyatt has never stopped looking for his killer. He's heard stories of the man over the years, and has even seen his name mentioned on the news a couple of times. By the time the Forever Road Dogs go to where he's been, he's already gone.

"Nothing," Wyatt says. "Just remembering an old friend is all."

Karen doesn't press him. Wyatt pulls on his helmet and leaves the house. His Harley is parked on the driveway. It stands outside the garage where his father lives and sleeps, and next to the truck that they share. Wyatt climbs on and revs it up. It's loud. There aren't any neighbours to annoy. Wyatt's home is secluded, an old ranch house on ten private acres, obscured from the road by a line of trees that offer privacy. He heads for the road now and goes to the clubhouse.

Decades back, the clubhouse used to be a mechanic's

garage. A friend of Vic's owned it. He'd worked there for a couple of years. When the friend was looking to retire, Vic bought it from him. He gutted the building. Expanded it. Installed a bar, and lounge area, and a meeting room for FRD business. Officially, the building is still a garage. People in town know who the FRD are, and they know better than to roll up looking for an oil change. The FRD work on their own bikes, but it's been a long, long time since a paying customer last had their vehicle serviced.

The outside of the clubhouse is showing signs of last night's party, though the prospect is out with a trash bag in hand, clearing up the crushed cans and emptied bottles. He waves as Wyatt rides past him, but Wyatt ignores him. He doesn't even know his name. Once upon a time, he used to bother learning the names of their prospects. Only one in ten ever graduate to becoming an actual Forever Road Dog. Wyatt stopped caring. If the prospect ever graduates, *then* Wyatt will learn his name.

Of course, if that day comes for the current prospect, Wyatt doesn't expect he'll still be in the area. Maybe he'll get to know him better via phone and video calls.

The inside of the clubhouse does not have the post-party low energy that Wyatt was expecting. Instead, there is a hum of tension. Glen Hurley, his vice-president, and Kurt Holyfield, his sergeant-at-arms, are sitting at the bar, nursing a hangover beer. They turn when they hear Wyatt enter. They don't look hung over. He's seen them hung over. He'd recognise it. This is something different. They look solemn.

Instantly, Wyatt is on alert. From where he stands, he looks around the rest of the clubhouse. On a sofa he sees Donnie, the birthday boy himself, sitting forward with his head in his hands. Others sit near him, or stand close by, arms folded and brows furrowed. He sees Dale McKenna leaning against the wall, chewing on a thumbnail.

"What the hell's happened?" Wyatt says. The women that were present last night have all gone. Wyatt isn't sure how this makes him feel. Ordinarily, they'd still be hanging around, sleeping off the effects of the night, stumbling on their heels with their hair wild. His mind jumps to the worst-case scenario. Someone got carried away. One of the girls got hurt. Maybe she died – an overdose, or at one of his boys' hands. Wyatt grits his teeth. "Don't tell me someone's dead."

Mark Logan is first to stand and answer him. He's as solemn as the others, but he's more alert. He's not slouched over, holding his head in his hands or chewing on his fingernails, looking like he fears the worst. "We just found out," he says. "We tried to call you. Figure you must've been riding over here."

Wyatt glances at his phone. He has six missed calls. The time stamps all correspond with his ride. "You just found out *what*?" he says. "What's happened?"

Glen clears his throat. "Nate," he says.

"Nate? Nathan Wood? What about him?"

"He got in a fight," Logan says, scratching at the side of his chin through his blond beard. "He got arrested in Utah. Cops are holding him."

"They found the meth, Wyatt," Kurt says.

Wyatt feels the world fall out from under him. His stomach sinks. His head spins. He bites his lip to focus up, and as the world settles he's surprised to find that his knees haven't buckled. That he's standing firm, resolute. That he hasn't shown any weakness. "Well," he says. "Shit."

"Uh-huh," Glen says, and he and Kurt nod in unison.

"How'd you find out?"

"He called us," Logan says.

"And no one else knows?" Wyatt says. They know who he's referring to.

"Just us," Logan says.

The dumb son of a bitch, Wyatt thinks, wishing Nathan was here now so he could punch him in his stupid face. The FRD do not need drama right now. They need things to be smooth. They don't need any kind of bullshit.

He runs his hands down his face and tugs at his beard. "He tell you what happened? In fact, scratch that – it doesn't fucking matter. I don't even care. I'm gonna go make a call."

He feels their eyes upon him. They're all waiting for him to erupt. They're surprised at his calm. Wyatt walks away. He goes to the right, into the club room. He closes the door. He takes a seat at the head of the table at which they conduct their business. His phone is still in his hand. He doesn't make the call straight away. He composes himself. Breathes deep. His eyes look to the left, to the wall, the framed pictures there of Brad Smithson, Kelvin Maynard, Willie Pence, Matt Harding, and 'Heavy' Henry Harding. Five dead brothers. Below them, stuck to the wall with a knife, is another picture. This one is not framed. A man in Army uniform – the only picture of him they were able to find online. There are stains on the picture where it has been spat upon, and gouges where his cheeks have been slashed. The eyes are X'd out. Damage has been done to the picture, but they all know the face. They've all committed it to memory, just as they've committed his name. The man who single-handedly killed the five brothers whose pictures hang in memoriam above him.

Tom Rollins.

Wyatt stares at the picture. Even with the X'd eyes, right

now he can feel it looking back at him. Mocking him. Wyatt balls his fists. He squeezes the phone. He turns away from Rollins and he dials a number that always fills him with dread.

He places a call through to Austin Myers.

7

"Heard you had a busy night last night."

Tom turns away from the river, looks back to see Lyle approaching him.

"Or should I say this morning?" Lyle says.

"It was a late one, that's for sure," Tom says.

"Surprised you made it out here at all."

"Wouldn't miss it for the world."

Lyle grins. "I appreciate your work ethic, Tom, but in light of what went down, I wouldn't have held it against you if I'd had to give you a day off. You slept yet?"

"Deputy Roach gave me a ride back to the bar," Tom says. "I was able to get a few hours before I needed to be out here."

"You're a damn machine." Lyle laughs, shaking his head. "Give me a few more like you, and hell, I don't know what I'd do. Probably have to expand or something. Buy another couple of boats."

Tom looks toward the nets. "You'd get sick of all the fights they'd keep getting into."

Lyle stands beside him at the railing, holding it in both hands.

"Who told you, anyway?" Tom says. "Valerie?"

Lyle nods. "Me and Val, we go way back. But I would've heard it one way or the other. Davenport is a small town, and what you did was a big story. Two guys, with knives?" Lyle whistles low, impressed. "And you reckon they were gonna try and rape those two girls?"

"That's what it seemed like."

Lyle looks disgusted. "Scum," he says, spitting out into the water. "Goddamn degenerates. Well, at least this story has a happy ending. Least you were there to see to that."

Tom nods, but he's not so sure this is the end of the story. After what Laila and Emma told him about being regularly followed and watched, he thinks it could be just the beginning.

When they take the boat back in, there is no sign of the two ecologists in the water today. Instead, as he gets off the boat, he spots Laila waiting at the road, standing beside her car. Tom says goodbye to Lyle and the rest of the crew and goes to her.

"I probably smell of fish," Tom says, stopping six paces back. "I apologise for that."

"You don't need to apologise," Laila says. "I don't mind the smell. And besides, it would be real silly for you to be apologising when I came out here to thank you, from me and Emma both."

"You don't need to thank me," Tom says. "Especially not when it's for doing the right thing."

"Uh-huh, but just because it was the right thing doesn't mean that everyone would have done it."

Tom notices that the car is empty. There's no sign of Emma. "How's she doing?" he says.

"She was shaken up," Laila says. "I gave her the day off. Truth be told, I was a little shaken myself. Decided to take the day off, too. Imagine my surprise when I went by the bar and Valerie told me you were out on the boat."

"I wasn't tired," Tom says.

Laila smiles. She looks beyond him, to the river and the boat. "Hey," she says, looking back at him like a thought has just occurred to her. "Would you like to go and get something to eat with me? My treat. As a thank you."

"I told you, you don't need to thank me."

"And I heard you, but I'd still like to."

There's still a few hours before Tom has to work at the bar. He looks into Laila's face, at her cheekbones and her sparkling eyes. He remembers how she laughed last night, covering her mouth with her hand like she was trying to keep it in. "All right," he says. "And I'd like to take you up on it. But I'll need to shower first, and change my clothes."

"Oh, of course," Laila says, playful. "You didn't think I was going to take you out looking and smelling like *that*, did you?"

8

Laila told Tom where to meet. After he'd showered and changed, he drove across town to the diner where she said she'd meet him. Tom drives a Ford. He's had it a while now. Since he was in Detroit. Cars don't always last very long for him. They tend to get totalled. He never gets attached. Just needs them to get him from A to B. As Tom gets out of the car, he sees her through the window, sitting in a booth, sipping from a soda. She waves at him.

"Been here long?" Tom says when he reaches the table.

"Five minutes," Laila says. "I would have ordered you a drink, but I wasn't sure what you'd want."

It doesn't take long for the waitress to come, and Tom asks for a water. He glances around the rest of the diner while she's gone. It's quiet. It's too early for the dinner rush.

"I don't usually come here at this time of day," Laila says, watching him. "It's normally busier than this. Maybe I should start coming earlier. It's easier to get a table, and the service is faster."

"You come here often?"

"Only sometimes. Friday nights, usually. Me and Emma. An end of work week treat. I pay for Emma. I'm going to do the same today, for you, and I'm not open for discussion so forget about it right now. Like I said, this is with my thanks."

Tom holds up his hands. "I promise I won't," he says. "You seem fond of Emma."

"She reminds me of my sister."

The waitress returns with Tom's water. While she's at the table, she takes their food order. Tom quickly looks at the menu. He gets a steak. Laila orders a salad.

"The service here *is* fast when there's hardly anyone in," Laila says when the waitress is gone.

"Are you a vegetarian?" Tom says.

"Most of the time I'm a vegan," Laila says. "But it's hard to stick to, especially when you're eating out, and sometimes I really just want cheese, or eggs. It kind of comes with the profession, though. Emma isn't quite there yet. She'd probably order a steak, too."

"Vegan, huh?" Tom says.

"Don't sound so surprised. What, if you'd heard in advance would you expect me to be pasty and skinny? That's a common misconception."

"I had no expectations," Tom says. He drinks some water. There's ice in the glass. It's cold against his lips, and feels good after a day on the boat, standing under the hot sun.

"You've cleaned up well," Laila says. There's a playful gleam in her eyes as she says this, then adds, "You got the fish smell out."

"I made sure I scrubbed extra hard," Tom says. "Since I knew I was meeting up with someone with such a discernible nose."

"I've been told many times that my nose is my best feature."

"Oh really? Not your cheekbones?"

"What, these old things?" Laila sucks in her cheeks in an exaggerated pout and turns her head side to side. She lets them out and laughs, covering her mouth with her hand.

Tom smiles. "Or maybe it's your eyes," he says. "Or maybe it's the way you cover your mouth like that whenever you laugh."

She glances down at her hand. "That's more of an action than a feature. Is that something I do a lot?"

Tom shrugs. "It's something I've noticed. Don't get self-conscious – I like it."

"I'm pleased to hear that, because until right now I didn't know it was something I did."

Tom looks out of the window. It's a regular habit. He checks the parking lot. Studies the cars. Commits their makes, models, and colours to memory. Makes sure they're all empty. He looks beyond the parking lot, too, to the road. Checks that no one has pulled over there and could be looking this way. No one is.

"What are you looking at?" Laila says.

"I'm just making sure no one's following you right now," he says.

"I haven't noticed anyone today."

Tom nods. "I've been thinking about what you said. About you and Emma being watched. We never had a chance to go into more detail. Why do you think that's happening? Do you know? Do you have any theories?"

The waitress returns with their food. She puts down their plates. Tom's steak comes with a jacket potato. He looks at Laila's salad.

"Should I have maybe ordered something else?" he says.

"No, no, of course not," she says. "I don't judge what people eat. I don't preach. If you ever hear me preaching, tell me straight away and I'll cut it out."

They eat. Between mouthfuls, when she's done chewing and swallowing, Laila speaks. "I work for a nonprofit called Mississippi Nature. Have you heard of them?"

Tom shakes his head.

"They cover the full length of the Mississippi River, from the mouth at Lake Itasca in Minnesota, all the way down to Louisiana, where it flows into the Gulf of Mexico. I've been in Davenport for three years now. Emma has been with me for fourteen months."

"You said you first started to notice these watchers and followers a couple of months back."

"That's right. Frankly, I'm surprised they didn't turn up sooner. Or maybe they did, and we just didn't notice. Maybe they *didn't* want us to notice then, and now they're ready to make their point. It's clear they were going to try and do something last night."

"Any idea of who *they* are?" Tom says.

Laila nods. "We think so. I'm getting to that. Have you ever heard of DuLac Chemicals?"

"No."

"As the name would suggest, they produce large quantities of chemicals for distribution to other businesses who in turn use them in the manufacturing of other products. Places that produce fuel products, or dyes, washing liquids – that kind of thing. The thing is, they don't have a great environmental track record. There's been spills and leaks from their factories. They've failed health and safety checks. But the thing is, they never get more than a slap on the wrist.

Despite their failings, they've never been at any kind of risk of closure."

"If they're as large a corporation as you're making them sound, that doesn't surprise me," Tom says.

"Well, unfortunately, yes. Their CEO, Martin DuLac, he's a very wealthy man. A billionaire. Any time that someone has protested them, or filed a report against them, the reason it falls quiet is likely because he's throwing around his cash. Paying people off. Bribing them into silence. No one's able to bring them to account. Every time they've had a health and safety issue, like a leak, their spokeswoman Carol Hardinge releases a statement about their endeavours to do better, and their guarantees that nothing like this will ever happen again – and then six months or a year later, one of their factories springs a new leak into a field, or a lake – once even into a town's water supply."

"That sounds serious," Tom says. "Sounds like it would be a big deal."

"And it would have been, except can you imagine who they must have paid off to keep that quiet? Mayors, councillors, even the local press and law enforcement. Barely anyone knows about it, and yet people are dying."

"From the water?"

Laila nods solemnly. "It's been a few years since the spill into the water supply happened, but now people are starting to get sick. Stomach issues, gastro-intestinal. People are developing rapidly spreading cancers. And yet no one knows, and no one can get the word out, because the authorities in that town are subduing the flow of news."

"But Mississippi Nature have found out about it?"

"Mississippi Nature launched their own investigation about seven months ago, and this is where it ties into Davenport. A lot of our funding has been put toward this investigation. Truth be told, most of it's going toward that as opposed to conservation right now, but this is important. We've hired private detectives, lawyers – even hackers."

"Hackers? Mississippi Nature isn't concerned about the legality of that?"

"These are desperate times. We need to do what we can. We're attacking a tank with a twig here – we need to do what we can. We know DuLac Chemicals don't concern themselves with legalities."

"Okay. So, what happened seven months ago?"

"That's when we found out DuLac Chemicals have gained the planning permission to build a factory here, right on the banks of the Mississippi."

The pieces are falling into place for Tom. "And you've been protesting it ever since."

"Every way we're able," Laila says. "We've issued circulars. We've lodged complaints and protests. Mississippi Nature is investigating the DuLac company's negligent history in the hope we can bring a case against them and cancel their application. Could you begin to imagine the damage they could do to this area? The untold damage they could wreak upon the local ecosystem? And it's not just local – they're planning on building right on the banks of the river. If they have another leak it'll go directly into the water, and from there it'll be carried down to the Gulf of Mexico, and from there?" She shakes her head. Laila speaks passionately. This is clearly something she cares a great deal about.

"The men watching you," Tom says, "the men following you, maybe even the two men from last night – you think they're from DuLac Chemicals?"

"That's what we believe," Laila says. "Emma and I are

right here, on the ground. We're the front line. We're the ones waging this fight directly. And now they're trying to intimidate us. To scare us away. Last night, who knows how far they would have taken things? They were trying to shut us up, because they know that's the only option they have. They can't pay us off. We can't be bought."

Tom finds his eyes drawn to the window again, once again checking the parking lot and beyond. There's nothing to see, but her story has raised his paranoia.

"If that's the case," he says, "I doubt the two from last night will be the end of it. You know that, right?"

Laila purses her lips, and Tom can see that she does. "They scare me," she says. "I won't deny it. Of course they do. But they won't scare me away. This is about more than just me."

"That's admirable," Tom says, "but you're going to have to keep your eyes wide and your head on a swivel. Don't take chances with anything. Anyone gives you a bad feeling, you need to listen to that feeling." He looks at her, worried for her, and for Emma. "You still have my number. Anything concerns you, you call me. Don't hesitate. Don't overthink it. Don't doubt yourself. Just call me."

Laila manages to smile at him. "You planning on joining us on the front lines?"

"You keep smiling at me like that, I think you could ask me to do just about anything."

9

Despite last night's excitement, and the stories that have no doubt spread through town off the back of it, the bar is surprisingly quiet.

Tom cleans glasses at the far end of the bar. There is no Laila and Emma tonight. There are no suspicious patrons he feels the need to keep an eye on. Instead, there are two occupied tables, one booth, and a friend of Valerie's at the other end of the counter, locked in conversation with her. Nine people total, not including Tom and Valerie.

He left the diner with Laila two hours ago. He walked her to her car, though it wasn't parked far from his own. Before they parted, Tom once again looked the area over.

"You don't have to worry about me, Tom," Laila said, seeing what he was doing. "I'm capable. I can take care of myself."

"I'm sure you can, but don't take any risks."

"I won't." Laila opened her car door. She patted her back pocket, where her phone was. "If I see anything I don't like the look of, I'll call you."

Over the last two hours, since they said goodbye and drove their separate ways, Tom has thought about Laila more than once. About her smile, and the sparkle in her eyes. About the way she patted her back pocket, and the way she popped her hip to do so. Tom grins, remembering. From the look on her face, he knew she'd done it on purpose. The action was likely designed to stick in his mind the way it has. Other than when they were talking serious matters, such as DuLac Chemicals, their conversation had leaned toward the flirtatious. She'd said she wanted to thank him for last night, but their eating together had felt almost like a date.

Tom dries his hands and serves a customer. Time passes. He watches the door, but no one else comes in. The bar remains quiet. Through the windows he looks out into the parking lot, but it's devoid of activity.

After a while, Valerie comes to join him. "Slow one," she says.

Tom nods.

"It happens," Valerie says with a shrug. "Can't ever judge it. One off night isn't going to make me worry just yet. I've gotta say, I *am* surprised though that the good people of Davenport wouldn't want to come here and hear the story of last night from the man himself, because I can guarantee you that the story has already spread."

"I don't doubt it," Tom says. "Lyle said as much earlier."

"I've lived in Davenport a long, long time. It's a quiet place, and I like that, and that's why I stick around. Everyone else who lives here is the same, I reckon. But we all love a little excitement now and then, you know? So when something happens, we all hear about it, and we're all eager to learn more."

Tom doesn't say anything. He's been in plenty of small towns. He grew up in one. He knows how it is.

"Maybe they just don't want to make it obvious," Valerie says. "They could come out en masse tomorrow night, so be ready for that. How are you feeling, anyway? You good? You don't look tired."

"I'm fine."

"You're a machine, is what you are."

Tom laughs. "Lyle said the same thing."

"Well, it's true! I keep waiting for you to burn out. How do you do it? What's your secret?"

"Healthy living."

Valerie looks him over. "I can believe that. I heard they both had knives. That right?"

Tom nods.

Valerie's eyes are wide. "Jesus," she says, under her breath. "Did they cut you? You look okay, but I can believe you'd hide it and not say a word."

"No, they didn't cut me."

"And you managed to disarm them both?"

Tom nods.

"What happened to them? To the weapons, I mean."

"Deputies took them."

Valerie nods. "And the men? They're in custody now, right?"

"Right."

"They're lucky you disarmed them before the cops turned up. If they were waving around knives when the sheriff's boys turned up they would've shot them."

"Then maybe I should've let them keep them," Tom says.

"Where'd you learn to fight, anyway? I always get the feeling there's a lot about yourself that you've never told me."

"I'm just trying to keep the mystery alive, Valerie. I don't want things to get stale between us."

She laughs and hits his arm playfully. She looks the bar over. A table of three are leaving, waving as they go. "I think I might get away myself, if that's all right with you. If you're okay to lock up. Unlike you, I don't live so healthily, and I need my beauty sleep."

"Sure," Tom says.

"If anyone comes bursting in with knives or swords tonight, don't call for me. I won't be any good."

"I'd never dream of putting you in danger like that, Valerie. I thought you'd give me more credit than that."

She hits him on the arm again then calls goodnight to her customers, and leaves the bar to walk around to her house at the back.

Another hour goes by. As the minutes tick off, the bar gradually empties out until Tom is alone. He wipes down the tables, and the counter. He clears away the glasses and puts the empty bottles into the recycling. He vacuums the carpeting, but since it was such a slow night it doesn't take long. Likewise when he mops the floor behind the bar.

Everything done, everything in its place, he turns off the lights and leaves the bar, locking the door after him.

It's quiet outside, and there is a chill in the night air. It's eleven at night, and Tom can't remember the last time he left the bar so early. Usually people will cling on until the very end. Long after midnight is when he's used to locking the door.

He walks around the back, to his room, enjoying the cold and the quiet. When he gets inside, he'll go straight to bed, and try to catch up on some of the hours he missed out on last night.

He doesn't make it to the bed.

As he puts the key in the lock, he feels a blow rock him from behind, a shot from something harder than a fist burying itself in his lower back, into his right kidney, the pain reverberating through his whole body. Tom battles to keep his feet, though his knees buckle beneath him. He falls against the door, trying to remain upright.

Then, a hand slams flat into the back of his skull and his forehead bounces off the door, hard. A trickle of blood runs down between Tom's eyes. He's spun around and whatever struck him in the lower back now buries itself under his ribs, emptying his lungs. A fist connects with his jaw from the right.

Tom can't keep his feet. He feels himself falling. Blood is in his eyes. Blinking it out, he sees three pairs of legs. They kick and stomp at him. Tom tries to cover up, to protect his head. He kicks back at them, but isn't able to connect. A boot heel breaks through his arms, plants itself on his cheek and bounces his head off the ground. Tom feels sick. Everything blurs.

The kicking stops. Tom tastes blood. Someone crouches down and takes a handful of hair at the back of his head and raises him up, twisting him so they can look into his face.

Tom remains on his side, his right arm turning numb under him, pain radiating up and down his body. His vision clears enough for him to make out the face of the man looking down at him. Tom has never seen him before, nor the two men flanking him, currently popping their knuckles and rolling their heads round on their necks.

"You with me?" the man holding him says. He has piercing blue eyes, and a greying crewcut. He slaps Tom's cheek. "There you are. Now listen up, and listen close. This is for involving yourself in things that don't concern you. Last night, the two men you had locked up, they're mine. Nobody touches my men. If somebody does, if they involve themselves in *our* business, then this is what happens to them. I feel like we've made ourselves very clear here, friend."

Tom spits blood.

"I'll take that to mean you understand. If you know what's good for you, stay away from Laila North and Emma Killick. If you ever stick your nose in again, we'll cut the fucking thing off." The man leans down closer. The corner of his mouth is twisted upward in a smirk. He's enjoying himself. "This is your one warning, friend. Next time, there will be no conversation."

He lets go of Tom's head. Tom manages to stop his skull from hitting the ground again. The three men turn and leave. Tom's head is swimming. His vision blurs again. He sees the men walking away, and then he sees nothing.

10

Nathan Wood has returned to Texas. Wyatt has summoned him, and has sent Dale, Logan, and Donnie out to escort him in directly. He waits for him in the clubhouse, sitting at the head of the table and smoking cigarette after cigarette. He's impatient. He's not sure how he's going to react when Nathan walks through the door. He's not sure what he's going to say. All he *does* know is that he's not happy, and neither are the people they're in business with.

There's a knock at the door. Glen pokes his head in. "They're coming through the gate now," he says.

Wyatt nods. "Send Nate straight in. No fucking around. I wanna talk to him *now*."

Glen nods and slips away. Wyatt blows smoke and stubs out the cigarette. He gets to his feet and paces, waiting. He soon sits back down. There is a tightly wound energy inside him. It tingles in his toes and his fingertips. It crackles across his skin like electricity. His hands fidget and he wants another cigarette, but he forces himself to wait.

Then there is a knock at the door. Nathan enters. He's alone. He's smiling.

"Take a seat," Wyatt says, sounding surprisingly calm to his own ears. While he's glad to have Nathan back, he's not happy to see the smile on his face. "I see your bail was paid."

Nathan drops into a seat close to Wyatt and nods. He blows air. "Came straight home," he says, then laughs. "Thanks for that, by the way. I appreciate it. I didn't wanna spend another second in a fucking Utah jail cell."

Wyatt stares at him. Nathan is too laid back. He slouches in the chair and there's a grin on his face, like this is all some big joke. It's no laughing matter. He's messed up. He's messed up big time.

Wyatt keeps his emotions in check. When he talks, his voice remains calm and level. "You wanna tell me what happened up there?"

Nathan pulls a face and waves his hands like it's no big deal. "Ah, just some bullshit."

"Uh-huh. What happened, though? Tell me."

"It was just a fight, that's all. It got blown way out of proportion."

"Who started it?"

Nathan hesitates. He sees the way that Wyatt stares at him. He's starting to doubt himself now. He clears his throat and straightens in the chair. "I'd just stopped for something to eat. That was all."

"Who started the fight?"

"Well...I mean, I guess – I did. It wasn't ever a big deal. Hell, and I was outnumbered, but it was still me that got carted away in the back of a cop car –"

"When they took you away, they didn't care so much about the fight anymore, did they?"

Nathan falls silent. "I guess not."

"No, by then they were more focussed on the meth you were transporting across state lines."

Nathan sits back and sucks his teeth, his eyes casting to the side, refusing to make contact.

"Why the hell would you start a fight, Nathan?"

Nathan shrugs.

"Look at me when I'm talking to you."

Wyatt's voice is icy cold, and Nathan jumps back to attention.

"I'm going to ask you once," Wyatt says. "What were you thinking?"

"Wyatt, Prez, listen – I'm sorry. Really. I am."

Wyatt stares.

Nathan stammers. "I – I wasn't fucking thinking, and that's the problem. There was this chick, and man, you should've seen her legs. You know how it is, right? And you know I'm a leg man. And she was just sitting there in her Daisy Dukes, and her boyfriend was this real asshole, a real piece of work, and I was just trying to be friendly, y'know? And, I mean, you know how it can get on the road when you're all on your own. I was just looking for some company."

Wyatt stares.

Nathan withers. He feels obliged to continue. "It was a stupid mistake – how was I supposed to know the cops were gonna look the bike over? The one that moved it, he must've been a rider. He must've been familiar with it, cos he knew like *that*." He clicks his fingers. "He knew something was wrong. It must have been the weight. But what are the fucking chances of that, right?"

Wyatt takes a deep breath. Nathan stops talking. "Do you have any idea of what you've done?"

Nathan doesn't answer.

"They paid your bail, Nathan, and they called in their lawyers, but they weren't happy about it." Wyatt leans closer. "They've got good lawyers, man, but even they might not be able to stop this from turning federal. You were crossing state lines. Do you get how serious that is? I never took you for a moron, Nate – have I overestimated you?"

Again, Nathan is not looking at him. Wyatt slams the flat of his hand down on the table, causing him to jolt in his seat.

"We're dealing with serious people," Wyatt says once he has his full attention again. "We can't afford any careless fuck-ups like this, and they won't tolerate them. Do you get that? You've nearly jeopardised this whole operation, all because you were horny and bored. You get how fucking stupid that is? And it's not just the operation, Nate, it's our *lives*. You've put all of us in danger."

Nathan frowns at this.

"Oh yeah," Wyatt says. "It's that serious. They can use us to transport their meth. We're a means to an end. But they don't *need* us. If we can't hold up our end of the arrangement, you think they're gonna keep us around?"

"We're Road Dogs, man," Nathan says, suddenly defiant. "We ain't scared of anyone."

Wyatt leans back. "Times change."

Nathan doesn't understand. He looks confused. "What are you talking about, man?"

Wyatt doesn't tell him. It wouldn't be right for the president to tell him how their business associates could crush them like bugs. It wouldn't be right for Wyatt to tell him that he *is* scared. Everyone in the FRD who needs to know about the true seriousness of their situation already does.

And while Wyatt may be afraid, he remains defiant. As defiant as Nathan wants to be.

"We've been summoned to Mississippi," Wyatt says. "To meet with our associates in person. It's been specified that we bring *you* with us."

Nathan doesn't look surprised. He doesn't protest or ask questions. He understands all too well. He's to be reprimanded. He shrugs one shoulder. "Okay," is all he says.

Wyatt remains surprised at how in control he's remained throughout this meeting, when in reality he'd like nothing more than to bust up Nathan's face and try to knock some sense into his stupid skull.

"All right then," he says. "You'll be leaving in a couple of days. You'll ride over with Glen and the rest. I've already told him you'll be sticking close to him until then. You don't go anywhere or do anything without his say-so."

Nathan tilts his head. "You make it sound like we're all going there separately."

Wyatt nods, once.

"You ain't riding with us?"

"I'll already be there," Wyatt says. "But you don't need to worry about that. You can leave now. Go and find Glen. You're his problem now."

11

Tom hurts, but he's undeterred.

The warning from his attackers wasn't enough to take him out. If anything, the beating has gotten him more involved, and fuelled a determination inside him.

Valerie found him, drifting in and out of consciousness, at the base of his door. She managed to rouse him, but before she could call for an ambulance Tom stopped her. He didn't want an ambulance. By then, he was wide awake. "Just get me some painkillers," he said. His head was throbbing, as were his limbs. His hands shook with the trauma. He managed to make it to the shower and wash the blood away. Cleaned up, he didn't look so bad. Multiple contusions on his limbs and torso, and some swelling in his face where the boot heel connected with him. Blood was caked in his hair, too, from when the boot stomped his head and it bounced off the ground. He had to pick gravel out of the wound. When he pissed, there was blood in it. Twisting to check his lower back on the right-hand side in the mirror, he could see the bruising there was worst of all.

But he was alive, and he was awake, and he had the face of the man who warned him off in his mind.

Valerie protested when he said he was going out. She'd aided him into his room and hung around while he washed and changed his clothes in the bathroom. She stood near the door, unable to sit, wringing her hands. "I really think you need to see a doctor, Tom," she said. "And if you won't, then you should at least rest."

"I don't need to rest," Tom said. *I need to find the men who did this*. He didn't say that last part out loud. He didn't want to worry her further, or have to deal with her protestations. "I don't need a doctor."

"You could have a concussion."

Tom didn't think he did. His vision had cleared, and his headache had receded into a dull throbbing. He hadn't thrown up, and didn't feel like he would, either. "If I start to feel too bad, I'll go to the hospital. How's that sound?"

He could tell from Valerie's face that it didn't sound too good to her, but it was clear to her that she wasn't going to be able to talk him out of anything. He grabbed his backpack and took it out with him. He didn't want Valerie to see him retrieve his Beretta and KA-BAR. Once in the car, he concealed both weapons on his person. He might not need them, but it's better safe than sorry.

Tom drives. He's called Lyle and told him he won't be on the boat today. His hands have stopped shaking. There are various aches in his body, especially his lower back, but the pain in his head has gone, replaced instead by a simmering anger. He goes to the county jail.

The jail is in the sheriff's station. It's only an hour away from Davenport. It's not a big building. Atlas County is not large, encompassing only a handful of small towns. The sheriff's department employs less than half a dozen people. Tom knows all of the deputies. Sometimes they stop by the bar while out of uniform, and sometimes they swing by while in uniform to make sure everything's okay.

Tom parks and heads inside. It looks like a lot of other sheriff stations Tom has been in. This one appears to have last been decorated in the eighties and hasn't felt the need to change anything since then. There's a front desk barring the way through to the rest of the building, and beyond that Tom can see the deputies' desks, and the back office with the sheriff's name on the door. There's another door opposite, leading through to the cells.

Deputy Shaun Roach is on the front desk. Tom has seen and spoken with him recently. Roach and another deputy came to Laila's to arrest the two men. "Rollins," he says, his eyes narrowing as he looks Tom over. "What happened to you? You didn't look this bad the other night."

"I'm fine," Tom says.

"You don't look fine," Roach says before Tom can continue. "There been more trouble at the bar? You here to make a report?"

"Nothing like that," Tom says. "The two men you arrested the other night, at Laila North's house, I'd like to talk to them."

Roach raises an eyebrow. "You want to *talk* to them?"

Tom nods. He holds Roach's eye.

Roach sighs. "Listen, Rollins, you know that's not allowed, right?"

"You can accompany us."

Roach is shaking his head. "Rollins, even if they were still here, I couldn't let you –"

"They're gone?" Tom says.

"Lawyered up. Paid bail." Roach holds out his hands in a what-you-gonna-do gesture.

"So they're gone, just like that?"

"I'm afraid so."

"When?"

"Early this morning." Roach checks the time. "About four hours ago, now."

"That doesn't bother you?"

Again, Roach holds out his hands. "What can we do? They paid bail. Their lawyers came and collected them." Roach looks around suddenly, then leans closer. "I don't know what you're not telling me, Rollins, but I can see from your face, and from the way you walked up here, that something more is going on. You don't wanna tell me, then fine. That's your choice. But whatever you want with those two men, be aware of this at least – I get the impression they've got powerful friends."

"Why do you say that?"

"Because of their lawyers. The two I arrested, they were just a couple of thugs, right? Well, these weren't thug lawyers. They weren't *cheap*, you understand? It didn't strike me that the two we released were paying these lawyers direct."

Tom grits his teeth. The throbbing in his head is coming back. "What about Laila and Emma?" he says. "They pose a risk to them both."

Roach doesn't respond straight away. He's not leaning close anymore. "Rollins, I'm sorry. I wish I could do more, but you know how it is. My hands are tied. All of our hands are tied. The two we arrested, they didn't actually *do* anything to Laila and Emma. They attacked *you*, and that's what we were holding them on. Unless something actually happens to those two women, there's nothing we can do. I hate it, I do, but that's how it is."

Tom doesn't hang around. Without another word, he turns and leaves the station.

12

Tom goes to Laila. He drives straight to her house, but she's not home. Tom goes to her work, and hopes she's in the building and not out in the field. If she's in the field, he's not sure how he'll find her. She has his number, but he doesn't have hers.

He reaches the building and her Honda is parked outside. Tom doesn't feel relief just yet. On foot, he mounts the steps and knocks on the door. The windows have venetian blinds, half-closed, and he can't see inside.

He hears footsteps hurrying to the door. It opens, and Laila is there. She's surprised to see him, but then she smiles, and then she leans forward to closer inspect his face and her smile turns into a frown. "Oh my God, Tom, what happened?"

"Can I come in?"

"Of course." Laila steps aside.

Tom enters the building. It's mostly work spaces, with microscopes and samples. Large refrigerators for storage. There are a couple of desks. One of them is neat and ordered, with papers piled in appropriate trays. The other is messy, papers scattered across it. Tom can guess which desk belongs to whom.

"Are you alone?" Tom says. There's no sign of Emma.

"Just me," Laila says. "Tom, are you going to tell me what's happened?"

Tom goes to a window and peers out through the blinds. "Have you seen anyone today? Anyone watching? Anyone following?"

"No, I haven't seen anyone."

Tom nods and turns back to her. "I took a beating after locking the bar last night. There isn't much more to it than that, but they made reference to the two men that came after you. And they made reference to you and Emma, too."

Laila covers her mouth with a hand. "What did they say?"

"They warned me off. Said to keep my nose out of their business – and that the two of you are part of their business."

"Who were they?"

Tom shakes his head. "I hadn't seen them before."

"They could have been sent by DuLac."

"That's what I'm thinking." He tells her how the two men are no longer in custody. "I'm guessing those lawyers came from DuLac, too."

Laila takes a seat. She stares at the ground, unblinking, her eyes moving left to right while she thinks. Slowly, she looks up. "I take it from your being here, you're not heeding their warning."

Tom forces a grin for her, to calm her, to reassure her. "Do you know how many times I've been warned off? I never listen."

She laughs at this, but it's a small laugh, and she doesn't cover her mouth.

"I'm not going to leave you, okay?" Tom says. "It's clear now that you're being targeted. We need to stick together. And with Emma. Where is she?"

"She's not hanging around," Laila says. "She was shaken after the other night, those two men. Everything happening with them, and with DuLac. I told her to leave town, to take some time off until hopefully things are resolved."

"That could take a long time."

"I know, but I couldn't keep her here with me and put her in danger like that."

Tom remembers how Laila said Emma reminds her of her sister. "Where's she going?"

"To stay with her parents," Laila says. "They live just outside of Memphis."

"Okay, that's good. Has she left already?"

"Not yet. She's going at the weekend. Her parents are going to come down and get her. Emma can't drive. I offered to take her but she said she didn't want to put me out."

"Where is she now? Home?"

Laila nods.

"Call her. Tell her we're coming to get her, and there's no discussion. We're taking her to Memphis. We stick together."

13

Austin Myers sits alone in his office, leaning back in his chair and staring at the ceiling. His hands rest, fingers laced, upon his taut stomach. He's lost in thought. He's been the head of security for DuLac Chemicals for ten years. Austin enjoys his work. He likes being in control. Giving orders, and dealing with problems. Sometimes, though, it feels like he spends a little too much of his time behind the desk. It can be a struggle to stay in shape when he's so sedentary all the time, but he manages it.

However, last night, getting out into the field and laying a beating on that bartender, it put the thrill back into the job. Too often he has to send others to do the dirty work. It's good to remind himself just how it feels to get his own hands dirty. He hasn't had the opportunity for a while.

He doesn't know the bartender's name, only that he was involving himself in DuLac business. Probably trying to impress the two women, Laila and Emma. In fairness to him, he did lay a pretty good beating on two of Austin's men, and they were both touting knives. Maybe the bartender succeeded? Maybe the two women *were* suitably impressed. Not now, though. Not once they get a look at him.

Austin grins to himself. He looks down at his hands. They're unmarked. There was little need to throw punches. Their boots did most of the work, as well as the blackjack he was swinging. No doubt the bartender is struggling to piss straight today. Austin almost laughs.

He has people looking into the man. To find out his name, his background. Just in case. Austin is confident they scared him off last night, but information is power, and it's always worthwhile to know more about your enemy than they know about you.

Due to the nature of his work, Austin is usually on the move, going wherever DuLac Chemicals has an issue. Austin has always worked in security. He started out his career as a lowly night watchman, back in North Dakota. He hated it. It bored him to tears. He was always looking for an opportunity to leave, to branch out. That opportunity finally arrived, though it was a few years coming. A friend of his had been in the Army. He'd made the transition into private security. He got in touch with Austin. Said there was a job opportunity if he wanted it. Austin did. There was training involved. Military-level training. Austin ate it up. Loved every second of it. It finally felt like he was doing something he was born for.

The security they provided wasn't just national. They worked overseas, too. They did a lot of work in Dubai. Austin developed a reputation. People liked him. He was efficient. He got the job done. He was reliable. And, when called for, he was *brutal*.

He enjoyed working private security. It felt like he'd

finally found his calling. Plus, he made a lot of contacts. Became friendly with a lot of people who were ex-military. He keeps in touch with them. Some of them work with him at DuLac.

DuLac Chemicals approached him directly. Austin never applied to work for them. He was headhunted. They told him they liked what they'd heard, and they were prepared to offer him a lot of money for his services. It was a *lot* of money. Austin couldn't turn them down. He brought some of his co-workers with him. Reached out to some of his newer ex-military friends, and invited them to join. Austin can't deny the rush he gets from having ex-military answer to him, a man who has never served a day in his life.

Currently, the new DuLac project in Mississippi sees him occupying an office in downtown Natchez. The building is a converted factory. Outside his door, the floor is an open space, the workers on computers with only dividers between them. There's a small kitchen area in the far corner where they can make coffee or tea, and microwave meals. Austin's office would have most likely been the factory foreman's. It gives him privacy. There's a CCTV screen on his desk, so he can watch the people outside working. They know he's watching. They keep their heads down. They behave themselves. None of Austin's men, his security team, are out there. His men are in the field. They're busy. Outside, at the desks, they're all tech geeks.

Austin's phone rings, tearing him from his blissful reverie. He glances at the screen. It's Terry, one of his men. Terry was with him last night when they went to see the bartender. Since then, Austin has had him watching Laila. He told him to keep his distance after recent events, to make sure he wasn't seen. Terry has been in the trees, lying flat, covered with a camouflage net and watching through binoculars. If he's calling, Austin thinks it must be important. Something could be happening.

He answers the phone. "What have you got for me?"

Terry is in a car. Austin can hear it. "Laila's on the move," he says.

"Where's she gone?"

"Two seconds," Terry says, and Austin hears the car quieten. "We're just parking up round the block, out of view."

Terry is not alone. He's with Kevin. Kevin was also present for last night's beating. Kevin is presumably driving. While Terry was in the trees, watching, Kevin would have stayed with the car.

"She's not alone," Terry says when he comes back on the line.

"Who's she with?"

"The guy from the other night who hurt Marshall and Jeremy," Terry says. "The one we laid a beating on last night. The bartender, fisherman, whatever he is. Guess the message didn't get through."

Austin frowns. They'd beat him good. It should have been more than enough. He doesn't jump to conclusions, though. "What are they doing?"

"They've just pulled up to Emma Killick's place. I'm gonna go check. Figured you'd want an update first. I'll call back."

Austin hangs up the phone and sits forward in his chair. He warned the bartender not to get involved. To stay away from Laila and Emma. Less than twelve hours later, he's with them both.

Austin gets to his feet and goes to his office door. He calls out onto the floor. "Who's working on the barman?"

The geek closest to him gives a start and turns in his chair. "I – I am, sir." He even raises his hand a little like he's in school.

Austin turns his eyes upon him. An icy stare, just to put some discomfort into him. "You got a name yet?"

"Uh, I uh, I had to –"

Austin narrows his eyes. "You had to *what*?"

The geek swallows. "Ms Hardinge e-mailed. She wanted me to –"

"Ms Hardinge isn't here," Austin says, cutting him off. "*I* am. Whatever she asked for, leave it for now. Get me the barman's name, history, anything else you can find. And *fast*. That clear?"

The geek nods. "Yes, sir. I'm right on it." He doesn't turn back to his computer.

Austin claps his hands together, causing him to start. "Then do it!"

The geek spins and starts typing.

Austin shakes his head and closes his office door. He returns to his desk, but Terry hasn't called back yet. He starts pacing, impatient for an update.

Ten minutes pass. After fifteen, Austin starts to think about calling Terry back, in case something has gone wrong. He already knows the damage the bartender is capable of wreaking. If he spotted Kevin and Terry, he might have gone in on them the same way he did the other night with Marshall and Jeremy, the two men he'd assigned to Laila and Emma then.

After twenty minutes, Terry calls back. Austin can hear

that they're on the move again. "That was a longer wait than I was expecting," Austin says.

"Sorry about that, but we had to be careful," Terry says.

"What did you see?"

"They're in Laila's car, the Honda, but the barman's driving. They came to Emma's place and they loaded some bags into the trunk."

"What kind of bags?"

"Travel bags."

Austin perks up at this. "Oh really?"

"Yeah. Couple of suitcases, and a few smaller ones. They loaded them up, then they got back on the road – all three of them this time."

"Sounds like maybe he *did* get the message," Austin says. "And maybe the message has extended to the women, too."

"Could be."

"Where are you now?"

"We're following. They're heading north. We've just left Davenport. You want us to stick with them, or turn around and come back?"

"Stick with them," Austin says. "It sounds like they're leaving town, but I want to know for sure. Follow and see where they go. But Terry, keep your distance. Don't let them see you. We know this guy's observant."

"Got it," Terry says. "We'll be in touch."

Austin puts the phone down and returns to his chair. He leans back again, thinking this time. Thinking how maybe their problems in Davenport have finally been resolved. If he's lucky, the three have split and he'll never have to think about them again.

Though at the same time, part of him *had* hoped for a little more pushback from the bartender. Another excuse to get out there and personally hand out a beating, get his hands dirty again. Maybe even bury the motherfucker. It's been a while since Austin last had to do anything like that.

Oh well, he thinks. Until the next time DuLac Chemicals encounters someone belligerent. He can be patient. He held out up to now, after all.

14

It's a five-hour drive from Davenport to Memphis. Tom settles in, clearing his head, focussing only on the road and the mirrors. It helps him to ignore his various pains, especially the one in his lower back. Every so often he shifts, uncomfortable in the seat, trying to find a position where the bruise doesn't burn or feel like a bed of nails driven directly into his kidney.

Laila sits beside him, her chin resting in her hand and her elbow on the arm rest. She stares out of the window, watching the scenery passing them by. She didn't protest at Tom driving her car. They dropped his Ford off at the bar on their way to get Emma. Tom said it was best if they stuck to one vehicle.

Emma sits in the back. Tom glances at her in the mirror. She's silent, distracted. Like Laila said, she's shaken. He doesn't blame her. She sits behind Laila, also staring out the window. When they first arrived to pick her up, she was horrified. She remarked on the bruises on his face and the scab on the right side of his head, mostly concealed by his hair. Tom and Laila brought her up to speed. They packed her bags. They hit the road. Since setting off, there hasn't been much conversation. They stopped at a gas station to fuel up, as well as grab snacks and water. None of them has eaten anything yet.

Laila turns away from the window. "How are you doing?" she says. "You holding up?"

Tom nods.

"I can drive if you need me to."

"I'm okay for now. Another couple of hours and we'll see where we're at."

Laila pauses a moment. She's watching him. He can feel her eyes. "It's more than just your face though, isn't it? I've noticed the way you wince. How you move. You keep shifting like your back hurts."

"That's because my back hurt," Tom says, and tries to smile at her but she doesn't smile back. She's concerned about him.

"What did they do?"

"They did a number to my kidney is what they did," Tom says. There's no reason to keep it secret.

"Just the one?"

"So far as I can tell."

"Which one?"

"The right."

"What did they do? Did they hit you with something?"

"I couldn't tell what it was. A pipe or a blackjack or whatever. Hell, could've just been a fist wrapped in something for all I know. I wasn't looking. They blindsided me. And they must have been good, because I'm careful."

"I've noticed that," Laila says.

"They got the drop on me." Tom shrugs. "They managed

to sneak up on me. It happened. It's done. It's frustrating, and I'm annoyed at myself that they were able to do that, but it's done now."

They drive in silence for a few miles, then Emma leans forward. "Kidneys are pretty serious though, right?"

"I've got two," Tom says.

Emma laughs at this. After seeing the solemn expression she's worn on her face up to this point, it's good to hear her laugh. To see her smile, however briefly. The same goes for Laila. "God, you're such a *guy*," Emma says. "I bet you're in agony right now, but you just *have* to tough it out. Is this for our benefit? Are you showing off?"

"I'm not that kind of guy," Tom says. "I have a high threshold for pain, that's all. *But*, once it reaches that threshold, I won't stop complaining. You'll know *all* about it, because I'll tell you. Over and over again."

Emma laughs again, and this time Laila joins in, covering her mouth with her hand.

"And plus, you should see what I'm like if I stub a toe. That's where my threshold goes out the window."

"I'm glad to hear that it's not just for our benefit," Emma says.

"I'd never assume either of you to be so easily impressed."

"I can't speak for Laila, but it would take a *hell* of a lot more than that to impress me. You'd have to lose the dick, for a start."

Now it's Tom's turn to laugh. "Well, if the urge to put the moves on you suddenly takes me while we're on this five-hour drive, fearing for our lives, and on our way to drop you off with your parents, consider that duly noted."

The atmosphere has lightened in the car. Tom is glad of

it. He's glad to hear Laila and Emma speaking. To sense that they're no longer choked by their worry and fear.

And then Tom looks at the mirror and sees that the Dodge Charger Sedan that he'd first noticed when they left Davenport is still behind them.

Laila picks up on how he falls quiet. "What is it?"

"Might be nothing," Tom says. "I'll keep an eye on it."

He first spotted it a few miles out of the town, before they'd reached the freeway. It kept its distance, but the road was quiet and there wasn't much for them to hide behind. Now, there are plenty of other vehicles, and it keeps its distance, but it's always there.

Tom has been riding comfortably in the slow lane. He speeds up now and overtakes the three cars ahead of him.

"What are you doing?" Laila says.

"Just checking," Tom says.

He sticks to the speed limit. He sees how Laila looks over, checking.

Behind them, the car waits a beat, until a van and a truck fill the space behind Laila's Honda, then they pull out, too. Tom pulls back into the slow lane. He slows all the way down, dropping twenty below the limit. The Dodge realises how much he's slowed. The Dodge quickly pulls back in, only one car between it and the Honda now. The manoeuvre was so abrupt, the truck they pulled in front of blares its horn. It swerves out to overtake, flipping the Dodge off as it goes. Tom can't see the Dodge's driver. He wonders how he reacts to the aggressive driver. The Dodge sticks in the slow lane. They slow down further so that the vehicles behind them are forced to pull out and go around them.

"They're following us," Tom says, sure now. "No doubt."

"Do you think they realised what you were doing?" Laila says.

"Hard to tell," Tom says. "It probably gave them some kind of idea. It's got them thinking."

"What if they kept coming when you slowed down and they tried to run us off the road?" Emma says.

"I was prepared," Tom says. "But I don't think they would have done that. They wouldn't have been so brazen. Whenever they've come at us in the past, it's been in the dark. It's been late at night. They don't want witnesses."

"What do we do?" Emma says. "I don't want them to follow us all the way to my parents' house. I don't want them involved with this."

"I won't let them," Tom says.

"What are you going to do?" Laila says.

Tom doesn't answer straight away. He keeps driving, accelerating back up to the speed limit. He looks ahead, watching the road, checking the turn-offs. They're following the satnav to Memphis, to Emma's parents. "Do you know an alternate route?" he says to Emma. "A quieter road."

Emma thinks, gauging where they are. "Yeah, I think so. It'll add about an hour to the journey."

"That's fine. If it's quiet enough, we won't be on it the whole way."

"What do you mean by that?"

Tom ignores the question. "Give me directions."

Emma looks ahead. "It's not this turn-off," she says. "It's the one after."

Tom nods. He checks the mirror. The Dodge remains behind, three cars between them now. When they reach the turn-off Emma has indicated, the Dodge follows. It slows down. Another car made the turn. There is one vehicle between them now. Already, Tom can see that this is a much quieter road. As they get further along it, there are nothing but fields either side of them. The car immediately behind turns off, heading toward a farmhouse. The Dodge stays with them, but it pulls back.

Laila is watching the side mirror. "What now?"

"Now we wait for an opportunity," Tom says. "And when I find it, I'll take it."

15

Wyatt is in Mississippi. He's a day early for his meeting. Nathan isn't with him. None of the other Road Dogs are, only his father.

Wyatt is not riding his bike, though he's brought it with him. It's parked up, safe and sound, at a cabin they'd already rented out ahead of time for the purpose of their upcoming unofficial business in Mississippi. Neither of them wears their kuttes. They keep a low profile. They ride in the truck. Wyatt has driven. Vic sits in the passenger seat, wincing while he rubs his stiff knees.

"You need anything?" Wyatt says. They're parked at the roadside. It's a quiet road, three miles out from Fort Ellicott. Fifteen miles from the cabin. They spent the night in the cabin. This morning, Vic had a flare. A minor one, so he claimed. Wyatt wanted to leave him, but he insisted on coming. Wyatt had to lift him from the bed and carry him through to the bathroom. Luckily, his father was fine after that. Said he could see to himself. Wyatt was glad. He didn't particularly like the idea of wiping his father's ass. He keeps this in mind – when this is all over, and they've made their payoff, he'll make sure to employ a carer for his father. Someone who can tend to his needs, especially when the point comes his bones have calcified so badly he *does* need help in the bathroom. He'll make sure to find a looker, though. His father would like that. He wouldn't except anything less. Some little Latin mami who isn't shy about earning a little extra in the bedroom. His father would like *that*, too.

"I just need soldier boy to hurry up," Vic says through his teeth.

"You need to get out the truck, stretch out? Walk it off?"

"I'm fine," Vic says, his tone close to biting.

"You want some weed?" Wyatt says. "Might numb the pain a little. Might make you more fucking bearable, too."

Vic forces himself to calm. "No," he says, taking a deep breath. "This is important. I need to be straight for this. We both do."

Wyatt looks down the road, the direction of Fort Ellicott. It's clear. Nothing coming. He has the window down. It's a still day. Quiet. He breathes it in deep. Wishes he'd been able to ride his bike over here, and back. A perfect day for riding.

Vic shifts his weight and grunts. "Dale gave him the time, right?"

Wyatt nods. "Dale also said that his cousin would get here *when* he could. He's a soldier. We can't just expect him to walk away from his duties. He'd be reprimanded or some shit, and then he might be no good to us. They could get suspicious or something."

"A soldier on a decommissioning base," Vic says. "What can there be to *do*? What's holding him up?"

Wyatt glances at the time. It's just after midday. They've

been here for forty minutes. "Dale said he'd get off duty at eleven. Would you rather he rushed straight here, maybe raised some eyebrows? It's better for us if he takes his time."

Vic grunts again, but doesn't protest further. He sighs heavily. "You think back when it was active, this road was busier?"

"I reckon someone would've been along to ask us what we we've been doing sitting here for so long," Wyatt says, then chuckles.

Vic sits forward suddenly, eyes narrowed. "Someone's coming," he says.

Wyatt sees them, too. A car coming their way. It slows as it draws near.

"That him?" Vic says.

Wyatt can't see the driver. He stares at the windshield, the sunlight reflecting off it. It pulls over, parks in front of them. A man gets out. He's not in uniform. Wyatt recognises him, though. Dale showed them a picture. Corporal Gil McKenna, cousin of Forever Road Dog Dale McKenna.

Gil nods as greeting then makes his way to them, tugging at his ear. He glances back down the road he's come. "Turn your engine on," he says. "If anyone comes down after me, we wanna be able to tell them that you've got lost, and I'm giving you directions."

Wyatt does so. He notices that Gil's car is still running.

Gil reaches through the window. "Pleasure to finally meet you face to face," he says.

Wyatt shakes. "Likewise," he says. All of their communication so far has been by burner phone.

Vic leans over to grasp his hand in turn. "Took your time," he says.

"You have any trouble finding the place?" Gil says, ignoring the comment.

Wyatt shakes his head. "How are things at Fort Ellicott?"

"Quiet," Gil says, again looking down the road.

"You expecting anyone?"

"No, but I'm not the only person who just came off duty."

"Where'd you say you were going?"

"Heading to Natchez for food."

"Food good there?"

Gil shrugs. "Better than on base."

Wyatt decides that's enough small-talk. "Let's get down to business," he says. The purpose of this trip has been to meet Gil McKenna in the flesh. The timing of their summoning to Mississippi due to Nathan's indiscretions is purely coincidental, but has worked out well for him and his father.

"The majority of troops on the base will be moved off tomorrow," Gil says. "After that, it's gonna be a skeleton crew. I'll be one of those skeletons, which you already know."

"And the armoury?" Wyatt says.

"It remains full. Transport has been arranged to clear the weaponry in a week, so we need to make sure we've cleared it out before then." Gil pauses. He glances down the road, quickly this time. His attention returns to Wyatt. "I'm sure I don't need to make it any clearer to you how much of a risk I'm taking with this."

"It's already clear as day," Wyatt says.

"And it needs to be worth my while."

"It'll be worth *all* our whiles."

Gil's jaw juts out while he thinks. "How many of your men do you have involved in this?"

"Only the inner circle," Wyatt says. "Higher ranking members of the FRD. And your cousin, of course, plus one more. Wouldn't be any kind of plan if Dale hadn't brought it to our attention, after all."

"Yeah, well, he wouldn't know a damn thing if I hadn't mentioned it to him."

"Of course. Once we sell the guns, there's going to be plenty to go around. We're all going to be very rich men once we pull this off."

"Who's the extra one?"

Wyatt waves a hand. "You don't need to worry about him. He won't be around for long."

Gil frowns. He doesn't understand. "I'm not sure I like the sound of that."

"Forget about it," Wyatt says. "Just trust us. It'll all make sense when we're done."

Gil nods, though hesitantly. "How long will it take to get the money?"

"Less than a week," Wyatt says. "We've put out feelers. I already have a buyer lined up."

"How long before I get my cut?"

"Best you wait a while," Wyatt says. "It'd look mighty suspicious if you suddenly came into a lot of money right after Fort Ellicott's armoury is robbed."

"Six months, I'm leaving the Army," Gil says. "My papers are all in order."

"And they'll probably be keeping an eye on you after that."

"I don't plan on hanging around. They won't know where I've gone."

"All right. Once you've disappeared, you get your cut. You don't wanna take any risks, but neither do we. After we send you that money, make sure you're sensible. We don't want them to be able to track us down through it. We'll keep in touch through Dale. We won't touch a dime of what's yours."

Gil nods. He looks between Wyatt and Vic. "And I hear you've been leaning how to drive boats?"

"We both have," Vic says. "We're prepared."

"You good at it?" Gil says.

"Like he said," Wyatt says. "We're prepared. We've put the practise in. Keep a cool head, Corporal McKenna. You don't need to worry about a thing."

"I'll stop worrying in six months," Gil says, "soon as I have that money." He pats his hands on the side of the truck as he straightens. "I better go. You best do the same."

"Pleasure to finally meet you," Wyatt says with a nod.

Gil goes to his car and pulls away. Wyatt waits a moment before he turns the truck around and does the same. The road further down in the direction of the base remains clear.

"Jittery fella," Vic says.

Wyatt grunts. "I thought the same."

"Y'know, something has just occurred to me after meeting that boy. Something you said, too."

"What?" Wyatt says.

"You said we wouldn't touch a dime of his cut. You mean that?"

Wyatt laughs. "Hell no." He straightens the truck and follows Gil out, keeping his distance.

"What about Dale? It's his family. He ain't gonna let us do that."

"*We're* his family," Wyatt says. "And if Dale wants to make a fuss..." Wyatt shrugs, driving away from Fort Ellicott. "I won't like it, but we'll do what needs to be done."

"Kill him?"

"You really gonna make me say it?"

"I ain't naïve." Vic nods grimly, agreeing. "If he can't see the bigger picture, that's just the way it'll have to be."

"We can't afford to be precious," Wyatt says. "Or sentimental. We've gotten ourselves in deep, and only we can dig our way out. This is our only opportunity to do that. If Dale can't see that, fuck him."

"Uh-huh." Vic waits a beat. "And what about Logan?"

Wyatt grins. "There's no sentiment there. You know how that's gonna go down."

Vic grunts. "When it does, I wanna be there."

16

The Dodge has kept back. It's allowed Tom space to think.

"This road is quiet enough," Emma says. "Why aren't they trying anything?"

"Middle of the day," Tom says. "Like I said earlier, last two times we've had run-ins with them it's been the middle of the night. That's all I can guess."

There's woodland up ahead. Tom has an idea. "This is our chance," he says, pointing at the trees. "When we get to the other side of the trees, I'm gonna pull in. The second I stop the car, I want the two of you to run into the woods and hide. Listen out for when I call. You got that?"

"What are you gonna do?" Emma says.

"Make sure they can't follow us anymore," Tom says.

The Dodge keeps its distance as they pass by the woodland, the trees thick on their left and right. They drive in shadow. Tom can see the clearing ahead. The road submerged in sunlight once again. He puts his foot down to buy themselves a little extra time, but he keeps the Dodge in view. He wants them to see where they go. Wants them to follow.

Clear of the trees, he turns right into the field, the car bouncing over the grass and dirt. He stops it close to the tree-line. Laila and Emma get out of the car and run for the trees, like Tom told them to. Tom gets out, too, but he doesn't follow them into the woodland. Instead, he runs toward the road, to where he pulled off it, and lies flat in the long grass, close to a tree, concealing himself from view. There are tyre tracks making it clear where he pulled in.

He hears the Dodge approach. It's slowed down. It's cautious. It doesn't follow straight into the field. The Dodge inches forward. Tom keeps his head low. He doesn't chance taking a look, but he can imagine the man – or men – inside craning their necks to look around.

They're likely deliberating, but at the same time they know they can't wait too long. If they do, they could lose track of where Tom and the women have gone. The Honda is clearly empty. They roll into the field. They pass close by. Tom can see them now, can see their tyres as they pass by just a couple of feet from where he lies. He follows at a crawl, remaining low.

The Dodge stops behind the Honda. The car doors open. There are two men. As Tom rises to his feet, pulling out his Beretta, he realises that he recognises them both. Two faces from last night, coming into focus. They're two-thirds of the group who attacked him outside the bar. The two who didn't talk.

Tom raises the gun. "Either of you armed?"

Both men spin at the sound of his voice. They see the gun and raise their hands.

"I asked a question." Tom remains outwardly calm, but

he feels his blood running hot. He wants to hurt them. He's not in the habit of taking a beating and not giving one in return.

"We're not armed," the man on his right says.

"That sucks for you, doesn't it?"

The man on the right swallows. The man on the left is sweating. His eyes flicker toward the Dodge.

"The guns are in the car," Tom says. It's not a question.

The man on the left nods. "Y-yeah."

"Throw me the keys."

The man on the right does so. Tom catches them, keeping the Beretta trained on them both. The driver's door is still open. Tom kicks it closed. He locks the car and keeps hold of the keys. He shoots out both tyres on the driver's side. The man on the left flinches as he does so.

Tom walks toward the Honda in a wide circle. He places the Beretta on the roof, then steps closer to the men. The keys to the Dodge have other keys attached. House keys, or motel or hotel room keys. Tom lets them slide between his fingers. "I'm facing you this time," he says. "You wanna take another swing?"

Both men glance at each other. They don't hesitate. They charge. The man now on Tom's right attempts to go around, to go for the Beretta, but Tom was prepared for this move. He placed the Beretta there on purpose, to give them something to go for. He's stayed close to the rear of the Honda, and he's able to easily cut him off with a kick across his torso, driving the wind out of him and dropping him to his knees. Tom spins as the man on his left comes up, and drives the back of his elbow into his face. He stumbles back, nose bloodied, but Tom follows, grabbing him by the back of the neck and punching him twice in the stomach, the keys protruding from his knuckles like small knives, puncturing him. He punches him across the face with the key, tearing a hole in his cheek.

The man on his knees is using the car to try and get back to his feet. Tom comes up behind and punches him in the kidneys. The man cries out. Tom punches him again, the key piercing flesh. He grabs a handful of hair and wrenches the man's head back. "I hope you enjoy pissing blood as much as I have." He slams his face into the back of the Honda, denting the metal, but also opening a cut above the man's right eyebrow. He's dazed and unsteady on his feet. Tom shoves him away and he falls over the other man.

Tom pockets the Dodge keys and calls for Laila and Emma. He conceals the Beretta again.

Emma emerges from the woodland first. "Holy shit," she says, looking at the two fallen men. She looks at Tom as Laila follows behind her. "You have a *gun*?"

"Just for emergencies," Tom says, and then gets back into the Honda. Laila and Emma get in after him. Tom turns the car around in a wide circle, and gets back onto the road. He drives until the Dodge and the trees and the two men are long gone behind them, and then he throws the Dodge's keys out of the window.

17

Austin gets a call from Terry. "I didn't expect to hear from you so soon." Austin is in his office still. He's in his chair now, but he's been doing push-ups. There's little call for him to have an office, really. It's little more than a base of operations. A place for him to sit while he co-ordinates his team on their various activities. Most of his work is done over the phone.

He supposes, though, they keep him in an office close to all the tech geeks to keep them in line. Carol has told him as much. "Keep them in line," she said. "People like this, who've spent all of their lives pissing about on computers, you have to make sure they stay focussed on the task in hand. You don't and they're liable to start messing around at a moment's notice and nothing gets done."

Terry's voice stounds strange, like his mouth is swollen, or his nose is broken. "He made us," he says. "The son of a bitch made us, and he remembered us from last night."

Austin sits upright. "What happened?"

"Motherfucker lured us in, put a beating on us. I ain't

gonna lie, he fucked us up, Austin. Put a key between his knuckles or something and he's tore a hole in my goddamn cheek when he punched me. He's messed up my whole damn face."

"I don't care about your face," Austin says, gripping the edge of the desk with his spare hand. "You were never that pretty to begin with. What about Kevin?"

"There's no hole in his face, but he's in a similar condition. He's punched holes in us with that damn key."

Austin rolls his eyes. He doesn't care that there was a key involved. He cares that the bartender gave them a beating. "Where is he now?"

"I don't know," Terry says. "He shot out our tyres and they took off."

Austin's eyes narrow. "He's armed?"

"Yeah. He took our keys, too. Locked the Dodge so we can't get at our guns. We've had to smash the window to get them out."

Austin takes a deep breath. "So you don't know where they are now?"

Terry doesn't respond. This is answer enough.

Austin has to take another deep breath. His arm trembles, gripping the table still like he's trying to tear a chunk out of it.

"We need picked up," Terry says finally, his voice quiet. "The Dodge is no good."

"Send me your location," Austin says. "I don't feel much like talking right now." He hangs up the phone. He pauses a moment, then slams his fists down on the desk.

There is the chance that it was a revenge beating. That the bartender realised they were being followed, lured Terry and Kevin in, and then once he saw who they were he lost his shit. It's a possibility, and the three could still be leaving town, never to return.

Except, it feels like more than that to Austin. If they were leaving, it wouldn't matter that someone was following. They could just keep going and that would be the end of it. Despite them driving away from Davenport, Austin doesn't feel that they've truly left. They're gone for now, but he senses that they're going to return. This isn't over. The bartender, and potentially the women, are going to become a bigger problem going forward.

The message from Terry comes through, giving their location. Austin ignores it for now. He'll let them sit for a while before he sends someone to get them.

He thinks on the bartender. He's a capable fighter, that much is clear – that's four of Austin's men he's beaten down now. That's too high a tally. And he spotted they were being followed. Austin's men are good. They're not careless. Austin can't remember the last time any of them were spotted while following someone, or while on a stakeout, unless they wanted to be seen. He thinks back to when he saw the bartender, barely fourteen hours ago. Remembers the beating he gave him. The bartender hadn't struck him as much of a threat then. A good-looking guy, sure, and it was clear he worked out, but nothing more to him than that. Austin didn't expect there to be any more trouble with him. Clearly, he was mistaken.

He gets to his feet and goes to his door, leaning out onto the work floor and zeroing in on the tech geek he spoke to earlier. "You!" he says, pointing. "What have you got for me?"

The geek gives a start, his eyes wide like he's a deer in headlights. "I was – I was just coming to see you, Mr. Myers," he says, his face blanching. "I – I – I've found him." He points back at his computer screen with his thumb.

Austin goes to the computer, pushing the geek aside. The bartender is on the screen. Except, in this picture, he isn't a bartender.

He's in uniform. He's a soldier.

Austin reads over what the geek has found, learning what is available to know about the man called Tom Rollins. Austin feels something shift inside him as he reads, and a sense of regret fills him up.

"Shit," he says.

He should have killed this guy when he had the chance.

18

It's getting late. Tom and Laila have found a motel on the outskirts of Memphis to spend the night. The motel is busy. There was only one room left.

"We can look somewhere else," Tom said.

"I don't mind sharing," Laila said.

She lies on the bed, resting after a day's travel. Tom is by the window. They're on the upper floor, and they have a clear view of the parking lot and the vehicles therein. Tom makes a mental note of them all. It's dark, and hard to tell, but he thinks they're all empty.

They left Emma with her parents a couple of hours ago. Tom and Laila said they'd be staying nearby for the night, in case anything happened. Emma is to call them if she sees something that doesn't look right. She hugged them each in turn as she departed. As she wrapped her arms around Tom, she spoke into his ear, "Look after Laila. Keep her safe."

"I intend to," Tom said.

"You think she'll be all right with her parents?" Laila says as if reading his mind, rolling onto her side and propping her head up on her hand.

Tom turns away from the window and takes a seat in the chair at the foot of the bed, gritting his teeth as the pain in his kidney shoots through his body. "I think so," he says. "We made sure they weren't following us here."

"What if they already know where her parents live?" Laila says. "DuLac Chemicals is a billion-dollar company. They have the means to gather this information."

Tom nods. He's already thought about this. "True, but it would involve attacking Emma and her parents in their home, in a residential neighbourhood."

"They tried that at my house."

Tom nods. "True, but is there really any need to go after Emma when she's no longer in Davenport? To them, it should appear like she's checked out. She's gone. She's no longer a factor. Would it really be worth it for them to go after her, when they've effectively already got what they wanted? And to bring her parents into things to boot?"

"I suppose not," Laila says. "I *hope* not." She pauses, looking at him. "Are we going to talk about the gun?"

"What's there to talk about?"

"It was a surprise to see it, is all. Who *are* you, Tom? Bartender, fisherman – but there's more, isn't there? I've seen you beat up four men now. It was impressive. You knew what you were doing. I'm not saying the everyday person on the street wouldn't know how to fight like that, but it feels like there's more than meets the eye."

"You saw the two today, huh?"

"Oh, I was watching. Don't think just because I was hiding that I wasn't."

"I was in the Army," Tom says.

Laila raises her eyebrows. "That where you learnt to fight?"

"Partly," Tom says. "My father taught me how to fight when I was young. He told me never to back down. He didn't know much in the way of technique, but he taught me to never be afraid to fight dirty." Her eyes on his, he doesn't want to keep anything from her. It would feel like a lie, even if only a lie of omission. "And I was CIA. Black ops. That was all a long time ago now."

"Ah," Laila says. "See, that makes sense. Now *all* of this makes sense. What brought you to Davenport?"

"Just passing through, and I needed work."

"And look at you now."

Tom laughs, pressing a finger to the scab on the side of his head, and feeling the pain in his kidney shoot through him again. "Everywhere I go, I have a knack for finding whatever trouble might pervade that place."

"You've found more than a little in Davenport."

Tom looks at her for a moment, lying on the bed, smiling, her hair hanging down from her propped head, her legs drawn beneath herself. He clears his throat. He gets to his feet. "I'm going to take a walk around the block," he says. "Check the area."

"Don't you want to lie down, Tom?" she says. "You look beat. You need to rest."

"I'll do a loop, and then I'll rest." She looks doubtful. "I promise."

Tom leaves the motel. It's getting late. The cool night air feels good on his face. He starts walking, ignoring the pain that shoots through him with every step. He thinks being sat in the car for so long, stuck in one position, may have aggravated his injuries, and not to mention the fight with the two heavies.

The block is clear. Tom makes his way back to the room, passing through the parking lot. None of the vehicles have moved. He can see inside them better from down here. They're all empty. He's glad of it.

When he gets inside the room, there's no sign of Laila, just the crumpled form on the duvet where she was previously lying. The shower is running. He goes to the bathroom door and calls through. "I'm back," he says. He waits to hear her voice, to know that it's her for sure.

"I'll be out soon," she says.

Tom goes to the window. He watches the road. The shower stops running. He glances back. Laila's clothes are nowhere to be seen. They must be in the bathroom with her. Neither of them has brought a change with them. They were so focussed on getting Emma out of Davenport and to the hopeful safety of her parents' home.

Tom turns back to the window. A few moments pass. Laila does not emerge from the bathroom. She'll be drying herself. Tom minds his business, and tries not to think about her in there.

The bathroom door opens. Tom doesn't turn. Laila says his name.

"Tom." She speaks it softly.

He turns. Her hair is wet. He sees droplets of water on her collarbone where they haven't been dried away. She's wrapped in a grey towel. Her clothes are in her hand. She drops them to one side. She stares at him.

Tom stares back. Neither of them says a word, not yet. Tom goes to her. She reaches out to him, her arms resting on his shoulders. Tom places his hands on her waist. They kiss. Tom pulls away long enough to ask, “Why?”

“Why not?” Laila says. “Things have been…everything has been so crazy. Let’s just take tonight for something normal.”

Tom kisses her again. Laila lets the towel drop.

19

Tom is already awake when Laila's phone begins to ring. He's in the chair, by the window, looking out as the sun streams down onto the parking lot and the nearby road, forcing himself to focus instead of spending all of his time watching Laila sleep. The phone sits atop the bedside table, vibrating loudly.

Laila wakes with a start and a deep breath. She turns to the sound, reaching for her phone. She holds it close to her face, squinting as she reads the screen. "Oh," she says, and pushes herself upright. She coughs and rubs at her eyes, and then she answers. "Hello?"

Tom watches. He can only hear her side of the conversation. It's not panicked. He wonders whom she's talking to. He waits to find out.

Laila's eyes lock with his across the room. "Got it," she says into the phone. "Got it. Right. We're on it. Uh – I'll tell you later." She hangs up. "That was Mississippi Nature," she says to Tom. She stretches, the blanket bunched up around her. "Have you been awake long?"

"About an hour."

"You were supposed to be resting."

"I was going to rest last night, but you had other ideas."

Laila laughs. "I didn't hear you complaining at the time."

Tom smiles. He tilts his chin toward the phone. "Why were they calling?"

"All that stuff I told you about DuLac Chemicals and their factories, you remember?"

"Of course."

"And how Mississippi Nature have been exploring their practices, trying to build a case to prevent the factory in Davenport? Well, they've gotten in touch with a farmer in Little Rock, Arkansas. His name's Pete Gannon. DuLac used to have a factory on the edge of his lands. If we can get out there, he's willing to talk to us."

"Little Rock," Tom says. "That's not too far from here, is it? Just a couple of hours."

"I'll get dressed," Laila says, stepping out of the bed. She's naked, but she moves around freely as she searches for where she dropped her clothes. They've already seen each other nude. There's no need for false modesty.

"What was that you were saying at the end of the call?" Tom says. "What are you telling Mississippi Nature later?"

Laila grins. "About you," she says. She starts pulling on her clothes. "I've mentioned you already, after what happened at the bar the other night. But I'm going to have to tell them that you're involved now. That you're all the way in." She has her underwear on. She pauses as she steps into her jeans. "Are you okay with that? You know you have a choice. I don't want you to feel like you're beholden to us – to me – or that last night was just to try and get you to hang around."

"No," Tom says. He shakes his head. "I already made it clear to you. I'm all in. Last night has nothing to do with that."

Laila nods once, satisfied. "I'm glad of that, because I'd hate for you to think I was a lady of loose morals." She winks.

"And I'd hate for you to think I'm a man who puts his life in danger just to get a woman into bed," Tom says. "A beautiful woman, sure, but that's an extreme way to go about it. I'd far rather rely on my charm."

"And your charm got you *very* far." Laila finishes dressing. She looks at her phone. "All right," she says. "Mississippi Nature have sent me the address. You ready?"

"Let's go."

20

Austin is in Davenport. He has Marshall and Jeremy with him. Marshall and Jeremy were following Laila and Emma at the bar when Rollins beat them up. They haven't recovered from the ignominy of their defeat, especially when it was two on one, and they had knives. Knives which are still in the possession of the sheriff's department. Austin's doesn't want them to recover from it. He doesn't want them to live it down. It's a failure they need to remember, and to keep hold of. It means they'll do better going forward.

Marshall tugs on the corner of his moustache. "That was my favourite knife," he says. "You know how many times I've used that knife? And now it's gone. I ain't ever gonna see it again."

Jeremy nods along. "I know how you feel."

"You know how you should feel?" Austin says. "You shouldn't be missing your fucking knives, you should be feeling the shame at a colossal failure. If the two of you had dealt with him then and there, none of this would be an issue right now."

He glares at them, and they don't respond. They know he's right.

Austin is in Davenport looking for Tom Rollins. It's been a night since he left town with the women. If he's coming back, he's surely coming back soon. He's coming back *here.* And if not, Austin intends to find out where he's gone, and where he could be. Austin read the man's history. He knows now the kind of person he is. He's not going to walk away. They need to be prepared for him, and the best way to do that is to get out ahead of him.

They know where Rollins works already. His two jobs. They found that out after he'd beat Marshall and Jeremy. Knowing already that he worked at the bar, Terry and Kevin came through and watched him. They saw him on the boat, too.

"He keeps busy," Terry had remarked at the time. "Kicks ass and then goes fishing."

Austin drives to the boatyard. It's early. The sun has not long risen. He parks and they wait. Terry and Kevin got the name of the boat Rollins was on. They know the owner's name – Lyle Bound – and what he looks like. The tech geeks found his driving record. Austin, Marshall, and Jeremy have committed Lyle's face to memory.

"We talk to Lyle first," Austin says while they wait. "Hopefully he'll get here soon. I've got more important things to be doing." Due to the repeated failures of his men, he's come out into the field, once again, personally. In a way, he supposes he should be grateful, and a part of him is. A part of him tingles with excitement. Rollins is proving to be a problem – a *big* problem. One that Austin is going to have to deal with himself.

He's going to get his hands dirty.

It brings a smile to his face. The only thing is, the only thing that has him impatient right now is that there's no sign of Rollins in Davenport. If he was here, fine, they could get down to business. But they have to *find* him. This is the source of his frustration. The waiting.

"Rollins is our priority," he says, as if to himself. "Don't forget that. And when we find him, I want him. He's mine."

An old beat-up truck rolls toward the boatyard. They all see it at the same time. Austin doesn't have to say a word. They all know it's Lyle. Austin gets out of the car and Marshall and Jeremy follow.

Lyle gets out of his truck. He doesn't see them coming. Only as he turns and realises they're upon him does he react. He takes a step back, bumping into the truck door, and places a hand over his chest. "Jesus, fellas," he says, laughing. "Didn't see you there. You almost gave an old man a heart attack."

"Lyle Bound," Austin says, just so Lyle knows that they know who he is. "We're looking for Tom Rollins. We understand he works on your boat."

Lyle frowns, turning his head. "And who might you be?"

"That's not important right now," Austin says. "We're looking for Rollins. Do you know where he is?"

Lyle doesn't answer. He looks the three men over.

Austin sighs, but it's for show. Inside he's smiling, because he knows what this reluctance to answer means. It means that they're about to get physical. He turns to Marshall and Jeremy and nods toward the road. Wordlessly, they do as he says. This has already been arranged. They understand what is about to happen. They go to the rear of Lyle's truck to keep an eye out, to ensure no one can interrupt what is about to happen.

Lyle sees them walk away. The corners of his mouth pinch.

"I'm only going to ask you one more time," Austin says. He holds up a finger. "Just once. Where is Tom Rollins?"

Lyle clenches his jaw. He says nothing.

Austin doesn't waste time. He drives a fist deep into Lyle's stomach. The old man groans and falls to his knees. Austin crouches beside him. "Does this need to get harder?"

Lyle spits into the grass. There's bile in it.

"Have it your way." Austin grabs him by the collar and drags him toward the water's edge. Lyle tries to struggle, but Austin is too strong for him. Austin dunks him into the water, holding him under. Lyle thrashes. Austin watches the bubbles that rise and burst on the surface, Lyle's breath leaving his lungs. Austin hauls him out. "Where is Rollins?"

Lyle gasps. Austin doesn't give him long to respond. He dunks him into the water again. He holds him under longer. Lyle's thrashing is weaker this time. There aren't so many bubbles. Austin looks around, both of his hands wet on the back of Lyle's head. It's quiet at the boatyard. It's still so early that there's no one else around yet. This is lucky. If there were, Marshall and Jeremy would have had to chase them off, to make sure they didn't see anything.

Austin breathes deep, inhaling the smell of the water and the wet grass. It's peaceful here. If he didn't have a job to do, he would stay and enjoy it a little longer.

He pulls Lyle out of the water. Lyle is limp in his hands. Austin spins him over and pounds him on the stomach. Lyle does a half sit-up and belches out water. He turns onto his side, coughing and gagging.

"Where is Rollins?" Austin says. "Next time, I keep you under. Next time, I hold you there until the bubbles stop, and face down in the river is how your crew will find you when they finally get here."

Lyle throws up into the grass. Austin waits. Lyle gulps down air. When enough time has passed, Austin reaches for him again, but Lyle begs off. "I don't know where he is," he says, holding up his hands. "I swear – all he told me was that he was going to be out of town for a couple of days. I swear..."

Austin watches him. Lyle is still struggling to breathe. Austin believes him. He pats Lyle on the chest. "See how easy that all could have been?" He straightens and whistles for Marshall and Jeremy to return. "You can tell him about this when he gets back, Lyle. You can tell him we're coming." Marshall and Jeremy hurry toward him like a pair of obedient dogs. Austin goes to the car and gets inside. They're not done yet. They're not done in Davenport. They have one more place to visit. The bar. Hopefully Rollins told the old bitch who owns it something more substantial.

"Did he know anything?" Marshall says.

"Nothing worthwhile," Austin says while he drives. "Rollins told him he'll be out of town a couple of days."

"Then we'll be here waiting for him," Jeremy says.

"Yes, we will," Austin says, "but if we can find out where he's gone and cut him off there, all the better."

They drive in silence to the bar. Marshall and Jeremy pick up on Austin's vibe. He doesn't want to talk. He's thinking about Rollins.

It's too early in the day for the bar to be open. They go

around the back, to where they know Valerie Reynolds live. They pass by the spot where they beat Rollins down. Austin smiles at the memory. There are still some drops of Rollins's blood on the ground, dark and dry. Austin almost wants to scoop the dirt up as a keepsake.

He knocks on the front door of Valerie's home. It takes her a while to answer. The old bitch is slow. When she finally opens the door, Austin smiles at her, but he doesn't waste any time. "Rollins," he says. "Where is he?"

Valerie steps back, thrown by his abrupt question. "Who – who are you?"

"Get the key to his room," Austin says. "Open it for us – *now.*"

Valerie recovers herself. She becomes defiant. "I won't do that," she says, standing her ground.

Austin waves to Marshall and Jeremy. They barrel into the house, shoving the old bitch out of the way, almost knocking her to the ground. They go through to the living room and upend the sofa. They start throwing things around.

"They'll find the key," Austin says. "But they'll tear your home apart before they do."

Valerie deliberates, looking back at the two men, and then again at Austin, and she knows she can't physically stop them. "I'll call the police!" she says.

"I have her phone," Marshall says. He holds up the cell. When Valerie turns to see, he hurls it to the ground, then smashes what survives the impact under his boot heel.

"She got a landline?" Austin calls.

"On it," Jeremy says, and they hear him tear it from the wall.

"You were saying?" Austin says.

Valerie takes a deep, shuddering breath. She bites her lip. "I'll get the key," she says.

"Hold it, boys," Austin calls.

Valerie waddles into the kitchen. Austin watches her walk away with disdain. When she returns, she's holding up the key. Silently, she leads the way to the room at the back of the bar. The room where Rollins has been staying.

When she unlocks the door, Marshall and Jeremy again barrel past. Austin remains outside with her. "You people really need to understand," he says, "that when a man like me asks for something, it's far better to just heed my demands straight off the bat."

Valerie can't meet his eye.

"Where is Rollins?"

"I don't know," she says. "Wherever he is, I begged him not to go. That beating he took...he was in no fit state. He needed a doctor."

Austin smiles at this. It's good to know.

When Marshall and Jeremy have tossed the room, they step back outside. "Nothing," Marshall says.

"Nothing personal, anyway," Jeremy says.

"Anything of his, he must've taken it with him."

"Are you sure you don't know where he is, Ms Reynolds?" Austin says, leaning in close.

She shies away from him, still refusing to look into his face. "I don't know where he is," she says.

Without a word, Austin walks away from her. Marshall and Jeremy follow. They get into the car. Marshall and Jeremy don't speak. They don't dare.

Austin starts the engine, then breaks the silence. He takes a deep breath. "Hard way it is, then," he says. "Hard way all round."

21

Tom and Laila reach Little Rock. They follow the directions to Pete Gannon's farm. Laila is driving. Tom didn't protest. His back aches. The pain is dimming, though. It's not as sharp as it was yesterday, on the drive up to Memphis. When he pees, there's no longer blood in it.

They reach the farm. Tom looks to the right, across the fields. They don't look like they're in use. They lie fallow. Some of them are overgrown. They're not being tended to. In the distance, he sees a building looming beyond the bushes that line the property. A patch of the bushes directly below the building is not in bloom. They're dead. Spindly branches of dried-out wood that make it look like winter. "That must be the factory."

Laila looks around. "I don't see anything else that matches the bill."

It's far away, but it looks out of use. No smoke or steam rises from it. There is a darkness about the exterior of the building that speaks of disrepair.

Down the road, Tom can see the farmhouse. As they get closer, he sees that it's an old wooden building. Like everything else around here, it has fallen into disrepair. Much like the fields, it doesn't appear as if anyone is tending to it.

"I don't see any workers," Tom says.

"I don't see *anyone*," Laila says, looking around. She stops the car in front of the slanted porch.

The front door to the farmhouse opens, and an older man steps out. He's thin and crooked, his right leg ramrod straight, dragged behind him in a tight brace. He steps up to the porch's railing and snorts, turning his head to the side to spit. When Tom and Laila get out of the Honda, he asks them, "Y'all from Mississippi Nature?"

"We are, sir," Laila says. "Are you Pete Gannon?"

"That's me," he says, turning. "Come on inside."

Tom and Laila exchange glances, then follow him in.

Inside, Pete drops into a chair, his right leg straight out in front of him. "Take a seat," he says, waving toward a sofa with its stuffing bursting out in places. A black cat walks slowly around the room, purring occasionally. Pete kicks at the cat, and it hurries outside through the cat flap in the door. "I'd offer y'all a drink, but I ain't got anything, unless you wanna help yourselves to tap water. I don't get guests."

They're in the living room. The television is on, but Pete has muted it. Everything in the room looks a few decades out of date. There are VHS tapes stacked on the floor in front of the boxy television. The flower-print wallpaper is peeling from the walls. There's a smell of meat hanging in the air. Cat food, or from Pete's own meals. There are porcelain models around the room, on the fireplace and windowsill. They look out of place for a man like Pete Gannon. Some of them are broken. Tom wonders if the cat knocked them over.

Pete notices Tom looking at a model of a young girl herding sheep. "My wife's," he says, "God rest her soul. Never liked the things, myself, but after she died I could never bring myself to throw them out." Pete sniffs, then turns to Laila. "They told me a woman would be coming to speak to me. Laila North. I'm guessing that's you. They never said anything about this fella."

"This is Tom Rollins," Laila says. "He's helping me."

Pete snorts. "With DuLac Chemicals, you're gonna need all the help you can get. You're gonna need more than this fella here, I can tell you that much."

"I was told you'd be willing to talk to us about DuLac," Laila says.

"Course I am. That's why I reached out, ain't it?"

"We know they had a factory on the edge of your farm."

Pete's face is sour. His lips draw in like he's tasted a lemon. "See it on the way in, did you?"

"We did. At least, we assume that's what it is."

Pete waves an arm in the vague direction of the road they've just driven down. "If you saw it coming down there, then you saw it. Goddamn eyesore."

"What happened, Mr. Gannon?"

"Pete," he says. "Just call me Pete."

"All right," Laila says. "What happened after DuLac Chemicals moved in, Pete?"

"They bought the land off McConnell. He used to have the farm next to mine, but it had belonged to his daddy first, and he was always desperate to sell that land. Always on the lookout for developers. Eventually, DuLac came to him. Course, he couldn't take them up on their offer soon enough. Soon as I heard about it, I didn't like it. Why would I? These assholes pumping chemicals into the air –

I'd heard about acid rain. What was it gonna do to my crops? Well, acid rain turned out to be the least of the problems. But what could I do about it? It wasn't my land. It was close, but it wasn't on my acreage, so I just had to take it. It didn't take long before things started to go wrong."

"In what way?" Laila says.

"You saw the factory, so I assume you saw the bushes too, right? Saw how they're dead? Well, starting from the edge of my field closest to the factory, *everything* was dying. I used to grow corn. It was withering on the stalk. Whatever was happening over there in that factory, whether it was the fumes, or they had a spill, or they were just generally careless with their waste, I can't say for sure. But it doesn't matter, because it was done. They were killing my crops.

"Well, I tried complaining to them direct, but that fell on deaf ears. I went to the law. They said there wasn't anything they could do about it. I raised as much hell as I could, but no one cared. So I hired a team. Ecologists, like yourself, right?"

Laila nods.

"They weren't from Mississippi Nature, though. From the sounds of it, if I'd known about them back then I'd have been better going to them. Anyway, the team tested the soil, and sure enough, it was poisoned."

"What with?" Laila says.

Pete smirks. "I don't remember everything they found, but I remember two things clearly. Ephedrine, and gasoline."

Tom frowns. "They go into meth," he says.

Pete points a finger at him. "Bingo. And I might not remember all the other chemicals they found in my soil, but I do remember that *they* went into meth, too."

"Meth?" Laila says, looking between both men. "From the factory? You're sure?"

"The team I hired sure was," Pete says. "Let me ask you something. How good of a look did you get at my field?"

"Just what was next to the road," Laila says.

"Uh-huh. And you didn't see any corn, did you?"

"Just dirt and weeds," Tom says.

"You head toward those dead bushes," Pete says, "and you won't even see the weeds. I don't know if you know this already, because I sure didn't, but since then I've found out that for every one pound of meth produced, it in turn produces up to *six pounds* of toxic waste. So you take a look at my dead fields, and that'll give you some kinda idea of how much they were putting out."

Laila looks at Tom. "Meth?" she repeats again, incredulous. "Could they really be manufacturing that?"

"Would you be surprised if they are?" Tom says.

It doesn't take Laila long to consider this. "I guess not," she says. She turns back to Pete. "What happened next?"

Pete breathes deep. "Well, figure I was making too much noise. Looking back, I maybe should've been a little more careful. Quieter. But I was mad as hell, you understand. I was goddamn furious. But anyway, one night I'm home, I'm in bed. My wife was already three years gone at that point and it's only been me and the cat in the house since then. Anyway, someone breaks into the house. And then they broke *this*." He pats his right leg and the brace. He sneers. "Warned me off. Said that if I didn't back off and keep my mouth shut, then they'd be back to do worse."

Pete laughs bitterly. "Worse? What worse can they do? Hell, look at me. Look at this place. I ain't got nothing to lose. But I get the feeling I wasn't the only person they visited.

The team I hired, they wouldn't answer my calls no more. Wouldn't call me back, either. No one would. Here's what I think happened, because I've had a long time to ponder over this and I've got two theories – either they were visited like I was, and they were warned off, and they had more to lose. If that's the case, I don't blame them. And that's probably what happened. But my other theory is that someone received a payoff – someone other than me. They figured I wasn't worth anything and they could get away without paying me a dime. Left me with nothing but a bum leg and a dead farm. But maybe a team of ecologists and lawyers, *they* might need their silence paid for. Like I say, they're just theories. I don't reckon I'll ever know for sure."

"I'm so sorry to hear that," Laila says. "How long ago did this happen?"

He taps his leg again. "They broke this four years ago now."

"The factory looks like it's no longer operational," Tom says.

Pete nods. "One year ago, they closed it down. I don't know what happened, but for them to leave it like that, it must have been something big."

"The official record is that there was a fire," Laila says. "It killed seven men. It rendered a lot of the machinery useless."

"I heard that too," Pete says. "Maybe I should have said I don't know what *really* happened. You believe the story?"

"It's their story," Laila says. "So, no."

"It's more likely it was an explosion," Tom says. "No matter how you cook it, whether it's in a trailer or a factory, meth is volatile. And if they were still manufacturing their legitimate products, whatever chemicals they were producing, then that could have made for a *very* lethal combination when the meth went boom."

Pete nods along. "When no one else would listen, I kept quiet. It wasn't that I was scared. There just wasn't anything else I could do. But when I heard about Mississippi Nature, and how they're standing up to DuLac, to them building a new factory, I knew it was time to speak up again."

"How'd you hear about that?" Laila says.

"I read the papers," Pete says. "About the only contact I still have with the outside world." He sits forward. "Listen – if there's a chance you can stick it to those bastards, I want to help. You need me to talk, I'll talk. They took everything from me. It's about damn time someone took something from *them*."

22

Tom and Laila leave Pete Gannon's farm. Laila is driving again. She doesn't speak for a while, digesting what Pete has told them.

"Well," she says finally, blowing out air. "That was a lot."

"Yet none of it surprising," Tom says. "Except, maybe, for the meth."

"Do you think it could be true?"

"I think you already know it is."

"You think they're still cooking it?"

"I'd be surprised if they'd stopped."

Laila nods. She blows air again. "This is a lot," she says. "Has it always been meth? Everywhere they've had issues, and leaks, could it be meth?"

"Maybe a combination," Tom says. "I'd assume they're still pursuing their legitimate business. There'll be a paper trail, a supply trail. It's a perfect front for them. A perfect way to launder the money they're making from the meth, too."

"I knew they were bad," Laila says. "But I – I wasn't

expecting *this*. I'm going to have to pull over. I need to call Mississippi Nature."

Tom feels his own phone buzzing. "Hold that thought," he says. He checks the call. It's Lyle's number. Except, when he answers, it's Valerie's voice on the other end. Out of nowhere, Tom feels his stomach sink. "Is everything okay?"

"I wish it was, Tom," she says. "Some men came by looking for you. They tore up my house, and your room. They went to see Lyle, too. I'm with him now. The bastards nearly drowned him, Tom."

Tom sits forward. "What do you mean? What happened? Is Lyle all right?"

Valerie tells him what happened. Tells him how after Lyle had recovered enough from the near-drowning he'd come straight to the bar, fearing that the men would go after Valerie, too. He was right, they had, but he got there too late to do anything about it. They've been able to comfort each other, at least.

Tom grits his teeth. He squeezes the phone. He sees how Laila steals glances while she drives.

"Lyle's all shook up," Valerie says, "but the doctor says he's going to be fine. He swallowed some water and he feels sick, he's breathing hard, but it's nothing a couple of beers and a good night's rest won't fix."

"What about you?" Tom says. "Did they hurt you?"

"Nothing like what they did to Lyle. I'm fine, Tom. Look, I'll admit, I'm shaken too, but it's just superficial for me. I can fix the furniture and buy a new phone. But they were looking for *you*, Tom, and I don't reckon they're gonna go so lightly on you."

Tom feels the corner of his mouth twitch. He's not going to go so light on them, either. "Have you called the cops?"

"Not yet. I'll call them once I'm off the phone with you."

"Do that, and then the two of you stick together. Are you at the bar? All right, I'm on my way. It's going to take a while, but I'll be as fast as I can." Tom hangs up.

"What's happened?" Laila says, concern in her voice.

"Pull over," Tom says. "I need to drive."

23

It's late afternoon by the time Tom and Laila get back to Davenport. They go straight to the bar. Tom is still driving. He got here as fast as he could. Out the corner of his eye he saw how Laila's hand tightly gripped the door's armrest as he cut in and out of traffic.

They find Valerie inside the bar, nursing a stiff drink. Tom is surprised to see Deputy Roach still around. There's no sign of Lyle.

"Rollins," Roach says as they enter, tipping his hat. "Ms. North."

"Where's Lyle?" Tom says.

"I've taken him home," Roach says. "We've been waiting here for y'all a while now. Figured it was best for Lyle to rest up. Thought it was best for Valerie to do the same, but she wouldn't go."

"They didn't hurt me like they hurt Lyle," Valerie says. "I'm fine. Just shook up is all, like I already told you."

"Where've you been?" Roach says. "Took you a good few hours to get back."

"Memphis," Tom says. He doesn't need to tell him everywhere they've been. "We took Emma to her parents."

"Is she all right?"

"She's better now she's out of town," Laila says.

"Who were the men?" Tom says.

Roach's face turns sour at this. He defers to Valerie, lets her tell them.

"The two men from the other night," Valerie says. "The ones who followed Laila and Emma home. I recognised them. Except for the third. I didn't know him."

"The two who were in custody?" Laila says, turning narrowed eyes upon Roach.

"Where are they now?" Tom says.

"We don't know," Roach says.

"Then maybe you shouldn't have let them out," Laila says.

"Now, you know that ain't fair," Roach says. "Our hands are tied. When their lawyers turn up with bail, what else are we supposed to do? We can't just say no because we get a bad feeling from them. None of us are happy about this."

"But now they've broken bail, you can re-arrest them, right?" Laila says. "And it doesn't matter what their lawyers say."

"They'll have to find them first," Tom says. "Reckon that's gonna be easier said than done."

"I've put out an APB," Roach says.

"You think that's gonna help?"

"Well, we haven't found them *yet*, but..." Roach trails off. He grumbles something they can't make out. It's clear he knows Tom is right.

Tom looks at Valerie, sitting at the bar, propping herself

against it to keep from slouching. "The third man," Tom says. "What did he look like? Crewcut?"

Valerie raises her eyebrows. "Greying," she says. "You know him? Was he one of the men who attacked you?"

Tom nods.

"Those men were sent by DuLac Chemicals," Laila says to Roach. "What are you going to do about that?"

Roach holds up his hands. "Now, slow down. I'll do what I can, of course, but there's no proof that they have anything to do with DuLac."

"Find out where their lawyers came from, and that'll be your proof," Laila says.

"Hold up, I said to slow down. Let me finish. You think I'm not going to do that? Laila, you and your organisation aren't the only people that don't want them building their damn factory here. This is a nice place. A good town. I grew up in Davenport. I've heard the stories of what's happened at some of DuLac's other factories. But I have to do everything by the book. You understand that, right? As much as I don't like their coming here, and what it looks like they're doing already, I'm constrained by the law. I'm *going* to look into the lawyers. I'm going to contact DuLac, and try to find the men responsible for what has happened to Lyle and Valerie – and to you, Rollins. But DuLac aren't in the county yet. It's out of our jurisdiction. We want to talk to them, we're going to have to reach out and ask them nicely, but there's nothing to say they'll agree to talk to us. And then we'll have to reach out to the FBI. Do you understand how long this is all going to take? I'm going to do what I can, but don't expect immediate results."

"I never do," Tom says. "Valerie, are you okay? Do you want me to hang around?"

"Do what you gotta do," Valerie says, and takes a sip of her drink.

Tom takes Laila by the elbow. "Let's go."

"Where are you going?" Roach says.

Tom pauses, looking back at the deputy. "It's a real shame you've got all those constraints," he says. "All those rules and regulations. All that red tape." He pauses a beat, then adds, "Good luck with all you try and do."

"Jesus Christ, Rollins, don't do anything regrettable."

"Regrettable?" Tom says. He smiles. "I wouldn't dream of it, Deputy Roach." He and Laila leave the bar.

24

Wyatt wears his kutte. He sits astride his Harley, the engine rumbling between his thighs.

His father is close by. He's in the truck. He's wearing his kutte, too. They wait, watching the road. After meeting with Corporal Gil McKenna yesterday, they got food then went back to the cabin and laid low. They've spent the day there, too. It's late evening now, and there's only about an hour of light left. The rest of the Forever Road Dogs Texas chapter is soon to arrive. Their associates only asked for a few of them to come for the meet, Nathan Wood prime amongst them, but Wyatt decided on a show of force. He knows it's not going to intimidate them, but it's worth showing their numbers.

The Texas chapter is comprised of sixteen members, not including the prospects. Wyatt and his father await the fourteen other men. The prospects have been left behind, to look after the clubhouse and to keep an eye on things in Texas.

Vic revs the truck's engine to get his son's attention.

Wyatt turns to him. Vic leans out the window to speak. "How you feeling?"

"Fine," Wyatt says. "You?"

Vic shrugs. "You ain't nervous?"

Wyatt thinks about this. "Not right now," he says. "If I thought this was something more serious, then maybe. As it is, it's just gonna be a slap on the wrist. And if it was serious, I wouldn't have brought everyone up here."

Vic nods. He stares down the road. They wait under the shade of a tree. It's a quiet road in the middle of nowhere. Wyatt sent detailed instructions on where to meet.

"Why do you ask?" Wyatt says. "You worried?"

"Everything worries me these days," Vic says. "Sooner we get out of here, the better."

Wyatt nods. He thinks again about getting his father a live-in carer, and grins to himself.

"What you smiling at?" Vic says.

"Nothing. How you feeling today? How's the arthritis?"

"Been better," Vic says. "But been worse, too. Sometimes, this is all I can hope for."

Wyatt cocks his head. He hears a familiar sound, still distant but coming closer. "You hear that?" he says.

Vic points. "I see it," he says.

Wyatt looks down the road. The Forever Road Dogs are on their way.

25

Tom paces the floor of Laila's office while Laila informs Mississippi Nature of what Pete Gannon told them. She's on the phone. She also alerts them to Rollins's involvement in things.

Tom isn't listening. He's angry. Angry that Lyle and Valerie have been dragged into this business. He forces himself to stop pacing and goes to the window, checking the road. He's already circled the building a couple of times, to make sure they're clear. His car was left at the bar when they went to Memphis. He checked it over when they left the bar after speaking with Deputy Roach. It was untouched. It's outside Laila's workplace now, next to her Honda. The building itself had not been broken into, either. Tom checked it, entered with his Beretta before he allowed Laila inside.

He breathes deep, composing himself. Laila is finished on the call. She's watching him. "How are you feeling?" she says.

"I'm fine," Tom says. He goes to her, leans against a desk opposite her. He folds his arms. "How'd the call go?"

"It's all worthwhile information," Laila says.

"How'd they take it?"

"It's intriguing, obviously. I wouldn't say they were *excited* at this discovery exactly, but it certainly helps our case. They're logging the information with our lawyers now. Giving them Pete's contact information. Obviously, we're going to need more proof of the meth."

"Where's the nearest DuLac factory to here?" Tom says. "Still in operation. We can go there, get inside, find out if they're cooking, too."

"I'll check." Laila turns on her computer. While it loads, she says, "If we find out who gave permission for the factory to be built here in Davenport, maybe we could take what we've found out to them. Especially if we go to another factory and find out for sure. More immediately, it might put a delay on things. Buy us some time."

Tom nods.

Laila types. She searches. "Oklahoma," she says after a moment. She types some more. She whistles. "According to the online map, it'll take us nine hours to drive there, give or take."

"Then we should get going," Tom says. "No time like the present."

Laila shuts down her computer. "We drive in shifts," she says, standing. "I don't care what you say, you need to rest."

"So do you."

"I've never denied it."

"That's fair."

They leave the small building. Laila locks the door. They get back into her car. Tom drives first. Laila brings up the map on her phone. It's going to be dark soon. They head out of Davenport. They don't get far.

"What's that sound?" Laila says. "Do you hear it?"

Tom does. "Sounds like motorcycles."

"Sounds like a *lot* of motorcycles, then," Laila says.

They reach a crossroads. Tom stops at the sign. From the left, they see the motorcycles approach. Fifteen bikers. A truck follows close behind. Tom's head turns with them, watching them go. They wear kuttes. This isn't a small group out for a recreational ride. They're a motorcycle gang.

From the back, Tom can see their patch. The snarling dog wearing a crown. Eyes of fire.

Tom grunts.

"What is it?" Laila says. She's been watching the bikers pass, too. They're continuing down the road, heading off into the distance.

"Those bikers," he says, "have you ever heard of the Forever Road Dogs?"

Laila thinks. "I don't think so."

"I have history with them," he says.

"Good or bad?"

"They're trouble," Tom says. He's still watching them go. They're far, now. Far enough for him to follow. "If DuLac Chemicals is involved with meth, then there's a chance the Forever Road Dogs are involved, too." He turns the car right, following the motorcycles and the truck. "Oklahoma will have to wait."

26

Tom follows. He keeps his distance. The road is quiet enough that he kills the Honda's lights. It's getting dark. He notices how Laila grips the armrest again, same as she did earlier on the way back from Arkansas, though he's not driving anywhere near as fast.

"I can't see anything," she says. "How are you driving like this?"

"I'm following their lights," Tom says. "I do what they do."

"Tell me how you know them. Tell me how they could play into all of this."

"I doubt you've heard of a town called Brenton, in Texas?"

"I can't say that I have."

"It's small. I'd have been more surprised if you had. Anyways, a few years ago, I was passing through, and I got into some trouble with a family by the name of McQuade. The McQuades were meth cooks, and they were in business with the Forever Road Dogs for distribution. They had a lab out in the middle of nowhere, in an abandoned factory. I put an end to their operation. During the course of that, I had a run-in with some of the Road Dogs."

"How many is some?"

"Five."

"Do I want to know what happened to them?"

"Probably not."

"How much trouble do you get into, Tom?"

"I've already told you," he says. "A lot."

"And you think the Forever Road Dogs could be involved with DuLac?"

"I don't know that for sure, but it's a fair bet. I already destroyed one of their sources for meth. They could be doing the same thing, but on a bigger scale this time. For now, let's see where they go. This could be nothing, but I'd rather know for sure."

The FRD ride around the outskirts of Davenport. In the distance, there is a wooded area. Tom can't see it through the dark, but he knows it's there.

"Do you think they're going camping?" Laila says. She knows it's there, too. More than likely, she's worked in it.

"You sound hopeful," Tom says.

"I *am* hopeful. I'm hopeful they're not doing anything that concerns us, or DuLac. There were a lot of them, Tom. Do we really need any more trouble?"

"Prepare yourself to be disappointed. I don't think they're the camping type, especially not when they're out in force like this."

"That's what I'm afraid of."

Trees are either side of the road now, making an already dark night even darker. Laila leans forward, struggling to see.

"They're slowing," Tom says, doing the same. He pulls to the side of the road, watching as the FRD do the same further down. The lights of the truck and their bikes die, turned off. Tom kills the Honda's engine so they can't hear it, and makes sure that the interior light doesn't come on and give them away. He watches. He can see dark shapes gathering, and then heading off road on foot, heading deep into the trees.

Laila looks around. "I think I know where we are," she says. "There's a clearing up ahead – where it looks like they're going. It's enclosed – rockface to the north and east, and trees all around. It's a make-out and hangout spot for teens from Davenport. We sometimes go there to clean it up, usually after a weekend, or at the end of whatever school vacation has just happened."

"A quiet spot," Tom says, thinking, wondering what they're doing. He looks around. He doesn't see any other vehicles nearby, parked at the side of the road. "I'm going to stash the car," he says, "and then we're going to follow them."

Laila doesn't respond. He knows she's not keen on the idea, but she isn't going to refuse, either. She's with him, and she knows he's right. This needs looking into.

Tom restarts the engine and turns the car around. He crosses to the other side of the road and drives down into a ditch below the trees, and behind a bush. He reverses up close to the bush. He gets out and quickly checks how it looks from the road. To anyone passing by from the direction the FRD have parked, the Honda is out of sight. The darkness helps, too.

Laila joins him and they run down the road. Tom checks the truck. It's empty, and locked. He follows the FRD trail for a little while through the trees. The FRD are not outdoorsmen, and they've moved clumsily through the underbrush, snapping branches and twigs, kicking up dead leaves and dirt. They're easy to follow. Soon after, Tom is close enough to hear them. He and Laila hold back again.

"The clearing is just up ahead," Laila whispers, her mouth close to his ear so as not to give anything away. "About fifty paces. They're starting to go downhill now, do you see? We keep following, we're going to be down there with them."

Tom understands. "Is there a vantage point?"

"If we go to the right, we're going to be on top of one of the eastern rockfaces. We'll be able to see down."

"We might not be able to hear them," Tom says. "We'll go to the top of the rockface, see how it looks."

Laila leads the way. She's careful not to make a sound, feeling her way through. The ground rises. They reach the top of the rockface. They edge carefully to the rim, not wanting to knock anything loose.

The Forever Road Dogs are gathered in the clearing below. They aren't alone. There's another group already present. They look like they've been waiting for the bikers to arrive. A couple of portable work lights have been placed to the east and west to light up the area so the two groups can see each other. There are seven men and one woman. The men wear suits. The woman, despite being out in nature, is in a pencil skirt. She's wearing flats but looks like she'd be more comfortable in heels.

"That's Carol Hardinge," Laila says, whispering, leaning close to Tom. "She's the spokeswoman for DuLac Chemicals."

Tom hears what she says, but someone else has caught

his attention. Of the seven men in suits, six of them stand back, their hands crossed in front of themselves. Tom can see the outline of handguns on at least two of them. He's sure all of them are armed. This isn't what he's noticed though. The seventh man stands at the front, with Carol Hardinge. The man with the greying crewcut who led the beatdown of Tom around the back of the bar. Of the other six men present, Tom doesn't recognise any of their faces. He doesn't see the two from the car, or the two from the initial night at the bar. For a big corporation, he imagines DuLac Chemicals has a large body of heavies it can call on when needed. No doubt there are others nearby, too, waiting in reserve should they be needed, hidden behind the northern rockface. Tom notices there's a gap between the two rock-faces, which is likely where DuLac came from. He'd wondered where their vehicles were. They must be parked further down the road, and have approached from the north.

Tom leans close to Laila. "The crewcut," he says. "That's who went after Lyle and Valerie."

"Who beat you down?"

Tom nods.

The two groups are talking. So far, it looks like they're doing little more than exchanging pleasantries. Two men from the FRD are at the front. A man with long hair and a thick beard whose kutte reads President, and an older man to his right with a patch that says Founder. Tom notices a familial similarity in the two men's faces. The president laughs about something. The older man smirks. On the opposing side, Carol is smiling politely. Crewcut's face is firm. He smiles a little, but it's a very small smile. His lips are pursed into a thin line.

Tom looks around, beyond the gathering of bikers.

Opposite their rockface, the trees are tightly bunched. There are bushes. At the base of the trees, the ground rises all the way up to the northern rockface. Through the trees, Tom can see only darkness, deepened perhaps by the shadows cast from the work lights.

"We can't hear them clearly from up here," he says to Laila. "We need to get closer." He points toward the hill. "We head for there. Follow me and stay close."

27

Austin Myers is the one who concerns Wyatt.

Motherfucker has *ice* for eyes. Wyatt cracks a joke and Austin smiles at it, but there's no humour there. Hell, it's barely a smile. Carol Hardinge – she's forcing herself to smile, that's clear, but Wyatt wouldn't expect anything less from her. It was a rude joke. She doesn't strike him as someone who enjoys dirty jokes. Shit, he's not sure she likes any kind of jokes at all. At a guess, Wyatt reckons Carol is in her forties, like him, but it's hard to tell if she's early, middle, or late. Her blonde hair is tied back in a severe bun, so tight it pulls the skin on her face taut. She clearly works out, but it looks like she goes to the point of exhaustion, like she uses the gym as a way to punish herself for something. It shows in her face, and in the veins that poke through on the sides of her neck. Wyatt can't see much of her body under her pencil skirt and blazer, but if he could see her arms he reckons they'd be muscular and veiny, just like her calves. She doesn't wear a wedding ring, and Wyatt isn't surprised. She's the kind of woman married to her work.

No time for men – or women – or for having and nurturing kids. He wonders when the last time she had a good fuck thrown into her was. If she had one now, it might lighten her up. Might put a genuine smile on her face. Of course, he's not offering. Next to Karen, it's like comparing a succulent, juicy, perfectly seasoned and cooked steak with a piece of chicken left in the oven too long so all the juices have run right out of it.

Wyatt watches Austin. He knows that some people joke when they're nervous. That's not what he was doing. Wyatt *is* nervous, sure, but he has his men at his back. His father is to his right, and immediately over his shoulder is VP Glen Hurley, and beside him is Sergeant-at-Arms Kurt Holyfield. Close to them are Donnie Willis, Dale McKenna, and Mark Logan. Wyatt told Nathan to hold back. Not to present himself unless he's asked to.

No, what Wyatt was trying to do was get a handle on Austin. To gauge the man. This is only their third time meeting face to face. Wyatt considers him well and truly gauged. They usually talk by phone, or video call. Just like on the phone, Austin is a hard ass. Doesn't have much of a sense of humour, nor the time for one. Austin doesn't wear a wedding ring, either. Wyatt wonders when the last time *he* fucked was, too. The way Austin and Carol are standing and staring back at him, their expressions blank, they look like they're made for each other. As Wyatt suspected, the Forever Road Dogs haven't been summoned here to be congratulated on all their hard work.

Wyatt doesn't let it sour his mood. He remains jovial. "That's enough greetings, huh? My ass is aching from riding all the way here, so what say we get straight into it?"

"We didn't expect you to bring everyone, Wyatt," Carol

says, casting a brief glance over the rest of the Texas chapter. "We only insisted upon Nathan Wood."

"It's been a while since we all got to go on a ride together," Wyatt says. He holds out his hands. "This felt like a good excuse. We've never rode as a group to Mississippi before. I don't believe I've ever been so close to the river before, neither."

"So you all came here to sightsee?" Carol says.

"We came here in all seriousness," Wyatt says. "But we're a brotherhood. You might not understand how that is, and that's fine. I respect that. Not everyone understands it, or else *everyone* would be clamouring to join a club. When we got the summons, we chose to ride here together. There's nothing to it. It's just how we are."

"Mm," Carol says. "And what about your business commitments?"

"We're still committed," Wyatt says. "Our deliveries are on time. We're only here overnight. Early tomorrow morning, we head back to Texas." This is a lie. Most of them will. Wyatt and a select other few will not. They're going to be in Mississippi for a little while longer. "There won't be any disruptions."

"None more than there have already been, I suspect," Carol says.

Wyatt glances at Austin. Austin is looking over the FRD. He pauses at each of the line behind Wyatt, like he's studying their faces. Wyatt wonders what he thought when he looked at Mark Logan. If he was surprised to see him. Wyatt doubts he would allow it to show. Austin is low-emotion as is, but also he's a professional. He knows how to act. He wouldn't give anything away.

Wyatt looks to the six men behind Austin. They stand

resolute, staring, unflinching. Their faces are as impassive as Austin's and Carol's.

Wyatt clears his throat, realising Carol is awaiting some kind of response. "Uh, yeah," he says. "All I can do is apologise about that. We promise it won't ever happen again."

"That goes without saying," Carol says. "And yet, I feel the overwhelming urge to *say* it." She stares at Wyatt. "Where *is* Nathan Wood? I doubt this is him." She motions toward Vic.

"This is my father," Wyatt says. "Founder of the Forever Road Dogs –"

"We know who he is," Austin says, speaking for the first time. "We know who all of you are. Ms. Hardinge was making a point."

"Indeed I was," Carol says. "When we specified to bring along Nathan Wood, we expected him to be presented front and centre, or at the very least at your side."

"Then I apologise again," Wyatt says. "But he's here."

"Then call him forward," Carol says.

"You ain't gotta call for me," Nathan says. He pushes his way through to the front, stopping at Wyatt's left. "I ain't a literal dog. You only gotta ask for me but once."

Carol stares at him. Wyatt can see the tendons wriggling in her cheek while she grinds her teeth together. "I'd assumed that asking for you *once* had been inferred."

"Inferred?" Nathan says.

Carol ignores him. "Do you care to explain your actions?"

Nathan rolls his eyes. Despite what Wyatt told him, he's belligerent. Nathan blows air. Wyatt nudges him hard with his elbow. He tilts his head toward the DuLac contingent, encouraging him to recite his lines.

"All right, all right," Nathan says. He holds up both hands and takes a step forward. "Look, I'm *sorry*, okay?" He pauses for a moment, thinking on what Wyatt told him to say. "What I did was foolish, and careless, and I understand that I jep – jep – that I put the whole operation in trouble. There are no excuses I can make – could make – that could be – that *are* – *could* be acceptable. Uh... Oh! And I'm also very grateful that you paid my bail, and sent the lawyer to get me out. I'm very, very, very, very, *very* sorry." Wyatt doesn't appreciate Nathan's flourishes. He especially doesn't appreciate it when he does a curtsey, hands splayed out to his side, and a flutter of laughter rises from the rear ranks of the Forever Road Dogs. Vic turns and shoots them all a look, and they quickly fall silent.

Carol isn't looking at Nathan. She's watching Wyatt. "I can see you coached him as best you could," she says.

Wyatt doesn't respond. He's not surprised Nathan's little apology speech came out as rehearsed – and poorly, at that. Wyatt has had him rehearsing it since before he came to Mississippi with Vic – once he was calm enough after their initial conversation, that is. He told Glen to make sure Nathan kept at it in his absence.

"I'm afraid *I'm* going to have to take over as coach for now," Carol says. "Perhaps viewing yourselves as a brotherhood has been to your detriment. Perhaps you're too careful about dealing out tough love when it's needed."

"I've never had that problem before," Wyatt says.

"Then why do you have it now? Why is this man, who is so clearly a moron, entrusted with our cargo to cross state lines into Utah?"

"Hey –" Nathan says, but Wyatt jabs him with his elbow again.

"And why was he stupid enough to get himself arrested?" Carol's eyes flare.

She pauses, but Wyatt isn't sure if she truly wants a response. The question felt rhetorical. She's letting it sink in, for all of them.

She goes on. "The business relationship between DuLac Chemicals and the Forever Road Dogs has been fruitful to both sides thus far. We've made each other a lot of money. We can't help but feel as though we've granted you access to more money than you could ever hope to grant to us. That's a fair assessment, is it not? What we put on the table was far greater than anything you could bring."

Wyatt nods. He knows she's right.

"And yet, with this in mind, we've been repaid with sloppiness, and carelessness. This is not an isolated incident."

"In fairness," Wyatt says, "it's been a long time since anything like this last happened. And those other times my boys got into fights, they never got arrested."

"No, but had the police gotten there in time they *would* have been," Carol says, shutting him down. She holds up a finger. "One careless fight," she says. "And yet, that's all it could take. One stupid mistake. There is no space for one stupid mistake. We have to be on top of our game *every single day*. Things are about to become much, much bigger for us. For all of us. We're preparing to go international. You're all aware of that. You're all aware of how much more money we will be making. And yet, on the eve of our embarking on something so big, just *one* mistake could bring it all tumbling down."

The lecture reminds Wyatt of being in school. Carol Hardinge reminds him of so many teachers who used to line him up in front of the chalkboard and attempt to dress him down for his tardiness, or his fighting, or his general attitude, or any number of other transgressions. He didn't like it then, and he doesn't like it now. He bites his tongue and forces himself to keep quiet and take it. It won't be like this for much longer. Sooner than they realise, he can tell DuLac Chemicals to go and fuck themselves.

"We take this matter very seriously," Carol says. She's still not finished. "I need to make this very clear – if anything like this ever happens again, we will be forced to sever our relationship with the Forever Road Dogs. Not just the Texas chapter – *all* of them. And, you see, therein lies our biggest problem. We don't have the kind of arrangement where we can simply shake hands and go our separate ways. You all understand that, I'm sure. No, we would need to be sure that the Forever Road Dogs, not a single member, would ever talk about what we all did together." She pauses. She wants the FRD to understand. She wants her words to sink in, to get through to them. She thinks they're idiots, this is clear, and she's going to talk to them as such. "If our relationship with the Forever Road Dogs comes to an end, then gentlemen, your days come to an end. I won't beat around the bush – there will cease to be a motorcycle club. Every single one of *you* will cease to exist. You'll disappear. It will be as if you were never upon this planet. You may think that you've experienced trouble, gentlemen, but you're not prepared for the trouble we can bring. We will come down on you so hard your heads won't have time to spin. I hope – I *sincerely* hope – that I have made myself clear, and in a manner you can understand. We will never permit anything like this recent arrest and seizure of our goods to ever happen again. There *will* be repercussions."

Wyatt realises he's been holding his breath. His mouth is

dry. He hates this feeling. In all his years as a member, and then leader, of the Forever Road Dogs, he's never felt like this. They are the ones who make *others* feel this anxiety. Getting involved with DuLac Chemicals was the biggest mistake he ever made.

"We understand," Wyatt says. "And if anyone doesn't understand right now, I'll make sure they understand when we get back to Texas. Nothing like this will ever happen again."

Nathan makes a sound, blowing out air, and Wyatt freezes. He feels a trickle of cold sweat run down his spine. On the DuLac side, everyone is looking at Nathan. Slowly, Wyatt turns and does the same.

"Why the hell are you letting her to talk to us like this?" Nathan says. He throws up his arms. "This is bullshit. They knew what they were getting into. They knew who we were, who we are. What – now they're gonna act surprised? They're gonna act tough?"

"Nate – shut the fuck up." It's Glen, reaching out for him to pull him back into line.

Nathan shrugs him off. "Nah, man. We're the fucking Forever Road Dogs. That's supposed to mean something. These corporate assholes can't talk to us like this."

Austin clears his throat. Everyone falls silent. Wyatt looks at him, feeling his blood run cold, knowing that something is about to happen.

"We never intended for Nathan Wood to return to your ranks," Austin says. "An example has to be set." He smiles now, and it's horrifying. It's the first time Wyatt has seen him smile genuinely. Austin raises a hand, and he flicks it forward.

There's a crack. A gunshot ringing out. Nathan's head

snaps back on his shoulders. The back of his skull explodes, spraying blood that splashes upon the men behind him. Nathan falls straight back, his eyes still open. He's dead before he hits the ground.

Wyatt looks beyond the DuLac men. He didn't see where the shot came from, but he thinks it was the rockface. There's a hidden shooter. A sniper.

"A demonstration of our seriousness," Carol says. Austin stares at the dead body. He's still smiling. "As he was your mess, we consider the cleanup of his body to be your responsibility. Make sure to do a thorough job." She turns to Austin. She speaks his name, to draw him away from the corpse. Austin snaps back to attention.

Wyatt doesn't speak. He can't. None of them can. He looks back at the rest of the FRD. They stare at Nathan's body. They don't move. Don't attempt to strike back. A few years ago, lack of immediate retaliation would have been unthinkable. They understand what is happening here. They understand what they're up against.

Carol and Austin turn and leave through the gap in the two rockfaces, disappearing through the trees and into the darkness. The six men behind them gradually break off and follow, until the FRD are left all alone.

Wyatt doesn't move straight away. They're not *entirely* alone. Probably. He looks toward the rockface. The sniper is likely still out there. Still watching. Covering them until they've cleaned up the Nathan mess.

Wyatt looks at his father. Vic looks back at him. He's thinking the same as Wyatt, about the sniper. "Let's just gather him up and get out of here," Vic says. "We don't wanna be here any longer than we need to."

28

Tom and Laila lie flat against the hillock. They've seen it all. Laila almost cried out when Nathan was shot. It was shock. She wasn't expecting it to happen. She was able to stop herself. She buried her face into the grass.

Tom has a name for the man with the crewcut, now. Austin. Austin who? He seems someone of importance. When they're done here, he'll get Laila to contact Mississippi Nature, see if they can find out who Austin is and his job description within DuLac Chemicals. Tom would guess he cleans up their messes. Would guess he was probably one of the men – or at least the one who sent them – who bust Pete Gannon's leg, and has visited whomever else has had issues with DuLac Chemicals over the years. With this in mind, there's a chance he won't be listed internally by the company. He doesn't seem to worry about showing his face, no matter what he's doing. He could be off the books, called in black ops style.

Tom knows where the sniper is. He saw the shot. When

Austin raised his hand, Tom was prepared for something to happen. He watched everything, everyone, and everywhere, unblinking. The sniper is on the northern rockface, concealed in the bushes there. He moved position after killing Nathan. Tom tracked him. He saw him move to the right, the bushes rustling ever so slightly as he made his way along, but moving too much to just be a breeze. Tom knows where he's stopped. He can still see the barrel of the disguised rifle poking out from the foliage, covering the FRD. The sniper himself is probably wearing a ghillie suit to better blend in with the bushes. He's practically invisible. Were it not for the earlier shot, Tom wouldn't know where he was.

Tom doesn't think the sniper saw him and Laila getting into position. If he did, he more than likely would have alerted Austin and the rest of the DuLac men. Or perhaps he did see, but didn't want to give away his position? He needed to remain silent for the killing of the Road Dog. Either could be a possibility.

DuLac have left their work lights behind. They continue to light the clearing. The FRD work by the lights. A couple of them have knelt over the body, inspecting it, making sure he's truly dead, though Tom saw the moment he was shot that there could be no doubt. The bikers mourn him quickly, knowing that they need to leave the area. They can't take time to fully lament his loss.

The FRD barely talk. They all know it's likely the sniper is still watching them. They don't want to risk him hearing anything they might have to say, especially if it's derogatory toward DuLac. Wyatt directs traffic. Tom remembers hearing his name, when he first had his own run-in with the Forever Road Dogs. He wonders if Wyatt heard his. If his men got in touch and explained who Rollins was and the trouble he was giving them.

Tom looks over the Road Dogs, committing as many of their faces to memory as he can. A couple of them leave the clearing, presumably heading back to their vehicles. They return shortly after with a tarp. They spread it out next to Nathan's body and roll him onto it. They wrap him up and carry him away. Tom reckons they'll carry him away in the back of the truck.

Wyatt points at something on the ground. A dark patch. Tom can't see it properly, hidden in the shadows where the work lights don't reach, but he knows what it will be. Blood, brain matter. Maybe some skull. "Clear this up," Wyatt says. "We need to clear everything."

One of his men stands over it, looking down with his hands on his hips. "What we supposed to do?" he says. "It ain't like we can just pick it up."

"Then dig it up, damn it," Wyatt says. "Do I gotta think of everything?"

The Road Dog hurries away and when he comes back he's carrying a shovel. He digs up the stained earth and carries it away.

"What about the lights?" someone says.

"Leave them," Wyatt says. "They ain't ours. The guy still watching us can take them away when he's done." He calls louder, for everyone else to here. "Mount up. Let's ride out."

Wyatt hangs back as the rest of the Road Dogs are leaving the clearing. He looks around. He looks up at the northern rockface, his brow knitted, his fists balled, then he turns and looks at the ground again, making sure they haven't missed anything. Then, he leaves. Tom can hear the engines of the motorcycles and the truck roaring into life.

They start moving, their sound growing dimmer as they get further away.

If Wyatt was right, and the sniper is going to come down and get the work lights, Tom is going to wait for him. He'll capture him. They can have a talk.

Except, the sniper doesn't come down. Tom stays low behind the hillock, keeping a hand pressed into Laila's lower back to make sure she does the same. He can see the end of the rifle. It's still poking out. The sniper has not moved.

"What's happening?" Laila says, keeping her voice low.

Tom doesn't answer straight away. He waits. The sniper doesn't move. "I think he knows we're here."

29

"What do we do?" Laila says.

Slowly, Tom takes out his Beretta. "We need to get out of here," he says. "I don't know when he might have seen us. He could have contacted the DuLac men who were here. They could be on their way back. We'll be sitting ducks." Tom looks at the work lights. They're battery powered. One of them flickers.

"Why hasn't he shot at us?" Laila says.

"Because he can't get a clear shot. We're in the dark, and we're behind this hill. Plus, he doesn't need to shoot. If he's called us in, he just needs to wait us out until the others get back."

"Do you think he knows you've seen him?"

"Probably. If he didn't know before, he's worked it out now when we didn't leave straight after the Road Dogs."

Laila looks back, through the trees behind them. "Could we go that way?"

Tom looks back. "If we got into the trees, I think we'd be

okay. It's dark, and there's a lot of cover. But I don't know if we'd be able to make it that far before he could pick us off."

Laila peers up at the rockface, trying to spot the sniper. "Where is he?"

"To the right. Where the bushes are thickest. All you'll see is the barrel."

"I can't see it."

"Then just trust that I do."

Laila motions to his Beretta with a nod. "Do you think you could get him from here?"

Tom shakes his head. "I'd maybe be able to spook him. But if he's a pro, he knows it's a shot I can't make and it wouldn't faze him." Tom looks around, thinking. "Do you know if there's another way up to that rockface? Could we get behind it from here?"

"Not from here," Laila says. She points to her left. "It's effectively just a flat wall that way. It's not climbable. The only way up is to go through the centre, the way DuLac left. It slopes behind there, like the rockface we were on top of."

Tom looks at the gap between the two rockfaces. It's narrow at the top. It's jumpable. Their only way out of this situation could be to kill the sniper. Tom looks around, to make sure there's no other way. He can't see any. What he does see, at the base of the hillock, is a thick branch in the shape of an L. He formulates an idea. It's weak, but it's all they have.

"I'm gonna kill the lights," Tom says. "Stay down."

He raises his head just enough to see the work lights. He fires into each, casting the clearing into darkness. As quickly as he looked up, he lowers his head again. The sniper does not fire.

They wait for their eyes to adjust to the new pitch blackness.

"Will that make it harder for him to see?" Laila says.

"I doubt it," Tom says. "He's probably got night vision up there. Maybe infra-red. But what it could do is stop something from catching his attention if the lights suddenly show up a shadow."

"What are you thinking?"

Tom slides backwards down the hillock, toward the thick branch. When he reaches it, he remains flat. He shrugs off his jacket. He drapes it onto the smaller part of the L-shaped branch, and then crawls back to Laila. "I'm going to go to the edge of the hillock," he says. When I'm in position, lie flat here, and move to the left. Hold the branch up so the top of my jacket is showing, like I'm crawling along, trying to get closer to the rockface."

"Do you think he'll fall for it?"

"I don't know. You're going to have to make it look good. We'll find out soon enough. And whatever you do, keep your head down."

Tom slides back down the hillock. He goes to the right, to the corner of it. He readies himself, lying flat on his stomach, the Beretta in front of him. He looks back at Laila. She's ready. She's down the hillock. She holds the shaft of the branch in both hands, ready to present it. Tom gives her a thumbs-up.

Laila starts moving to the left. She takes her time. She doesn't rush things. She's smart about it. Makes it look realistic, like Tom is trying to be sneaky but he's growing careless, like he isn't aware of his position. She works the branch along, gradually pushing it higher and higher up the hillock, until only part of it shows over the top.

Tom waits. He holds his breath, hoping that the sniper will see. Hoping that the sniper will believe it.

Laila gets closer and closer to the rockface. If she reaches it, then it's a bust. The sniper has not fallen for it, and Tom needs to think of a new plan *fast*. Laila gets closer. Tom is losing hope. He's already thinking what they could attempt instead.

There's a shot. Tom is already moving. He crawls through the darkness, on his elbows and knees, flat to the ground, going as fast as he can. He keeps expecting to hear another shot. To feel a bullet tear through his side and rip through his innards. The east rockface is close. He's almost at it. Almost under cover.

There is not another shot. Tom reaches the rockface. He hurries behind it, catching his breath. He doesn't stop for long. He keeps moving. He runs now, staying low, moving carefully through the bushes and trees to avoid making sounds. He gets to the top of the rockface and he drops down into another crawl. He looks toward the northern rockface. He can't see the rifle's barrel anymore. Since he shot out the work lights he hasn't been able to see the barrel. Looking down into the clearing, toward the hillock, he can't see Laila. She's staying low.

Tom gets close to the gap. He waits. He stares at the bushes, searching for the barrel, or waiting for some kind of movement. He finds the barrel first. It's moved again. The sniper has gone to his right, Tom's left, closer to the hillock now.

Keeping the barrel in sight, Tom gets to his feet and he runs. He jumps across the gap and rolls through when he reaches the other side. Peering out over the rockface, he sees the barrel has not moved from its new position. Tom makes his way through the bushes, going wide. He stays low, peering through. He reaches the sniper. He lies flat, looking through the rifle's scope. As Tom suspected, he wears a ghillie suit. From behind, it's easier for Tom to see, the bottom half of the sniper's body stark against the rocks. The rifle is an M24 SWS. Tom is familiar with it. He's fired them himself, when he was with the CIA. Right now, the rifle covers the hillock, waiting for more movement.

Tom gets closer. He reaches for his KA-BAR. The sniper's head rises from the scope, only by a couple of centimetres. Tom freezes. The sniper's head turns to the left, just a little. Tom hasn't made a sound, but the sniper has become aware of something. Tom doesn't hesitate. There's no point in continuing to sneak forward. Laila is below, in danger. Tom needs to end this now, and get them both out of here.

The sniper begins to spin, rolling onto his side, swinging the rifle to bear. Tom fires first. The bullet goes through the sniper's left forearm and hits his collarbone. He convulses on the ground, the M24 going limp in his grip, the barrel falling across his chest and pointing to the right of Tom. Tom fires again. This bullet hits the sniper between the eyes.

Tom keeps him covered as he approaches. He makes sure he's dead, though he has little doubt. He pats the sniper down. From inside a chest pocket of the ghillie suit he hears a low burst of static. A radio. Tom pulls it out, catches the tail end of someone speaking. "*– come in, you read? We're two minutes out, keep them covered.*"

The DuLac men are on their way back. Tom is surprised it's taken them so long. All he can surmise is that the sniper spotted Tom and Laila late, toward the end of the FRD clearing up. It's all that would make sense. It would have given the DuLac team long enough to get far away.

Tom doesn't dwell on it. He calls to Laila from the edge of the rockface. "We're clear," he says. "You good?"

Tentatively, she looks over the hillock. "I'm good."

"Then get to the car – they're on their way back. I'll meet you there."

30

Austin calls Wyatt. He says he hopes he's caught him before he's too far gone to Texas.

"I'm close enough," Wyatt says. It's not long after Austin has killed Nathan Wood. Killed one of Wyatt's men right in front of him, and there wasn't a damn thing he could do about it.

"Come to Natchez," Austin says. "I'll send you the address. It's my office. I need to speak with you. It's urgent."

Wyatt figures it must be pretty damn urgent if Austin is contacting him just a couple of hours after what he's done. "All right," Wyatt says. "I'll be there as soon as I can. Just me?"

Austin pauses a beat, like he's thinking. "Just you for the meeting. Keep some of your men handy. You might need them. Find somewhere they can hide out until we've spoken."

"Sure," Wyatt says, grinning as he looks over the men he has already kept handy, hiding out in the cabin he and his father have stayed in the last few nights. "That shouldn't be a problem."

Wyatt never had any intention of leaving Mississippi. Not until he has the guns from Fort Ellicott, anyway. That's still a couple of nights away, so for now he has to go to Austin, find out what's so urgent.

In the cabin, as well as his father, there is Glen Hurley, Kurt Holyfield, Dale McKenna, and Mark Logan. In the morning, Karen will make her way up to Mississippi to meet with them. Right now, she's probably packing their bags. The rest of the FRD are on their way to Texas with Nathan's body. They know about the men who have stayed behind, but they believe it's just business. DuLac business. They don't know anything about Fort Ellicott and the guns.

"What was that?" Vic says.

"Austin," Wyatt says.

"He's got a lotta nerve to be calling you right now," Kurt says.

"What'd he want?" Glen says.

Wyatt tells them.

"When?" Vic says.

"Right now."

Vic cocks an eyebrow. "You gonna go?"

"Reckon I gotta," Wyatt says.

"Alone?"

Wyatt nods.

"You think he knows what we've got planned?" Dale says.

"Don't see why he should."

"It's late," Kurt says. "You gonna ride?"

Wyatt shakes his head. "Gonna take the truck." His father passes him the keys. Wyatt heads for the door. "Y'all sit tight. I'm gonna be a while – I gotta make it look good and take my time. Soon as I know what's happening, I'll call."

Wyatt gets in the truck and drives north to Natchez. He takes his time. Pulls over at an all-night drive-thru to get a burger. Doesn't want to reach Natchez fast enough for Austin to get suspicious. Wyatt knows he would. He gets there too early and Austin is gonna want to know where he was when Austin called, then he'll probably work out how long it would have taken to realistically get back from there. Maybe start asking math problems, like what time Wyatt got turned around and what speed he was going.

Wyatt makes himself comfortable in the drive-thru parking lot. Lets the time pass, working it out for himself in his mind. Ninety minutes go by. He continues to wait. Better to take too long than to be too fast. If he's late, and Austin asks, Wyatt can always say they needed to pull over while they swapped vehicles, and that they had to get Nathan's body out the back of the truck and strap him tight to the back of Donnie Willis's Harley. Had to make it up so it didn't look like they were transporting a dead body.

This part's true, at least. This *is* something they had to do, before the rest of the FRD set out back to Texas, riding through the night so the body wrapped in tarp would be harder to see.

While Wyatt waits, he thinks about Nathan. The stupid son of a bitch. Wyatt had coached him through his apology, but even if he'd delivered it with all sincerity, Wyatt doubts it would have made a difference. He went into that meeting a dead man. Austin and the rest of DuLac had already made up their minds. Nathan was always going to die this night.

Wyatt sighs. Two hours have passed. He resumes the drive to Natchez.

It's quiet in the office. He sees rows of computers, all turned off. The only other people present are a few of the men he saw at the clearing. They point him toward Austin's office. Wyatt knocks. Austin calls him in.

Austin doesn't ask anything about the journey, or the time it took. Doesn't mention anything at all about Nathan Wood.

"We have a problem," he says. His face is flushed red. He's angry. This is the most animated Wyatt has ever seen him.

Wyatt takes a seat without being offered. Austin leans on his desk with his forearms, his fingers interlocked and clasped tight. Wyatt can see his arms and shoulders shaking. "What's the problem?" Wyatt says.

Austin forces his hands to break apart. He raises a hand. His fingers are pale from how tight he's been squeezing. "Before we get into it, I have a question for you, now that we're in private."

"Okay."

"I saw Mark Logan among your ranks tonight."

"I figured you would."

"When will he be dealt with?"

"Very soon," Wyatt says.

"When I passed you the information we found on him, I expected him to be dealt with immediately."

"Uh-huh, and there's nothing I would've liked more. But we've been using him, you understand? Throw the Feds off our scent. But we're gonna deal with him real soon, and we're gonna do it *our* way."

"He saw what happened tonight."

"Nothing you did will get back to anyone," Wyatt says.

"Men I trust are watching him. They ain't leaving his side. He won't even be able to piss solo."

Austin watches him, silent, then says, "Make sure that's the case." He stares at Wyatt with his icy blue eyes. The red is fading from his face now. "There's an issue in Davenport," he says. "A man. He's causing us problems. Got himself involved with a couple of ecologists, and now he's making their battle *his* battle."

"Okay," Wyatt says. He assumes this is the urgent issue Austin summoned him here for.

"He's risen from a minor nuisance to a major one," Austin says. "I've looked into him. Found some details. He's a serious hitter. Ex-Army. Ex-black ops. We want him dead." He points at Wyatt. "This is your chance to redeem your mistakes. To make up for Nathan Wood. Find this man, and kill him."

"I'm surprised you can't handle this yourself."

Austin gives a brief summary of what happened at the clearing after the FRD had left. Wyatt can't say he's sorry to hear that the sniper is dead, but he keeps it to himself. Austin also explains about their run-in with the cops, and two of his men being arrested. "We need to keep a low profile in Davenport," Austin says. "You and your men, minus your jackets and motorcycles – no one will bat an eyelid when they see you. You look like all the other fishermen in that place. You can get in, deal with him, and go back to Texas."

Wyatt nods along. He has no intention of finding this man, whoever he is. It's not their problem. The main players in the FRD won't be around long enough to find him. Wyatt will be *glad* to sail into the sunset and leave DuLac Chemicals with a nightmare ex-soldier on their hands. Fuck them.

"Can you deal with this?" Austin says, awaiting a response.

"Sure," Wyatt says, but he makes it sound good. Like he means it. "Of course. Thank you for the opportunity. We won't let you down. You have a name for this guy? A picture?"

And then Austin says, "His name is Tom Rollins. We have an image, though it's –"

Wyatt cuts him off. "Say that again. His name." He needs to know he heard it right. That he didn't imagine it. That it isn't wishful thinking.

Austin raises an eyebrow. "Tom Rollins."

Wyatt stares, waiting to see if there's a punchline. If this is some kind of a joke. None comes. Austin stares back at him. He's serious.

"We don't need a picture," Wyatt says. "We're on it." And he means it. This is personal.

31

They have a name for Austin. A full name, and a job title.

Austin Myers. Head of security for DuLac Chemicals.

Austin *is* listed internally as being part of DuLac, but there's no picture of him on their site. Tom isn't surprised by this. Mississippi Nature was able to look deeper, to find mention of his name in other places, like a bogeyman that emerges whenever the company encounters any form of issue or pushback. They were able to find an image of him too, but only one.

Tom and Laila hide out in a motel on the outskirts of Davenport. The Honda is parked around the back, out of view of the road. Unlike the motel they stayed in in Memphis, this one is quiet. There are only a couple of other vehicles in the parking lot, and only a few other rooms occupied. It's not a big motel.

When they first arrived, Tom got on the phone and called the sheriff's department. While he did that, Laila called Mississippi Nature and got them to look into Austin. She told them what they'd seen, too. Tom spoke with Deputy Roach. He told him what had happened out at the clearing.

"A *sniper*?" Roach said.

Roach said he knew where the clearing was. Said he'd head out to investigate. He'd call the sheriff in advance, to get some extra men to accompany him.

Tom and Laila wait. Tom stands by the window, watching the road. It's late, and it's quiet.

"Do you think they'll find anything out there?" Laila says.

"I don't know," Tom says. It's been three hours since he spoke to Roach. "Austin and his men were on their way back. They've probably cleaned the place up."

Laila stifles a yawn. "What happens if the cops don't find anything?"

"I don't know," Tom says. "Maybe nothing. If there's no evidence of a crime, what can they do? And it's not like the Forever Road Dogs are gonna come forward and spill about the murder."

"Do you think the bikers are gone now?"

"It sounded like they were leaving."

"That's probably good news for us, right?"

"For now. We've got enough problems on our hands as is. We don't need them adding to it."

"You think they're still looking for you?"

Tom shrugs. "Probably. It wouldn't surprise me if they are. From what I know about motorcycle gangs, they take the killing of their members seriously. Especially if it was caused by an outsider, as opposed to infighting."

"You don't sound very worried."

"I've dealt with them before." Tom turns away from the window. "What worries me is your wellbeing."

"I can take care of myself."

"I know. You proved it tonight. That's not going to stop me from worrying."

"I'm glad you care."

"I'd be heartless not to."

Laila sits on the end of the bed. Tom takes a seat beside her. The mattress feels hard beneath them, but he's so tired it doesn't matter.

"Why don't you rest?" Laila says.

"I'm not the one yawning," Tom says.

She laughs at him, covering her mouth with her hand. She nudges him with her shoulder. Despite everything they've been through tonight, she's managing to smile. To joke. She's tough. She's probably also relieved to still be alive.

"When I was talking with Mississippi Nature," she says, "I asked them to look into who granted DuLac permission to build their factory near Davenport."

"Did they have an answer?"

"No. They said it could take a while. They told us to sit tight."

Tom grunts.

"I'm surprised we haven't heard back from Roach yet," Laila says.

"Mm," Tom says. "It's been long enough for them to search the area."

"Do you think anything's happened to them?"

"It would be a big step for DuLac to go to war with local law enforcement."

"We can't put it past them, though."

"I suppose we can't. But I don't think that's happened." He looks at Laila. He strokes the back of her neck. She closes her eyes. "You should sleep," he says. "It's late. Mississippi

Nature probably aren't going to get back to us tonight. I'll wait up for Roach's call."

Laila opens her eyes. "No," she says. "I'll wait too."

"And if he doesn't call?"

"Then we'll suffer together."

Tom puts on the television. It plays an old black and white movie. Humphrey Bogart is on the screen. Gloria Grahame is with him. Tom realises the movie is *In A Lonely Place*. He hasn't seen it in a long time.

"Bogie," Laila says. She's smiling.

"One of the best."

They watch the movie. When it ends, they still haven't heard from Roach. It's after one in the morning. Too many hours have passed to expect a call tonight.

"We should sleep," Tom says.

As if on cue, his phone rings. It's Roach. "I'd about given up," Tom says when he answers.

"Rollins, listen to me," Roach says. "I'm outside the station right now, in my cruiser, so I'm gonna make this quick. We went out to the clearing and there was nothing there, nor any sign there was ever anything or anyone there tonight."

"That doesn't surprise me."

"Sure, but listen. We get back from the station, and there's a whole team of DuLac lawyers waiting for us. They've lodged formal complaints against you and Laila for harassment and trespassing."

"Trespassing where?"

"Does it matter? Listen, this whole thing stinks to high heaven. I'll do my best to keep pushing, but unless there's a body or a murder weapon, what can we do? I ain't even supposed to be talking to you right now, but I don't like this.

I don't like DuLac. I don't like their sleazy lawyers. If anyone sees you, we're supposed to give you a formal warning and slap you with a restraining order. It sounds to me like they just want an excuse to arrest the two of you, to get you both out of the way. Whatever the two of you are up to, you've clearly got them spooked."

"What we saw tonight spooked them."

"I don't doubt it. Rollins – Tom – I'll do the best I can. But the two of you need to keep your heads low. They're coming for you, and they're coming hard."

"Thanks for the warning, Roach," Tom says. "We appreciate it." He hangs up. He looks at Laila. "Did you hear that?"

She nods.

"We're on our own."

She laughs. It's without humour, and she doesn't bother covering her mouth. "What's new?"

32

Wyatt called the rest of the FRD back to Davenport.

"Rollins is here," he told them. He didn't need to explain further. They turned their bikes around and returned.

It's morning. Wyatt has met with the returnees away from the cabin. The others have come with him. Wyatt called Karen, told her to expect the cabin empty when she arrives. He told her what had come up.

"Son of a bitch," she said. "*Here*? Are you sure?"

"Austin sounded pretty damn sure," Wyatt said. "And he had a picture. Same one we have, from his Army days."

The Forever Road Dogs are back together, after a brief separation. The men are tired after their long ride back and forth. They try not to let it show. They want to begin the search. The *hunt*. If Rollins is here, they'll find him, and when they do, they'll tear him apart.

There's an order of business needs attending to first. They still have Nathan's body. They need to bury him.

They'd have rather done it in Texas, but they need to make do right now. They can't keep carrying him around, and there's nowhere else to store him. The sun is hot, and it won't take long for him to get ripe.

They find a quiet spot of woodland and bury him under a tree. They stand silent to pay their respects. Wyatt stands at the head of the makeshift grave. He needs to say some words.

"Nathan wasn't perfect," he says, "but who is? If he was, he probably wouldn't have been a Road Dog, am I right?"

"Speak for yourself," Kurt says, and there's general laughter at this.

Wyatt smiles. "I don't know that this is the kind of place that Nathan would have wanted to be buried. I think we all know he'd rather be under Texas soil than where he is, but we've gotta make do. It's a pretty enough place, right?"

"Under the tree like this, he can always just pretend he's looking up a skirt," Glen says.

"He always was a leg man," Kurt says.

There's more laughter.

Wyatt lowers his hands for them to bring it down. "I wanna get serious," he says. "We've lost a brother. A good brother. There might not be anything we can do about that right now, but Nathan isn't the only brother we've ever lost. Brad Smithson. Kelvin Maynard. Willie Pence. The Harding Brothers. We lost them, too, and it looks like there's finally something we can do about it. The man who killed them, he's here. We don't know where, but he's here somewhere, and we're gonna find him."

Shouts of agreement go up.

"What we feel for Nathan, we're gonna take it out by finding this asshole," Wyatt says. "We've waited a long damn time for him. We all know what he looks like. We don't need a picture for him. There's a woman with him. Name of Laila North. Vic's got her picture and he's gonna pass copies of it around. Everyone memorise it. You see her, you're gonna find *him*, too."

Vic starts handing out the pictures of Laila.

"Now listen good," Wyatt says, "because this is important. We're gonna split this town and the surrounding areas into quadrants, and we're gonna split the MC into two-man teams. Everyone gets a quadrant. Anyone finds them, they call it in. Now, Rollins is aware of us, so it's gonna be kuttes *off*. No bikes, either. I've spoke with Austin, and he's gonna supply us with rentals. We *drive*. We ain't looking to draw attention, and we don't want him to know we're here. That all clear?"

Murmurs of acknowledgement.

"Good. And one final thing – bring them in *alive*. You all got that? I want him alive, and we want the girl, too. Anyone gets cute and decides to just pick them off from a distance, they're gonna have to answer to me. This motherfucker don't deserve a quick death. We're gonna make sure he gets exactly what's coming to him, and it's gonna be *slow*. He's got five Road Dogs he needs to make amends for. You know it's gonna get bloody."

Wyatt looks around. Their faces are set. They're ready for this. It's been a long time coming. They nod at him. They mutter – agreeing with Wyatt, and cursing Rollins.

"All right," Wyatt says, pleased with what he sees. "Kuttes off, and let's get to it."

33

Carol Hardinge is in Austin's Natchez office. She sits opposite him, on the other side of his desk. Austin is bringing her up to date. After the meeting with the Forever Road Dogs in the clearing last night, Austin and his men escorted her back to her car and then they went their separate ways. She wasn't with them when Austin received the radio call from his sniper, telling him and the others to come back and help deal with a couple of unwanted watchers. The sniper knew it was Rollins and Laila, of course. Their pictures have been well circulated.

Austin feels calmer than he did last night. His initial fury has receded into a sizzling burn. It's always present, but it's no longer overwhelming him. He grabbed a few hours' sleep in his office after he spoke with Wyatt and then called Carol, impressing upon her that they needed to speak immediately. She came straight over. Carol is currently staying in a hotel in Natchez. It didn't take her long to get here. Austin didn't want to tell her what had happened over the phone. His office is clear, as is the work floor. He has his men sweep both regularly.

Carol is concerned about what happened to the sniper. “This is serious, Austin,” she says. “They saw what happened? They saw the biker killed?”

“We have to assume so,” Austin says. “They were gone by the time we got there, but we swept the area. We were thorough. We made sure nothing was left behind that could raise an eyebrow.”

“Apart from the witnesses.”

“We’re working on them. I sent our lawyers to the sheriff’s department. That oughtta put them on the backfoot.”

“It’s not enough.”

“I know it’s not enough, Carol,” Austin says. “And I’m dealing with it. They’ll be in the ground before the end of this week.”

“Mr. DuLac is eager to get the new factory up and running ASAP. For that to happen, we need these loose ends tied up.”

Austin just looks at her. He’s already said he’s dealing with it.

Carol sighs. “Your men are out looking?”

Austin tells her about his meeting with Wyatt. How he has called the Forever Road Dogs back in to find Rollins and Laila.

“Is that wise?” Carol says, her expression twisting with concern. “After last night?”

Austin grins. “First of all, the Road Dogs understand how their bread is buttered. More than that, you made it abundantly clear to them last night that the very last thing they ever want to do is go against us.”

She nods.

Austin sits back in his seat. "Secondly, they have a preexisting hard-on for this Rollins."

"How so?"

"Turns out they have history. Their paths have crossed before, and the Road Dogs already have a hit out on him."

"That's convenient for us," Carol says, her grin mirroring Austin's own.

"Their blood is *hot*," Austin says. "I think they might even want this son of a bitch more than we do. It's personal for them."

"What did he do to them?"

Austin tells her.

She chuckles when he finishes. "Well," she says. "It sounds like these brutish thugs might finally prove to be of some use after all."

There's a knock at the door. It's frantic. Austin and Carol look at each other. "What is it?" Austin says, annoyed.

The door opens. It's one of the tech geeks. The one who found out about Rollins and his past. Austin looks past him, to the men he has outside his door. They stand aside, watching. Their faces betray nothing, but Austin figures it must be bad news for them to have let the geek knock himself. "Sir, something's happening," he says, breathless, like he ran a mile to get here.

"What is it?" Austin says. "Spit it out. Can't you see I'm in a meeting?"

The geek points back over his shoulder with his thumb. "There's a hacker," he says. "Cyber security are shutting them down."

Austin gets to his feet. He strides out onto the work floor, pushing the geek ahead of him. "Where?"

The geek hurries ahead, leading the way. Austin follows.

Cyber security are at the front of the room. There's three of them. They type wildly, fingers dancing frantically over the keys. Austin stares at their screens, but it doesn't make any sense to him. "What's happening?" he says.

None of the three answers. The geek speaks for them. He's chewing a thumbnail. "We have to leave them to it," he says.

Austin grits his teeth, impatient for results and frustrated at how little sense this makes to him.

Carol joins them. "I hope this isn't more bad news," she says.

Austin doesn't respond.

Minutes pass. Eventually, the cyber security team sit back, sighing with relief. They exchange high fives.

"Before you start celebrating too much," Austin says, and they freeze, their shoulders almost touching their ears as they seize up. "Explain to me what has happened."

The man in the middle turns. He clears his throat. "Uh, we, uh, we became aware that someone was using a brute-force attack to get into our systems –"

"A brute-force attack?" Austin says, suddenly alert and looking toward the door. "Are they in the building?"

"Uh, no – it means they were guessing at our passwords."

"All right," Austin says. "Keep it in layman terms."

The man nods. "Yes, sir. So, we, uh, we picked up on what they were doing. They probably had a machine that was running through all of the different combinations, and it got through. The whole thing was pretty clumsy and we've managed to close them down fast, but they, uh, they did manage to get into some files."

Austin's eyes narrow. "What files?"

"I'm looking into it now," the man on Austin's left says.

He hasn't turned around. Nor has the man on the right. His fingers are back to typing, too. "What's he doing?" Austin nods at the man on the right.

He knows he's being talked about. "I'm tracing them back," he says. "Finding out who it was."

"That's good," Austin says, pleased to finally hear someone using their initiative.

A few minutes pass. The man on the left is first to turn. "It looks like..." He glances back to the screen, reading again, checking to be sure. "The file they got into, it has information on the new factory that's going to be built in Davenport. They went through it, all the way back to the beginning."

"What's at the beginning?"

The man checks again. "I'm not sure. I guess the earliest record we would have in this file would be who granted permission for the building of the factory in the first place? Like, the name of the official?"

Austin considers this, thinking what it could mean. He looks back at the man on the right. "What have you found?"

The man doesn't answer straight away. Two minutes pass. He finally turns, eyebrows raised, looking not at all surprised. "The building it came from," he says, "it's registered to Mississippi Nature."

"And they've looked up who gave permission to build the factory?" Carol says.

"That's correct," the man on the left says.

Austin has an idea what it could mean. "I need to make a call," he says. He goes to his office and Carol follows. She doesn't ask what he's thinking. She waits to find out.

Austin calls Wyatt. "I'm going to send you an address," he says when Wyatt answers. "It's in Natchez. Get plenty of your boys up here. Make sure you have men covering it."

34

Ted Brand lives in a suburb on the outskirts of Natchez. He works in the city, for the department of zoning and planning.

Tom and Laila are in Natchez. Mississippi Nature got back to them. Ted Brand gave permission for DuLac Chemicals to build their factory in Davenport, and all despite their poor reputation for ecological damage and a recent fire in Little Rock, Arkansas.

Tom and Laila went by Ted's house first. He wasn't home. No one was. It was empty. They drove into the city. They stopped at a thrift store first for Tom to buy a new jacket, then they continued on to Ted Brand's office building. Mississippi Nature was able to get his car details. Tom and Laila have spotted it in the parking lot around the back of the building. It's not a private lot. Laila was able to drive straight in and park. Tom pointed out the bay for her to pull into. There's an exit nearby. A perfect vantage point for them to watch both the exit, and the car.

"Make yourself comfortable," Tom says. "Unless he

heads out for lunch, we're probably going to be here for a few hours."

"I'm getting used to being in this car," Laila says. She settles herself into the seat. She's behind the steering wheel. She drove here. If they have to chase Ted, Tom wants to make sure he's able to get out fast and run after him. "I don't think I've ever spent so long in it before. Usually I only use it to get to work." She trails off, likely thinking of how much simpler things used to be. "How are your kidneys, by the way? I saw the bruises this morning, after you showered. They look better."

"Feeling better," Tom says. "The pain's still there, but nowhere near as bad as it was."

Tom checks the time. It's eleven thirty. If Ted Brand goes out for his lunch, and if he takes his car, he could be leaving at any point in the next hour and half – unless he takes a late lunch, of course.

"What do you think was with the boats?" Laila says.

Before Mississippi Nature were kicked out of the DuLac Chemicals database, as well as finding out about Ted Brand, they also saw details for the recent purchase of two trawlers and two motorboats. They passed this information on to Tom and Laila, too, unsure if it was worth anything.

"You think they're planning on doing some fishing while they poison the water?" Laila says. "Or do you reckon they're gonna use those boats to dump meth waste further out to sea?"

"Or another way to transport meth," Tom says. "Could be they're planning on shifting it further afield. Expanding their operation internationally."

"Via trawlers and motorboats? That wouldn't get them very far. Central America, South America maybe."

Tom grunts. "And they produce enough meth of their own," he says. "I'm not sure."

"Maybe the boats are a smokescreen," Laila says. "Against the damage they're doing. Like, if they sponsor a couple of fishing boats to fish in the water, that means the water can't be bad, right? Like they're proving a point."

Tom isn't so sure. "A company as big as they are, if that's what they were wanting to do, they could prove their point with a lot more trawlers. And the motorboats are no good for fishing. Not commercially, anyway."

They lapse into silence, watching and waiting. It passes twelve. The sun is shining down, and it's hot in the car. They roll the windows down, but they keep the engine off so as not to draw attention to themselves, which means they can't have the A/C. Tom is used to uncomfortable situations. He focusses on the task in hand. Laila toughs it out. She doesn't complain. She wipes sweat out of her eyes and keeps watch.

A couple of people leave the rear of the building. They get into cars and drive. No one gives Tom and Laila a second glance. None of the people were Ted Brand. Mississippi Nature sent them a picture. A small man, middle-aged, a bald pate with dark hair around the sides.

At twelve-thirty, Ted Brand leaves the building.

Tom taps Laila's leg to get her attention. She was watching the entrance to the parking lot, making sure he didn't come from the front of the building. She turns and sees him.

Ted crosses the parking lot. He isn't in a rush. He wears a grey suit, but he's taken off the jacket and carries it draped over his forearm. "Start the engine," Tom says. "Roll up next to him."

Laila does. She gets beside Ted. Tom is next to him. "Ted Brand," he says.

Ted gives a start, lost in a world of his own. He looks into the car. "Y-yes?"

"Get in the car," Tom says.

Ted doesn't move. "Uh," is all he manages.

Tom gets out of the car. He flashes the Beretta as he stands. He closes the passenger door behind him. Ted doesn't attempt to run. He looks up at Tom. A trickle of sweat runs down his cheek. "We're not looking for trouble," Tom says. "We just want to talk to you. Get in the car. In the back."

Ted hesitates. He swallows. He does as he's told. Tom gets in beside him. Laila drives, leaving the parking lot.

35

Ted sits rigid in the back of the car, staring at Tom sitting next to him. He looks toward where he saw the Beretta, concealed under Tom's jacket.

"I'm not sure who you think I am," Ted says.

"You're Ted Brand," Tom says. "You work for the department of zoning and planning. That right?"

Ted nods.

"Then you're exactly who we think you are."

Laila is still driving. While they travel, Tom notices how Ted nervously plays with his wedding ring, twirling it round and round on his finger. Laila doesn't leave the city. She pulls into the basement of a parking lot, and stops the car in a quiet corner.

Ted looks around. He checks the rest of the basement, looking to see if there's anyone who could help him. There's only a handful of other cars, and they're all empty. They're alone down here. "What – what do you want from me?"

Laila has turned around in her seat, looking back at him. "DuLac Chemicals are going to build a factory down in

Davenport," she says. "Right on the banks of the Mississippi River. DuLac don't have a stellar track record when it comes to environmental safety."

"So why'd you grant them permission to build?" Tom says.

Ted's eyes widen at this. A sense of understanding comes over his face. "You're not *with* DuLac Chemicals?" he says.

"The opposite," Laila says.

"What are you – cops? Private detectives?"

"I'm an ecologist," Laila says.

"And right now I'm a bartender," Tom says.

"Don't sell yourself short," Laila says. To Ted she adds, "He's also a fisherman."

Ted blinks. "I don't – I'm sorry, I don't understand."

"Why did you grant DuLac Chemicals permission to build their factory?" Tom says.

Ted shifts in his seat. "Listen, before I answer, I need to be very clear about something. The two of you, you're in trouble with DuLac?"

"You could call it that."

Ted looks toward the entrance of the parking lot. "How much trouble?" he says. "They could be following you. If they're following you, I can't be seen talking to you. I have a family. I –" He's looking suddenly very panicked. More so than when Tom and Laila first picked him up. He's growing frantic.

"Just calm down," Tom says. "Calm down, answer our questions, and then we'll take you back to your office. No one's going to see you with us."

"How can you be sure?"

"Because we're careful," Tom says. "No one's followed us."

Ted looks at Tom. Looks him in the eye. He sees enough to reassure him. “Okay,” he says, taking a deep breath. “Okay. Listen, if you’re in trouble with DuLac, then it sounds like we’re in the same boat.”

“You’ve upset them?” Laila says.

Ted sighs. “I’m well aware of DuLac’s history,” he says. “You’re asking me why I granted them permission to build, like it was no big deal. Like I shrugged and said, ‘Sure,’ and signed my name to a piece of paper without a care. That’s not what happened.”

“So tell us what did.”

“I turned them down,” Ted says. He shakes his head. “It wasn’t accepted. You know who Austin Myers is?”

“We’re familiar with him,” Tom says.

Ted looks at Tom as if he’s seeing the fading bruises on his face for the first time. He winces when he spots the scab on the side of Tom’s head, mostly concealed by his hair. “I can see you are. He turned up to my office with a couple of his goons. He didn’t hurt me, but he made it very clear that he could. He leaned on me, and he threatened my family, too. He knew everything about me – about my wife, and my kids. Where we live. Where we work. Where the kids go to school. He made it very clear that turning down DuLac Chemicals was not an option.”

“I’m so sorry to hear that,” Laila says.

“So I signed it off,” Ted says, staring bitterly at the back of the driver’s seat in front of him. “I couldn’t run the risk of him following through on his threats, especially for the sake of my kids. You’ve met him, right? He’d do it. I didn’t doubt for a second that he would.” He continues to stare. His face is dark.

Tom and Laila look at each other. This trip has been a

bust. They can't persuade this man to overturn his original permission when he already didn't want to give it in the first place. At this point, Tom isn't sure it's worth telling him about the meth production. The less he knows, the better, for both his and his family's sake.

Ted starts talking again, surprising them both. "And then the mayor came to see me." He's looking up again, looking at them both.

"The mayor?" Laila says.

"You know him, too? Mayor Oswald Goode. He *really* wanted me to push that permission through. He's been greasing the wheels ever since, hot-shotting that factory. They'll start building it soon. He's working hard for it, to expedite the whole process. So far as he's concerned, the sooner they get it built, the better."

"You think he's been threatened, too?" Tom says.

"No," Ted says. "I don't. If anything, I think he's been *bribed*. I think the completion of the factory is in his interests. The way he goes on, it wouldn't surprise me if he has a vested interest in it – like, an investment. He's waiting for a return on his money. That's how it strikes me."

"Jesus," Laila says.

Ted grunts.

"Thank you for the information, Ted," Tom says. "We're sorry to take you out of your day like this, but it sounds like you understand what we're up against."

"Do *you* understand what you're up against?" Ted says. "DuLac Chemicals will either pay off or threaten everyone in their way to get what they want. Who's gonna stop them? They're too rich and powerful to stand up to. If you wanna survive, you just have to do as they say and keep your heads down. I don't know how deep the two of you are in, but if you have the option, back down now and get out. Just run. You're gonna end up dead otherwise."

Tom speaks to Laila. "Let's take Ted back to his building."

"Did you hear what I said?" Ted says.

"I heard you," Tom says as Laila reverses the car and points it toward the exit. "And we appreciate the concern. But we're already in too deep. You know what that means?"

Ted shakes his head.

"It means we're going to have to be the exception."

36

Wyatt is outside of Natchez, sitting up in the front passenger seat of a van that Austin supplied for them. Vic is behind the steering wheel. In the back, there's Kurt Holyfield, Dale McKenna, and Mark Logan. They sit tight, waiting.

Wyatt is on the phone. They keep the line live. Glen Hurley is on the other end. He's in Natchez. Donnie Willis is with him. They're parked on the opposite side of the road to the building where Ted Brand works. Austin sent them all the information he has on Ted. There was a lot. Wyatt pared out the relevant details. They know what Ted looks like. They know where he lives, and where he works, and they know what he drives. Wyatt has a couple of men watching Ted's home, too. Vic is on the line with them, but it's just as quiet as it is with Glen and Donnie.

Glen can see Ted's car, but there's been no sign of the man himself. "What time's he gonna finish working?" Glen says.

Wyatt brings the phone to his ear. "Austin's file says he finishes at five thirty, but he doesn't usually leave until six. Sometimes later."

He hears Glen whistle through his teeth. "Jesus – so we're gonna have to sit here all day long?"

"We've gotta do what it takes."

"We can't just go in and find him?"

"We don't want *Ted*," Wyatt says. "We want *Rollins*. What is going inside going to accomplish?"

Glen mumbles something about using Ted to lure them in. Wyatt can tell he's already realised it's a stupid idea.

"You know what's at stake here, Glen," Wyatt says. "How many years has it taken us to get an opportunity like this? We ain't gonna let it slip through our fingers."

When they first lost their brothers to Tom Rollins, they tried hard to find him. It was like he'd disappeared, though. They couldn't go straight to Brenton, where it had happened. There was too much going on. It was too hot. When they were finally able to get out there, they couldn't find anyone who knew where he'd gone. They spoke to the woman who owned the hotel in town, but she was a hard bitch and wouldn't give them the time of day. Wyatt would have liked to press harder, but her new husband was the recently elected sheriff, and the last thing the Forever Road Dogs needed then was for a lawman to start hassling them. All they knew for sure was that Rollins was no longer in Brenton. That meant he could have been anywhere.

And now he's in Mississippi. He's been in Davenport. He's potentially in Natchez right now, same as they are. So close, Wyatt can already taste their forthcoming vengeance.

Except, not so fast. Their vengeance will come in time. First, Wyatt may have some use for Tom Rollins. A man with the talents of Rollins – they can't just let that go to waste. They can use him to their own ends. Wyatt is going to draw this out. Their revenge will be sweet, and it will be long. He glances into the back of the van, pretends to be looking at all three of the men there. He's not. He's looking at Logan. He has plans for *him*, too.

Double the fun.

But there's the woman, too. Laila North. Triple the fun, in that case.

Wyatt turns back around, grinning to himself.

Glen speaks again. "Hey – hey, you there?"

"I'm here," Wyatt says, lifting the phone back to his ear.

"Someone's just pulled into the parking lot," he says. "It's the woman's car – the Honda. Donnie's just checked, and it's the same plates that Austin told us."

Wyatt grips the phone tighter. "They've just arrived? What're they doing?"

"I'm not so sure they've just arrived," Glen says. "Ted's getting out of the car. They're dropping him off. It looks like they've already spoken to him. We must've just missed them when we first got here."

"What's happening?"

"Ted is speaking to them through the window. He's walking away now. He's going inside the building."

"Rollins? The woman?"

"They're still in the car. It's turning around. Hold on, they're leaving the parking lot." Glen falls silent. Wyatt hears movement, like he's sliding down in the chair to avoid being seen. "All right, they're gone." Wyatt hears their car start up and start moving. "We're turning around and going after them."

"Which way are they coming?" The Forever Road Dogs have every exit out of Natchez covered.

"Right now, they're coming your way," Glen says. "We'll update you if that changes."

Wyatt smiles. He turns to Kurt. "Call the others. We know where they are."

37

Tom is driving now. They make their way out of Natchez. He's spotted a car potentially following them. He hasn't said anything to Laila yet. It's too early to tell.

"What's our next move?" Laila says.

"They're coming at us," Tom says. "It's time we turn it around and hit back at them."

"How do we go about that?"

"We don't have the numbers, so we keep it quiet and we keep it careful. A friend of mine is good with computers. She could potentially get into their network, the way your organisation did, and find the information we need to go public."

"But their security team kicked our guys out," Laila says. "Why would it be different for her?"

"No offense to your guys, but she's better than them. When we're out of Natchez I'll give her a call. While she's doing that, we go back to our original plan of heading out to Oklahoma, to their factory, and we find physical evidence of the meth operation. All of this should be enough to shut it down."

"What about Austin?" Laila says. "Do you think that'll be enough? Do you think he'll stop once the FBI or whoever gets involved?"

Tom smirks. "I hope not. He and I are due a rematch. I owe him more than one. I owe him for Lyle, too."

"We can't forget about the Forever Road Dogs."

Tom sits at a traffic light. In the mirror, he watches the car that's following. It's three vehicles back, but he sees how it's crept over the line a little so it can see them, and see which way they go through the light. "I haven't forgotten about them," Tom says. "I assume they've held a grudge, but they might not know I'm here. They could be gone by now. If we're lucky, they're not a problem for us at all." The light changes to green. Tom goes straight. The following car does the same. "I was surprised at their lack of retaliation when the sniper killed one of them."

"They must be terrified of DuLac," Laila says. "And what they said they would do to them." They heard enough of the discussion to work out what had happened. "Do you think they'll stay in line, like Carol wanted?"

"If we play things right, I don't think they'll have long enough to mess up."

Tom gets out of Natchez and heads south on the freeway. The car is still following. If it's Austin's men, they're a sloppier pair than the two Tom dealt with the other day on the way to Memphis. This car keeps its distance, but not so much as the other. It's a little more overt in its intentions.

Tom tells Laila what he thinks. She doesn't question if he's sure. "Do you think they've been watching Ted Brand?"

"Probably," Tom says. "Except they didn't follow us to the

parking lot basement. They weren't behind us earlier, I'm sure of it. No one was following us."

"So they spotted us after we dropped him back off?"

"Or they waited for us to return. Though that wouldn't make sense. I don't imagine they'd want us to talk to Ted."

"So they turned up late, after we'd already got him?"

Tom doesn't answer. He doesn't know. He maintains a steady pace and keeps an eye on the car. They travel a few miles down the road. There are turns, but the car doesn't take any of them.

"What are you going to do?"

"Same as I did last time," Tom says. "Lure them in, and make sure they can't follow us anymore. I just need to find somewhere suitable first."

The car begins to slow. It pulls back. Tom frowns, watching it. A black van comes up fast from behind, taking its place, bearing down on Tom and Laila in the Honda. On the other side of the road, Tom sees a similar van there, driving the opposite direction. The van behind flashes its lights. Tom looks in the mirror.

Laila shrieks. She points. "Look out!"

Tom turns. The van from the other lane swings left, coming over the grass divider. It's ahead of them. Tom slams the brakes. He's unable to slow in time. The van from the opposite lane slams into the side of the Honda. Tom hears the door crunch beside him. Glass shatters. He's not in control. The van drives them across the lane and toward the verge. The Honda starts rolling.

38

Vic stops the van close to the crash. Wyatt leans out of his open window and waves at the other van. It drives away.

Behind, Glen and Donnie skid their car so that it's sideways across the lanes, blocking them both. A handful of cars slam to a halt, skidding across the lanes, almost crashing into each other.

"Get them!" Wyatt says.

Kurt, Dale, and Logan hop out the back of the van and hurry to the crash. Wyatt follows them. Vic stays in the van. He pulls it closer so there's less distance for them to carry the two.

The Honda is on its roof. Dale and Logan go to the driver's side and cut Rollins out of his seatbelt, then drag him onto the road. Rollins is still half-conscious. There's a cut above his right eye. He's blinking the blood out of his sight. Wyatt looks down at him. He wishes there was more time to savour this, but they need to go. Wordless, he stamps Rollins in the face, knocking him out.

Kurt appears from the other side of the Honda. He's carrying the woman. She's limp. "She still alive?" Wyatt says.

Kurt nods. "Just out."

Dale binds their ankles and wrists with plastic ties, and then they carry them to the back of the van. They bundle them inside. Wyatt gets back into the passenger seat. "We good?"

"We're good!" Kurt says.

Vic drives.

39

Austin is in his office. It's getting late. Some of the geeks are still out on the floor, at their computers. Austin has kept them working twenty-four seven. Mississippi Nature getting into their files has spooked him. They shouldn't have been able to do that. Austin isn't going to run the risk of them getting in again just because his computer geeks have gone home for the night.

Austin is on the work floor, standing at the window. He watches Natchez getting dark. There are no windows in his office. It's quiet outside. He stands with his hands clasped behind him. He breathes deep, controlling his patience. He's waiting to hear from Wyatt. He's hoping for good news. It's been hours now since he sent the Forever Road Dogs the information about Ted Brand.

Austin thinks it's been long enough for the Road Dogs to have either failed or succeeded. He doesn't understand why he hasn't heard from them yet. About an hour ago, he called them himself. Called Wyatt. He checks his cell phone to be sure how long ago it was. One hour and seven minutes. Wyatt hasn't called back.

Austin leaves the window. He returns to his office. On his way, he notices how the geeks still working watch him go out the corner of their eyes. In the office, Austin takes a seat. He leans back in his chair, laces his fingers on his stomach, and closes his eyes. He doesn't plan on sleeping for long. When there's a lot going on like this, when he's waiting on important updates, he grabs power naps when he can.

It feels like no sooner has he closed his eyes than his phone begins to ring. He glances at the screen before he answers it. He's been asleep for thirty minutes. The caller is Wyatt. "It's taken you a long time to call."

"We've been busy," Wyatt says.

"Do you have good news for me?"

"Oh, I'm calling with the *best* news for you," Wyatt says. From his tone, Austin can imagine the smug look on his face.

"I'm waiting."

"You can say goodbye to your problems. They're dead. We've killed them."

"I'm glad to hear that, Wyatt. What did you do?"

"Took them somewhere nice and quiet, out into some woods, and popped them each in the back of the skull. Execution style."

"From the way you reacted to Rollins' name and what you told me about him, I assumed you were going to take your time with him."

"We did," Wyatt says. "That's why I'm calling so late. We beat him bad. Popped his eyeballs. Tore his tongue out. Made the bitch watch. She was crying." Wyatt laughs.

"I'm glad you had your fun," Austin says. He's glad that Rollins and Laila are dead. The only thing he's not glad about is that he wasn't a part of it. "But I believe I asked you to bring them in alive."

"By the time we were through with Rollins he was half-dead and there wasn't much of him left anyway. And with the woman...well, I guess we got carried away and just did her the same way we did him. Didn't seem much point in bringing back half of a package deal."

"That was my choice to make," Austin says. "You should have run it by me."

Wyatt pauses. "You're right. I should've done. My apologies. Like I said, we got carried away. Honestly, I didn't think you'd mind. We dealt with your problem. That's what matters, right?"

"Where are the bodies?"

Wyatt doesn't answer straight away.

"Well?" Austin says.

"We got rid of them."

Austin takes a sharp breath. "I need proof of death, Wyatt."

"You have my word."

"That's not enough."

"It's all I can give."

"Where are the bodies?"

"We dumped them in the Gulf of Mexico."

Austin frowns. "How did you manage that?"

"We borrowed a boat."

"One of ours?"

"No – we went to a boatyard and took one from there. Weighed down the bodies and dumped them in the water. They won't be found. You don't gotta worry about that."

That isn't what Austin's worried about. Something

doesn't feel right to him. Something is off. "What did you do with the boat?"

"We returned it. Whoever owns it, they'll never know it was ever gone."

"In Natchez?"

"No – in Davenport."

"I didn't know you could sail."

"My dad does. Hobby of his, since he can't ride anymore."

"I wanted them alive, Wyatt. And if I couldn't have them alive, I at least wanted their bodies."

"I get it," Wyatt says. "I'm sorry. But hey, look on the bright side. No more problems, right? It's plain sailing from here on out."

Austin hangs up. Something niggles at him, but he can't put his finger on it. It doesn't feel right, but he can't understand why not. Wyatt – and all of the Forever Road Dogs – wanted Rollins dead. He saw it in Wyatt's face. He saw a hatred that can't be faked.

So, with that in mind, Rollins must be dead. And Laila, too.

Why would Wyatt lie about that?

40

Tom feels himself jostled side to side, dragging him from the depths of a deep sleep and wide awake into a throbbing, migraine-like headache. He coughs hard, which sends a fresh bolt of pain shooting through his skull. He tastes blood.

Dimly, he becomes aware of his name being spoken, over and over. "Tom – Tom, *Tom*. Are you awake? Can you hear me?"

The jostling continues, slowing only when he's able to force his eyes open. The voice is a woman's. Familiar. Laila.

Tom manages to raise his head, which sends a wave of nausea through him. As well as blood, he can taste bile now, too.

"Tom, speak to me," Laila says. "How do you feel? Can you keep your eyes open?"

"I feel like shit," Tom says. He manages to keep his eyes open long enough to see that they're held in darkness. When his eyes adjust he might be able to work out what kind of room they're in. He shifts and finds that his wrists are bound behind him, his weight on top of his stinging arms. When he moves his legs, he feels himself bound at the ankles, too.

He shuffles to the side until he feels wall, and manages to sit himself up with his back resting against it. The blood runs back into his arms, and his fingers begin to tingle. He can see through the dark enough to see that Laila is similarly bound and had rolled over close to him in order to jostle him with her knees. She shimmies up now so she's sitting beside him. "I think we're in a basement," she says.

"What do you remember?" Tom says.

"I remember being run off the road. I remember hitting my head pretty hard, and then everything went black. When I came to, I was down here next to you. You've got a lot of blood on your face. I started to worry you might have a head injury. You're not supposed to leave people sleeping if they have a head injury, right? So I tried to wake you up."

"It take long?"

"A few minutes. How do you feel?"

"Like I might have a head injury." The intensity of the migraine pain is beginning to fade now that he's upright and breathing deep. Instead, there is a constant throb, like the bassline in a nightclub song. He still feels sick. He swallows, trying to keep it down. "I don't suppose you saw who got us?"

"I haven't seen anyone since the crash," Laila says. "Just you."

Tom blinks, his eyes gradually adjusting. He looks around. Laila was right – it's a basement. It's empty. No boxes, no storage, no gardening tools. Not even a television or a pool table. The room is bare. To their left is a staircase, leading up to a door which is no doubt locked.

Tom works at the bind on his wrists. It feels like plastic ties. They dig into his skin, rubbing it raw.

"What are you doing?" Laila says, feeling his movements beside him. "Are you having a seizure? Tom?"

"I'm trying to get loose," Tom says. "We can't just sit here and wait."

The door at the top of the stairs to their left opens suddenly, filling the basement with dim light from the room beyond. A man descends the steps. He takes his time. His front is cast in darkness, and Tom can't see who he is. All he can make out from his silhouette is his long hair and his beard, and Tom understands that they have not been captured by Austin Myers and his men.

A light comes on in the basement. It's bright and stabs into Tom's eyes. Small knives penetrate his already tender brain. He throws up into his mouth. He spits it to the side.

"Looks like the two of you have made yourselves comfortable," the man says. There's laughter in his voice. He's enjoying this.

Squinting, Tom is able to look up. Beside him, Laila is wincing away from the light. Tom sees the man's motorcycle boots. His scuffed jeans. His kutte, which reads President above the pocket over his heart. Tom looks into the face of Wyatt, the leader of the Forever Road Dogs.

"You're looking a little worse for wear," Wyatt says. "The both of you. How you feeling? That crash looked painful. But hey, you're still alive, right?" He chuckles.

Wyatt looks at Tom most of all. He lowers himself down to a squat, and tugs at the plastic tie holding Tom's ankles together. "Tom Rollins," he says, drawing the name out and shaking his head like he almost can't believe it's true. "We've been looking for you for a long, *long* damn time. You know why, don't you?"

"No clue," Tom says.

Wyatt is taken aback by this, but he manages to recover himself. "Those men you killed," he says. "They were friends of mine. Brothers. Brad Smithson, sergeant-at-arms – you remember him?"

Tom doesn't answer.

"He was my best friend," Wyatt says. "My oldest friend. You killed him, motherfucker. I've thought about that every day for the last few years, ever since it happened."

Tom shrugs. "I don't think about it at all."

Wyatt is furious. He looks like he wants to lunge for Tom. His dangling hands open and close into fists. He straightens in order to control himself. He forces himself to laugh. "I'm sure you think you're real tough, Rollins. Those men were my friends. Brad Smithson, Kelvin Maynard, Willie Pence, Matt Harding, and Henry Harding. You killed them. *You* did that, you son of a bitch. And you might wanna play cute and act like you don't remember who they are, fine. But you're gonna. Believe me, you're gonna remember their names."

"I'll be sure to remember your name, too," Tom says. "Or maybe I'll forget it. Just like all the rest."

Wyatt smirks. "Keep it up. You ain't in a position to be cracking wise right now. Keep running your mouth like that and I'll stitch it closed." He goes to the base of the stairs and calls up, summoning his men to him.

Tom watches. Five other bikers descend the stairs and stand around in the basement. Three of them have sewn-in labels above their hearts, same as Wyatt. One says Founder, another says Vice-President, and the third is the new

Sergeant-at-Arms. Brad Smithson's replacement, presumably. The five new arrivals glare at him. Moving as little as he can, Tom continues to work at the binds at his wrists. He feels blood running down his hands and fingers.

Wyatt squats in front of Laila now. He reaches to his side and pulls out a bowie knife. He's grinning. Tom sits up.

"Relax," Wyatt says, seeing how he reacts. He reaches down between Laila's ankles and cuts the plastic tie away. "We just want her to be able to walk." He straightens back up and motions to two of the bikers. "Dale, Logan. Take her away."

Laila struggles against the two men, but they heave her to her feet and drag her up the stairs. Laila calls back for Tom.

"What are you doing with her?" Tom says, scared of the answer. "If you hurt her, I swear –"

"Whatever threat you're gonna make, I'm sure you mean it," Wyatt says. "But you can save it. You ain't in a position to do anything. And more than that, she ain't in any danger. We're gonna keep her safe." He leans in and pats Tom on the cheek. Tom tries to bite his fingers. Wyatt snatches his hand back, laughing. The three remaining bikers join in. "Feisty, ain't ya?" Wyatt says. "We're gonna hold on to Laila, so you just behave yourself down here."

Wyatt looks back at the other bikers and nods. They head for the stairs, going back up.

"Rollins, I want you to remember something," Wyatt says before he departs. "I could kill you right now. Hell, I *want* to. But I haven't. You remember that, Rollins. You just keep that right at the front of your mind."

With that, Wyatt kills the basement's light, and then he

leaves too, closing the door behind him, plunging Tom back into darkness.

Tom doesn't understand what Wyatt meant, or why he hasn't killed him. It doesn't really matter. They have Laila. Tom doesn't trust Wyatt's reassurances that they're not going to hurt her. He continues to work at the plastic tie, ignoring the blood that spills from the front and backs of his wrists.

41

Austin hasn't been able to shake the niggling feeling. Instead of ignoring it, he's acting upon it.

Wyatt said they used a boat from a boatyard in Davenport. Austin has checked – there are only three. One of them is where Austin visited Lyle Bound and dunked him in the river. He sent a couple of men there to ask around the boat owners, see if any of them were suddenly low on fuel or if they'd noticed their boats being tampered with. They called him back and said they'd pretended to be cops and talked to everyone present and the boat owners all said things were how they left them. Austin visited one of the other yards himself. This one was a little more hi-tech. It had security cameras. Austin talked his way into taking a look at them. There was no sign of Wyatt last night, nor any of the other Forever Road Dogs.

There's only one boatyard left. It's south of Davenport.

Austin goes there alone. He drives in silence, just he and his thoughts. Pondering why Wyatt would potentially lie to him about killing Rollins and Laila and disposing of their bodies. Why would he keep them alive? When Austin first gave him the assignment he seemed eager enough to put Rollins in the ground. It was genuine, too. A genuine hatred. A genuine desire to kill that man.

So what could have changed? Austin has wondered if Wyatt chose to keep Rollins alive. To draw out his punishment and eventual demise, but if so, that wouldn't have been a problem. Austin just needed to see proof of that. What does he care if the Road Dogs want to cut the man into pieces, as Wyatt claimed they did on the phone. He doesn't care. Hell, more power to them. Just send him the snapshots of it happening.

If Austin had known this was going to become an issue and fill him with doubts, he would have rather done it himself. Even without the issues, he would have rather done it himself. It's been all the damn noise lately that necessitated sending the bikers in his stead, especially since the snatch happened just outside of Natchez. DuLac Chemicals had made a promise to Mayor Oswald Goode that they wouldn't bring any trouble to his doorstep.

Austin reaches the boatyard. It's small. There aren't any fishing boats moored here. These look more like pleasure craft, though none of them are mega-yachts like the one Martin DuLac owns. These are for sailing leisurely up and down the Mississippi River.

Austin parks his car at the side of the road and continues on foot. There's a barrier blocking the way in. He can see an older man in a hut a little further down, reading a tatty old paperback. Austin ducks under the barrier. The older man doesn't notice him until Austin is standing right in front of him. He gives a start. He puts the book down. *The Old Man*

And The Sea, Ernest Hemingway. Austin feels unsurprised by it. It's fitting.

"Help you?" the man says. He looks past him, toward the barrier. "You know, you ain't supposed to just walk on in."

Austin ignores the question, and the advice. Behind the man there is a doorway. Austin saw cameras on the way in. He assumes they must feed through into the room beyond. "You have a break-in last night?"

The older man tilts his head. "A break-in? No..."

"You sure? You've been through the security footage?"

"Well, when I got here the gate was still locked, and everything looks how it's supposed to. None of the boats are gone, so if someone broke in I'm not sure what they would've taken."

"Show me the footage," Austin says.

The man frowns. "I'm not sure why I would do that. Who are you?"

"Show me the footage and you never have to find out."

"I – I don't understand."

Austin reaches back and pulls out his Glock. "I've asked you nicely," he says. "Now I'm telling you – we're going to go and look at the security footage together."

The older man's eyes bulge. He stumbles back, knocking over his chair as he gets to his feet. He raises his hands. "All right," he says. "S-sure."

They go into the back room. There's a single computer, and a couple of old, boxy televisions behind it hooked up to the CCTV.

"Sophisticated," Austin says.

The older man doesn't respond. He no doubt knows already that their setup is a piece of shit. On the computer, he brings up the footage from last night. There are eight cameras at the yard, and they fill the screen in quadrants. It's not high quality. Everything is blocky and distorted. There is a lot of static. It is, however, clear enough to see if anyone breaks in.

"Skim through it," Austin says, watching.

The older man does as he's told. "What are you looking for?"

"I told you," Austin says. "A break-in."

The older man skims through, from late last night to dawn this morning. "I don't think anyone's gonna have come once it was light."

"Keep going," Austin says. "Bring it up to date."

The older man doesn't complain. Just does as he's told, very aware of the gun still in Austin's hand. The first person that appears on the footage appears to be the older man himself, when he first arrives for the day. It's staticky, but Austin thinks it's him.

Austin takes a step back.

"No one," the older man says. "I didn't think there'd been a break-in..."

"Forget we had this conversation," Austin says, pressing the cold barrel of the Glock into the back of the man's neck. "You tell anyone about this, you try to call the cops, anything, I'll know. And I'll be back to see you. You'll never know I'm coming. Me, or my friends."

The older man doesn't respond. He sits frozen. Austin hears a dry click as he swallows. Without another word, Austin turns and leaves the boatyard.

Wyatt has lied to him. Even after their demonstration the other night with Nathan Wood, Wyatt has seen fit to lie. Austin doesn't like it. He feels the anger rising within him from deep in the pit of his stomach soon engulfing him.

He's going to find out *why* Wyatt has lied to him. He's going to find out what has happened to Rollins and Laila. For now, he's going to be smart about it. He doesn't want to spook the Road Dogs and send them running. Doesn't want them to know that *he* knows.

But once he has the information, he's going to destroy their club, just like Carol told them they would.

42

Wyatt has sent most of the Forever Road Dogs back to Texas. The only members remaining in Davenport are those involved in the forthcoming Fort Ellicott heist – plus one. He's told Donnie Willis to hang around. Donnie doesn't know anything about Fort Ellicott. Probably doesn't even know it exists.

Donnie is with Karen. Karen is staying at another cabin, just three miles from the one Wyatt and the others are hiding out in. Donnie didn't ask any questions. He's good like that. Does as he's told. They told him to stay with Karen, to make sure she's all right and to keep her company. He hasn't asked why she's in Davenport at all. Hasn't asked why the others are still hanging around, or why they've kept Tom Rollins and Laila North alive.

Wyatt and Vic drive to Karen and Donnie now. Laila is in the back of the van. She's tied up and gagged. The van is not one of Austin's. It doesn't belong to the Road Dogs, either. It's a rental. They picked it up this morning, under an assumed name and forged documents, for the heist. Austin doesn't know they have it. They already returned his vehicles to him before the rest of the Road Dogs made their return to Texas.

"You think Donnie's gonna get suspicious?" Vic says, tilting his head back toward Laila. "All he thinks is he's here to keep your wife company. Now he's gotta babysit this bitch, too?"

"I don't think he'll ask us anything," Wyatt says. "Donnie ain't like that. Besides, Karen will keep him in line. He suddenly decides to get talkative, she'll feed him some bullshit and he'll swallow it whole. How's the arthritis, anyway? Big night coming up."

"I'm pilled up, I've taken my injections, and I'm good to go. Calcifying bones ain't gonna stop me. I know what's on the line."

They reach Karen's cabin. Vic heads up the porch and to the door while Wyatt goes to the back of the van and gets Laila out. She's wriggling, trying to struggle, but she's tied up tight. Wyatt slings her over his shoulder and carries her into the cabin.

"This who I'm looking after?" Karen says as he drops Laila down onto the sofa.

Donnie stands to the side. He looks at the woman and scratches the side of his nose.

"This is her," Wyatt says, wrapping an arm around Karen's waist and kissing her. "How's Donnie? He behaving himself?"

"Donnie always is."

Donnie is still staring at Laila. She's an attractive woman. She's distracting him. "Ms. North isn't a plaything," Wyatt says. "For now, anyway. So keep your hands to yourself, Donnie."

Donnie grins, knowing Wyatt has read his mind.

"Not in here, especially," Karen says. "That's nothing I wanna hear. You do that on your own time and in your own space."

Laila watches them, eyes fearful, prone and helpless on the sofa.

Vic goes into the kitchen and gets himself a glass of water. He drops a couple of pills. Wyatt doesn't question him on them in front of Donnie, out of respect. The FRD might know Vic has arthritis and that's why he had to step down and why he doesn't ride anymore, but under no circumstances should he ever be made to look weak in front of them.

"How, uh, how long do we gotta look after this chick for?" Donnie says.

"Look at that," Vic says, turning from the kitchen sink. "A question."

Wyatt ignores his father. "Until we tell you otherwise," Wyatt says. "And I don't want anyone to know she's here, Donnie. That clear?"

Donnie looks thrown by this. "Like, do you mean *any*one, or any of the other Dogs?"

"Both," Wyatt says. "Just keep your mouth shut and don't worry about it."

Donnie hesitates. "I ain't used to keeping secrets from the other Dogs," he says. He clears his throat.

"Don't be ridiculous, Donnie," Vic says. "We ain't the Boy Scouts. We all keep secrets when we gotta."

"You already know what he wants," Karen says to Wyatt as an aside.

Wyatt grunts. "Keep your mouth shut, Donnie, and you get dibs when the time comes." He tilts his head toward Laila.

"All right," Donnie says, brightening. "I suppose I can keep *one* little secret."

"Make sure he does," Wyatt says to Karen. "We've gotta go."

Donnie nods at this. He doesn't question where they're going, or what they're doing. Doesn't ask why they're still hanging around in Davenport. Laila made him curious, but he was easily sated. Now, he's back to being a good soldier. Back to being obedient.

Wyatt kisses Karen goodbye. He and Vic leave the cabin and get back into the van.

"You think Donnie *will* keep quiet?" Vic says. He's in the passenger seat, stretching his legs out into the footwell.

Wyatt starts the van's engine. "Even if he doesn't, does it really matter? Any of the other Road Dogs want to question what we've been doing, we're not gonna be around to answer."

43

Tom has worked at freeing himself, wrenching and twisting his wrists back and forth, side to side. The skin on his wrists is raw and bloody. His head still aches. The sickness has passed, though, and he's glad. He hasn't thrown up again. If he had, he'd be concerned about a concussion. He's no longer dazed, and he doesn't feel sleepy. He's confident he doesn't have a concussion.

Tom manages to work his way up to his feet. The basement is in darkness still, but his eyes are well-adjusted now. He grinds the plastic tie against exposed brickwork. He feels it catch on a corner. Finding the corner again, he continues scraping at it. The tie snaps.

Tom shakes out his cramping, bloodied wrists, then lies on his back and raises his bound legs, searching out another brick corner again with the tie holding his ankles together. It's difficult to hook on. He sits up and grabs at the tie at the back, forcing it into place. Gripping tight, he scrapes it up and down against the corner, thinning it out. He yanks down with his legs. The tie snaps.

He rolls to the side and gets back to his feet, looking around. There are no windows in the basement. The only way out is through the door at the top of the stairs. No doubt there is someone on the other side, standing guard. Tom ponders his next move, wondering if he should wait in ambush for when they next come into the basement, or if he should try to get into the house. He needs to think about Laila, and what is best for her. If he breaks free, they could kill her. He has no idea where they've taken her. For all he knows, they could have just moved her to another room upstairs, just to mess with him, to make him think that something worse is happening to her. He thinks about where he could be right now. If it's a house, it can't be in a residential area. They haven't bothered to gag him. If he were to shout, it clearly wouldn't make a difference. More likely he's being held in the basement somewhere secluded. Somewhere like a cabin.

Tom doesn't get to think for long. The door at the top of the stairs begins to open. He hears voices. He drops back to where he was, draping the broken tie over his ankles so it looks like he's still bound. He sits on the other tie and holds his hands behind himself. He looks toward the stairs.

Two men descend. He doesn't know their names, but they're the two lower ranking members of the Forever Road Dogs he saw earlier. The two without titles. One of them has a brown beard, and the other's is blond. They close the door at the top of the stairs and then turn on the basement light when they get to the bottom.

The blond one is talking. "Wyatt said to check in on him regularly. You think this is *too* regular?"

Tom watches them both, waiting for them to get closer. His decision has been made for him. He'll catch them by surprise. Find out who is still in the house/cabin, and find out where Laila has been taken.

"Well, I just think, what's he gonna do?" the other biker says. "You know how hard it is to break those things? I've seen TV shows where they make like it's no big deal and they just bust them with strength, but that's bullshit. That ain't gonna happen, and especially not when he's all beat up like this. He'd need a tool or something to cut through, and there's nothing down here for him. We don't need to be down here every five minutes or whatever."

"It's hardly been five minutes. Wyatt said we still need to check him, Dale. He don't wanna take any chances."

Dale looks down at Tom, posing in his captive position. "Well, there he is," he says. "We've seen him. We've done our due diligence. Now let's go back – I'm getting hungry."

The blond biker stops Dale before he can turn. "Not so fast," he says. "We should check those binds. Get in and have a closer look."

Tom braces himself, preparing.

"Why me?" Dale says. "You do it."

"Because you're the one on watch, that's why," the blond biker says. "I'm just accompanying you down because I'm a nice guy like that. What's the matter? You scared? You said yourself he's still bound."

"He tried to bite Wyatt – you see when he did that?"

"Yeah, but he missed. Just be careful." The blond biker shoves Dale.

Dale shrugs him off. "All right, all right. Don't push me, man. I'm doing it." He shakes his head and takes a step closer to Tom.

Tom is ready for him. He's waiting. Just a little closer...

Before Tom has the chance to do anything, he hears a

thud, and then Dale falls forward, his face hitting the wall close to where Tom is, scraping the brickwork on his way down.

Tom looks up, surprised. The blond biker is shaking out his fist. "Easy there, buddy," he says to Tom. "I can see that you've freed yourself, so just take it easy and keep quiet. We don't want the fellas upstairs to hear us."

Tom gets to his feet, eyes narrowed.

"Name's Mark Logan," the biker says. "Contrary to how it looks, I ain't FRD. I'm FBI. Undercover. Five years with the Road Dogs, now."

"I'm supposed to take you at face value?"

"You think I'm carrying proof? Knocking Dale out is all I can offer you."

Tom looks at Dale, fallen and unconscious. "This you calling it a day on being undercover?"

"Not quite," Logan says. "I'm gonna blame this on you."

Tom raises an eyebrow.

"A head trauma like that, he's not gonna remember exactly how fast you blindsided him."

Tom looks toward the door at the top of the stairs. "I assume we don't have long," he says, "so whatever it is you wanna talk to me about, we better get to it."

"You're probably wondering why Wyatt hasn't killed you," Logan says.

"Still being alive caught me by surprise, I'm not gonna lie."

"Same. I've seen firsthand how much he's been jonesing for you the last few years."

"Then what changed his mind? He finally saw me up close and decided it would be a waste of my pretty face? We got to talking and my sparkling personality won him over?"

Logan smirks. "He wants your help."

Tom isn't sure he heard right. "My help?"

"Help might be a little strong. He wants to use you." Logan tells him about Fort Ellicott, and the armoury. Tells him about the upcoming heist, organised by the man lying on the ground's cousin. Tells him about Wyatt wanting an out from DuLac Chemicals. "He knows you were in the Army. Figures that knowledge could come in useful. Plus, if he sends you in, it means he doesn't have to put one of the other Road Dogs at risk. You're expendable. Of course, he'd like to deal with you himself, but right now he's got bigger problems. Imagine that! All these years he's been looking for you, waiting for you, and then you finally come along and it turns out he needs to run away from DuLac Chemicals and can't do you the way he'd like."

"He got himself in deep, huh? I saw what happened out at the clearing with the sniper."

"You did?" Logan says. "Well, shit. You *have* been active. But if you saw what happened, then you've got a damn good idea of why Wyatt and his inner circle are planning on getting out."

"How'd he get in with DuLac Chemicals in the first place?"

Logan checks on Dale before he answers. He gives Tom a look. "That's on you."

Tom doesn't react. He waits.

"When you shut down the McQuades in Brenton, you left the Road Dogs in need of a new hookup. Enter DuLac Chemicals. DuLac are manufacturing meth on an industrial scale, all across America, and the Road Dogs are distributing it. And now, they've got plans for further afield. They're going global."

"The factory in Davenport," Tom says, thinking. "The boats..."

"Bingo," Logan says. "The boats are to sail it down to the Gulf of Mexico, and from there to a Central American country where Austin has contacts. They're gonna fly it over to Europe."

"Which Central American country?"

"I don't know. The Road Dogs aren't the ones who are gonna be doing the sailing or the flying, so we've never been told."

Tom digests this. "Where's Laila?"

"She's with Wyatt's wife. Karen. Donnie's out there, too. He's not part of this heist, so I ain't sure what they've told him."

"Where they at?"

"Another cabin. Few miles away."

"What they gonna do with her?"

"They ain't gonna hurt her – not yet. She's their leverage over you. They've gotta make sure you play nice. But listen to me, Rollins – I don't doubt for a second that Wyatt's planning on killing you both soon as he's got what he wants from Fort Ellicott."

"When's the heist?"

"Three nights. It's been difficult, but I've got word out to the Bureau. Out here, we're all close together, all the time. Feels like we're always on top of each other. Barely get a minute to myself. As you can see, I manage workarounds." He motions toward Dale. "The night of the heist, there's going to be an FBI team out at Fort Ellicott, waiting. I've alerted them to yours and Laila's presence, too, and I've made sure they don't say anything to the base – we don't want to spook Dale's cousin. Listen, when Wyatt talks to you, agree with whatever demands he makes. Make it look good. I've got your back. Before we get close to Fort Ellicott, a Bureau team will swoop in and get you and Laila out, safe and sound."

"And you?"

"I'll be arrested, too. Don't want to waste my cover. When we're in lock-up, that's when we'll be split and I'll be sent out to my next assignment. Then, it's the end of the Forever Road Dogs, and we'll make our move on DuLac Chemicals, too. It's been hard for me to get anything on DuLac – they're careful – but the Road Dogs have talked openly enough about their connection. I have recordings. We can make a start. Definitely enough to shut down the building of the Davenport factory in the short term, and a start to closing them down permanently in the long term."

Dale is beginning to stir. Both men notice.

"So now you tie me back up," Tom says.

"Now I tie you back up," Logan says. "Except, that's not going to be enough."

"I figured."

Logan shakes his head, loosening up his neck. "Do me first."

Without warning, Tom hits him across the face. He doesn't hold back. Logan stumbles back, but he remains upright. He spits blood, pressing a hand to his cheek. "That wasn't no love tap."

"You looked like you could handle it," Tom says.

"Yeah, well, so do you." Logan rears back.

Tom holds up a hand, stopping him. "You *could* hit me," he says, "but I'm already pretty beat up." He points at his face. "Is anything your knuckles can do gonna get any traction with what's already going on?"

Logan laughs. “You son of a bitch.”

Tom shrugs and turns around. Logan wraps a plastic tie around his wrists again. “If you ain’t gonna take a punch, then make sure your acting’s good enough,” he says.

Tom sits back down while Logan does his ankles. “I’m trusting you,” Tom says to him. “Laila is trusting you. I’ll make it look good.”

44

Austin doesn't call Carol. He arranges a meeting and goes to see her direct. She's in her hotel room. She doesn't have an office in Natchez. Austin has told her she's free to share with him, or take up some space on the floor, but her job necessitates her always being on the move, and so she's chosen not to occupy a desk and computer that could be taken by someone more static.

She's on her cell when Austin arrives. She holds up a finger to let him know she won't be much longer.

Austin doesn't take a seat. He goes to the window. Carol is staying in the Hampton. Her room is on the front of the building. There's what looks like a monument opposite, a shape just bigger than a semi-circle of marble columns and in the centre a circle with trees and the American flag. Austin can't tell what it's a monument for, though he sees a couple of cars drive in and go around it slowly.

Carol's room is as neat and tidy as Austin would expect it to be. Her double bed is made, and he has a feeling this was likely done by her as opposed to the maids. There is no sign of her suitcase, and he assumes it's tucked away in the wardrobe. On the desk close to the window, illuminated by the lamp there, she has work out but it is separated into neat and orderly piles.

Carol finishes her call and takes a seat on the bottom of the bed, crossing one leg over the other. Despite working from her room, she wears a suit with a pencil skirt, her legs clad in tights. She's wearing pumps with a sensible two-inch heel. She looks ready to walk into a boardroom meeting. Austin has never seen her dressed down.

"What can I do for you, Mr. Myers?" she says. "I assume, since you wanted to meet face to face, that it's important."

"Could be," Austin says. He remains standing with his back to the window. "Apparently, Rollins and North are dead." He arches an eyebrow.

Carol picks up on the brow, and his tone. "You have doubts?"

He tells her about the lack of proof. How Wyatt claims the FRD took a boat down to the Gulf of Mexico and dropped the weighted bodies overboard.

"I'm surprised to hear that they sail," Carol says.

"So was I," Austin says. "If it's true, that is. And if it is, if they can sail, it's noted." He taps the side of his head.

"You sound concerned."

"They've lied to me." He tells her about his checking the boat yards. "I *know* they've lied. And so soon after we showed them what we're capable of."

"Mm." Carol nods, a curled finger covering her mouth while she thinks. "Perhaps the bikers wanted some alone time with the two?"

"It's crossed my mind."

"Laila North was an attractive woman, and I've heard

stories about these outlaw bikers." She rolls her eyes. "I pity her."

"*If* that's what's happening," Austin says. "Why would they need to hide that from us? They want to partake in some torture, why would I have a problem with that? Just show me the proof. This whole thing is feeling too secretive on their behalf. They're claiming they've *killed* them, and dumped the bodies where we'll never find them. That's suspicious to me."

"And to me, too," Carol says. "I understand your concerns. What are you thinking?"

"I wanted to bring it to your attention, first of all," Austin says. "But going forward... I'm gonna have my people keep an eye on the Road Dogs. I'm going to ensure my own men are aware of what's been happening, and that they're extra vigilant in turn. And if they're lying to me..."

"If you find out they've put a step wrong," Carol says, "call me. We'll make the decision on how to handle them together."

"And if they need dealt with?"

Carol holds his eye. "Then I'll give you my permission to wipe them out."

45

Tom is dragged upstairs. The biker's kutte says Sergeant-at-Arms. The sergeant doesn't say a word. He's backed up by the vice-president.

They sit Tom down in the kitchen. He looks around, blinking against the light. Gets a good look at the cabin Logan told him they're holding him in. Out the windows, he can see the greenery of trees. A lot of trees. The cabin is out the way, isolated, as he suspected.

There are six Forever Road Dogs present, and another man whom Tom doesn't recognise. He has an Army haircut, and Tom assumes this is Dale McKenna's cousin. Tom stares at the man long enough for it to be clear he's wondering who he is and why he's here.

Wyatt sits directly opposite Tom on the other side of the table. He's grinning. Behind him, he's flanked by his sergeant-at-arms and his vice-president. The founder leans against the refrigerator with his arms folded. He's wincing about something, clearly in some kind of pain. Further back,

Dale McKenna and Mark Logan stand by the door, blocking the way out. Tom doesn't look at Logan for long, but he notices the deep bruise on his face. He sees the scrape on Dale's face from where he took a ride down the brickwork. He rubs at the back of his neck.

"I heard about your escape attempt," Wyatt says.

Tom shrugs. "Shame it was just an attempt."

"You've upset Dale," Wyatt says, jabbing a thumb back toward the biker. Dale glares. "Says you've given him one *hell* of a headache. Good thing Logan was there to keep you subdued, huh?"

"Guess I wasn't as ready to run as I thought I was," Tom says. "Time spent tied up on your ass will do that, I suppose."

"Sure." Wyatt places both hands flat on the table and drums his fingers. "I'm sure you're wondering why I've kept you alive."

"I've thought about nothing else."

Wyatt laughs. "I've done my research on you, Rollins. Ex-Army, huh? And then a period of time where your whole existence was blacked out. What was happening there, huh? I don't expect you to answer. I've got my theories. Needless to say, I know you ain't a joke. You're a serious guy. You're a *risk*. So, to keep you alive, I must be real stupid, huh?"

"Where's Laila?" Tom says. "If you've hurt her, you'll find out how stupid you've been."

"She's fine," Wyatt says. "I've told you already – you don't need to worry about her. Hell, she's safer than you are. She's good and comfortable, keeping my old lady company. You ever heard of Fort Ellicott, Rollins?"

"No."

Wyatt turns to the out-of-uniform soldier. "This here is

Corporal Gil McKenna. He's the cousin of Dale there, but don't worry. He's not holding a grudge against you."

Gil stares at Tom like maybe the opposite is true.

"He's stationed on Fort Ellicott," Wyatt says. "The base is being decommissioned, but it still has a nice, full armoury. Gil here is our inside man."

Tom says nothing.

"We're gonna hit that armoury, Rollins," Wyatt says. "And you're gonna do it for us."

Tom says nothing.

"Look at this guy," Wyatt says, turning to the other Road Dogs. "Stoic, or what? Not a goddamn word out of him." He turns back to Tom. "You at least got a question?"

"Sure, I got a question," Tom says. "What the hell makes you think I'm gonna rob an armoury for you?"

"Because we have Laila. And while I assure you she's comfortable right now, it ain't always gonna be that way. My old lady, she's a stone-cold killer when she needs to be. I give her the call, she'll slit Laila's throat like it's nothing. I got Donnie out there too, though, and I could see in his eyes that he took a real shine to little Miss North. Maybe I'll let him have some fun with her first, huh?" He waits a beat, smiling. "*That's* why you're gonna rob an armoury for us."

"You make a compelling argument," Tom says.

Wyatt laughs. "You're damn right I do."

"But what then? What happens after the heist?"

"After the heist, we let you go. You and Laila."

"You expect me to believe that?"

"Not particularly, but what choice do you have? You're just gonna have to trust that you'll do such a good job, and I'll be so fucking satisfied, that I'm gonna be in the best damn mood of my life and I'll forget all about my five friends you killed. And I'll let you go."

Tom says nothing. They sit in silence for a while. Tom feels all eyes on him.

Wyatt breaks the silence. "We got a deal?"

"It ain't much of a deal," Tom says. "But I don't see any other option."

"Well, so long as you're compliant," Wyatt says. "That's what I like to hear."

The other Road Dogs chuckle. Tom notices how the older man, the founder, doesn't join in. He's wincing still. Distracted by his pain.

"Now I've got questions," Tom says.

"As expected. I don't expect you to go in completely blind."

"What's in the armoury?"

Gil starts listing off weapons and ammunition, looking upward and counting off on his fingers, remembering. "M4s. M16s. Sig Sauers – automatic and handgun. Berettas. Glocks. M550s. M240s. RPGs. All the relevant ammo. Grenades – M84s, M18s, M67s. There's more of everything, but you get the picture. The armoury is full."

"Fort Ellicott planning on going to war sometime soon?"

"Target practice," Gil says.

"That's a lot," Tom says to Wyatt. "What are *you* planning on doing with it?"

"That don't concern you," Wyatt says.

"Sure, it doesn't concern me," Tom says. "But I'm curious. I saw what happened at the clearing, Wyatt. I saw what happened to Nathan."

Wyatt stares at him.

"DuLac Chemicals know about this heist?"

Wyatt says nothing.

"DuLac Chemicals got you scared, Wyatt?" Tom tilts his chin toward the other bikers. "I notice this isn't a full chapter. Everyone else know about this? They know what's happening at Fort Ellicott? I don't need you to tell me what you're planning on doing with the haul, Wyatt, cos I can already work it out for myself. You're scared, and you're running away. You're gonna sell those guns and live the easy life somewhere you don't think they'll ever find you. And you wanna keep as much of the profits from this sale as you can, and that's why the rest of the chapter isn't present. But that's why you need me – because you're worried you're still a couple of bodies short."

"We're using you because I don't give a fuck what happens to you," Wyatt says.

"Except, you do," Tom says. "You don't want some random soldier to shoot me. *You* wanna do it. And not with a gun, hell no. You want something more personal. A knife. Your fists."

"I'm getting real close to using my fists right now if you keep running your damn mouth."

"I need to see the base," Tom says.

Wyatt blinks, surprised by the sudden change. "Sure," Wyatt says.

"And I need to know some names," Tom says. "Ugly One through Five ain't gonna cut it." He counts off the five bikers behind Wyatt, starting with Logan.

"No time like the present," Wyatt says, standing. "We'll take you out to the base now." He motions to Logan and Dale. "Cut his ankles free. Rollins, you need to be on your best behaviour. You try anything, we ain't gonna hesitate.

Laila is dead. You remember that. Keep it real fresh in your mind."

"It's all I'm thinking about."

"Good," Wyatt says. "Get him out to the van. Kurt, Vic, Gil – you're coming with us." He looks down at Tom while Logan holds him still and Dale cuts the tie at his ankles. "We can make our introductions on the way."

46

Tom sits up front in the van, in the passenger seat. Wyatt drives. Vic is in the middle seat. Gil and Kurt are in the back. Kurt crouches directly behind Tom, his Glock pressed into the base of Tom's skull.

"You just be careful where you keep that finger," Tom calls back to him. "I don't wanna see my brains over the inside of this windshield just because we hit a pothole."

"You ain't gotta worry about my finger," Kurt says. "It's nice and steady. You just make sure you behave yourself and there ain't gonna be any problems."

Tom does behave himself. He has to think about Laila's wellbeing, but also he's aware of what Logan has told him. Of the FBI's plan to capture the Forever Road Dogs when they make their move on Fort Ellicott. And, once they have the Road Dogs, the trail will lead them directly back to DuLac Chemicals. The FBI will complete what Laila and he started.

So Tom sits tight. He watches the road. He glances in the mirror, and he spots someone that could be following them.

He doesn't say anything to the Road Dogs. He doesn't make it obvious that he's seen something, but he keeps watching, glancing at the mirror from time to time to check that the black Mercedes is still behind them. It always is.

He hasn't seen Wyatt look at the mirrors too much. Not more so than he should, anyway. They've made no mention of a convoy, and the Mercedes is keeping its distance, like it doesn't want to be seen.

"Once you've got these guns –" Tom says, "– and it's going to be a *lot* of guns, not to mention the ammo – how you gonna get them to your buyer? If you're on the run from DuLac, I imagine you're going far. Over borders. You really think you can get that amount of guns over a border without raising suspicion?"

"None of your concern," Vic says. He's grimacing. His teeth are gritted. He's trying to hide it. He doesn't want anyone to know he's in pain. So far as Tom can see, there's no obvious ailment. Cancer? A bum hip? Something that isn't clear to the eye, whatever it is.

"You just keep your mouth shut and think about Laila," Wyatt says. "That's all that needs to concern you. We get the guns out, and then we go our separate ways."

"Sure," Tom says.

In the mirror, Tom can see the Mercedes still. It's too far back to make out the drivers. He wonders if it's anyone he's already met. If they could be from DuLac. He reckons it's most likely that they're from DuLac. That maybe the Forever Road Dogs aren't being as inconspicuous as they think they are.

Tom won't tell the FRD about the Mercedes. He'll have to try and get a message to Logan somehow. It could be difficult. From what Tom has seen, the FRD are never solo, especially not around him. Logan had to go to extreme measures in order for them to speak. He took a great risk revealing himself to Tom.

Wyatt turns the van down a quiet country road. There are fields either side, and a few trees. The road stretches down as far as Tom can see. There's nothing coming from the other direction. The van slows. Tom checks the mirror. The Mercedes hesitates. It chooses not to follow them down the road. It keeps going. Wyatt doesn't notice.

"This is one of those bumpy roads I warned you about," Tom says to Kurt.

"No need to worry," Wyatt says. "We're stopping." He pulls over into a layby and kills the engine. "We go the rest of the way on foot. Nothing stupid, Rollins. We've made ourselves clear on that."

"Like crystal," Tom says.

"We're gonna have to cut you loose," Vic says. "But Kurt's gonna be sticking real close, and he's gonna have that Glock on you at all times. You get an urge to try something stupid, you just remember that he's the fastest shot in the Dogs. And if you *still* feel like trying something stupid, you just think about little Laila and what we can do to her if you don't play nice."

Tom holds up his bound hands. "Playing nice."

Vic cuts Tom loose. They all get out of the van, apart from Vic. He stays behind. No one remarks upon it. Whatever pain he's in, it seems to Tom that the others are aware of it.

Gil seems shifty on the road. He keeps looking down it, making sure no one is coming. They don't stay on the road for long. They go into the field. Gil leads the way, taking big steps through the overgrown grass. Tom is behind him, with

Kurt at his side. Kurt holds his elbow and keeps the Glock pointed at him. Wyatt follows from the rear.

They turn toward the north through the field. It begins to ascend. Gil takes bigger, stretching steps. At the top of the hill is a crop of trees. They're heading toward them.

They've been walking for just over a mile when they reach the trees. The van is still visible behind and below them. Beyond it, Tom can't see any sign of the Mercedes, though he's not able to look for long. He doesn't want to give it away. He's not trying to do any favours for the FRD. He wonders where it's gone, if perhaps the people inside have parked up somewhere and they too are crossing carefully through the field. If they are, he can't see them. Perhaps they're watching from afar, through binoculars, though he sees no gleam from the lenses catching the sunlight.

Kurt jostles him forward. "What you looking at?"

"Just looking," Tom says. "Wondering why Vic hasn't joined us. Doesn't look like he's on watch."

Kurt doesn't answer. "Through the trees," he says. "Follow the corporal."

Tom does. He finds Gil crouching low at the treeline. He points when Tom gets near. Below them is Fort Ellicott. "That's the armoury," he says.

Tom looks the base over. It's quiet. He doesn't see any troops running drills, or performing target practice. The only life Tom sees is in the watch tower.

"There's only six men remaining on the base," Gil says. "Of which I am one."

"Where do they think you're at right now?" Tom says.

"Off-duty."

"And you regularly go off-base?"

"Since it got decommissioned, yes. Things have gotten slack. They think I'm at a diner in Natchez right now."

"You realise the risk you're taking doing this?"

"It's only a risk if I'm caught."

"And you ain't concerned at what Wyatt and his men might do to your buddies?"

"They're not my buddies," Gil says. "They're my co-workers."

Tom looks to the base. Gil starts to point things out but Tom stops him. He knows what's what. Tom has seen bigger bases. Fort Ellicott has likely shrunk while they've been decommissioning it. A chain-link fence topped with barbed wire marks the perimeter. The armoury is to the northwest. To the rear of the camp is thick woodland. There is one watchtower beside the main gate. The mess hall is north, at the rear, and to the east are the barracks. It's a small building. At most, it probably only holds a couple dozen men.

"Tell me who'll be where," Tom says.

"All right," Gil says. "On the night we go in, there'll be four men on duty, and two will be in the barracks. We're going late, so they should be sleeping. I'll be in the armoury. One man will be up the watchtower. Two will be on patrol. They'll do a sweep of the base every fifteen minutes. When they're not on patrol they'll be in the mess hall."

"You listening close, Rollins?" Wyatt says.

"Uh-huh," Tom says. "And I want you to listen to *this* – we don't hurt those men down there." He doesn't know when Logan's FBI team will move in. Doesn't know if they'll swoop in before anything can happen, or if they'll wait until it's in progress. He has to be prepared for either. If they get through the gate, he can't run the risk of the soldiers being harmed.

Wyatt snorts. "We don't hurt them? What, you think we're just gonna walk in and politely ask them to lie down until we're done?"

"That's not what I mean and you know it," Tom says. "No killing. No maiming."

Wyatt snorts again.

"I'm serious."

"Sure."

Wyatt is noncommittal. Tom will need to keep this in mind. He doesn't want the soldiers getting hurt. He won't allow it.

Tom watches the base, thinking of how best to approach it. Again, if the FBI are in position (and Tom thinks they'll probably hide out in the trees to the rear of the base) then there shouldn't be any need to think about what they'll do. He has to make it look good for the Road Dogs though.

"You planning?" Wyatt says.

"You got one already?" Tom says.

"Of course. But I'm willing to compare notes."

"If you're sending me in first, then we're doing it my way."

"That what you think?"

"That's what I know. That's how it is. I'm on point, so we do it how I say."

"Like I said, I'm willing to compare notes."

"Sure, we'll do that, and you'll see my notes are better." Tom turns. "We don't need to be here anymore. I've seen all I need to."

47

Terry and Marshall were following the Forever Road Dogs. They call Austin to tell him what they've seen.

"We couldn't follow them down the road," Terry says. "It was too quiet, and it looked like they were pulling over. We held back so they wouldn't make us."

Austin is in his office. He sits at his desk. He's alone. "Were you able to double back?"

"We pulled further down the road, and we were able to get a good enough look at them. They were trudging through a field."

Austin frowns. "A field?"

"Yeah. But Austin, listen – they weren't alone. There were two of them who weren't bikers. I don't know who one of the guys was, but the other was *real* familiar."

Austin feels a cold hand clench in his guts. "Who?" he says, though he feels he already knows the answer.

"Tom Rollins," Terry says.

Austin sucks his teeth. He stares at the door. "You're sure?"

"I've seen him up close and personal," Terry says. "We both have. I still got a hole in my face to show for it. It was him, no doubt."

"Did you see them return? Did they go back to the van?"

"Yeah."

"And Rollins was still with them?"

"Live and in colour."

"Son of a bitch," Austin says under his breath, grinding his jaw. Now he knows. He knows for sure. After this call, he'll inform Carol of what he's learned. Wyatt, the Road Dogs, they've kept Rollins alive. But why? He wishes he knew. "What about Laila North? Any sign of her?"

"None."

"Did you see where the road led?"

"Yeah – some Army base. Fort Ellicott. You heard of it?"

Austin has. "It's decommissioning. Before long, there won't be anything out there." Why would the Forever Road Dogs take an interest in an Army base? Why would they keep Tom Rollins alive and take him to see it? It doesn't make sense.

"What do you want us to do?" Terry says.

"Stay on them. Don't let them see you, and report back to me if anything happens." He hangs up and calls Carol.

"You know," she says as she answers, "I don't think we've ever talked so much before. Especially not with such regularity."

"We've never had so many issues before," Austin says.

"More bad news?"

"Rollins is alive." He tells her what Terry has just told him.

Like him, Carol is confused about Fort Ellicott. "What do you make of that?"

"I don't know," Austin says. "It doesn't make sense to me. I doubt they're looking to enrol."

"And from what you've told me, Rollins left that life behind a long time ago. Could he have some kind of connection on that base? An old friend? A relative?"

"Not a relative," Austin says. "His mother is dead. His father is in New Mexico, in some doomsday prepping commune. His brother is in Chicago, running a gang or some shit."

Carol laughs. "This Rollins has proven to be a very colourful individual."

"I'm sick of his colours. He should be dead. I was promised he was dead."

"What are you going to do about the bikers?"

"I don't know just yet. I'm going to have my team ready. Make sure they're armed to the teeth and ready to move at a moment's notice. If the Forever Road Dogs are planning something, I want to know what it is. If it affects us in some way, we need to be prepared for that. I won't allow a bunch of filthy bikers to ruin what we've built, and what we're building."

"Are you going to talk to Wyatt?"

Austin is silent. He's thinking. "I'll arrange a meeting," he says.

"Are you going to ask him for an explanation?"

Again, Austin thinks. "Not directly, no. He'll lie. But I'll offer him an opportunity to explain himself. If he doesn't take it, then as far as I'm concerned, when the time comes it'll be open season on the Road Dogs."

48

Tom doesn't know the time, but he thinks it's late. It's dark in the basement. It's cold, too. The chill runs through him. He breathes deep and ignores it. He's bound again, and it's hard for him to get comfortable on the rough, uncovered floor. He sits propped up with his back to the brickwork. It sounds quiet upstairs in the cabin.

Tom can't sleep. He thinks about Laila. He hopes she's all right. He knows he needs to rest. He's still beat up, and he needs his energy for everything that's coming. When the FBI make their move, he doubts the Road Dogs are going to go down without a fight. He's prepared for that. He and Logan will be in the middle, in the thick of it. It could come down to them to subdue the FRD, to encourage them to surrender. Except Logan said he's planning on getting arrested too so as not to blow his cover. Tom supposes that's if they go quietly.

As he finally begins to doze, he hears the door at the top of the basement steps slowly open. Through one half-closed eye, he looks toward it, wondering who it could be. The kitchen beyond, through the open door, is in darkness. One biker descends. He doesn't turn on the basement light. He's moving carefully, quietly. "Rollins?" he whispers.

It's Logan. "I'm awake," Tom says.

Logan creeps forward and drops to a knee in front of Tom. "Everyone's asleep upstairs," he says. "I had to wait a long damn time for them to pass out. How was today?"

"I got a look at the base," Tom says.

"I heard you made a plan."

"It has to look good. You said to make it believable."

"Yeah. Wyatt's gonna do things your way, not that it should matter."

"There was a Mercedes following us today," Tom says. "One of your guys?"

"No," Logan says. "My people are holding back until the night of the heist. They wanna get them in the act. Did you see who it was?"

"They kept their distance. They were careful. DuLac, potentially."

Logan doesn't speak for a moment. Tom can't see his face through the dark. He's probably thinking. "I wonder if they know what Wyatt is planning."

"Or else they're suspicious."

"Yeah," Logan says. "I found out where we're supposed to be sailing to – Nicaragua. Wyatt said today, when he was going through the plan. He and Vic have been learning how to sail. They've appropriated DuLac's plan for transporting the meth down to the Gulf of Mexico. They're planning on taking the boats that DuLac have purchased, using those. Once they have the guns from Fort Ellicott, they'll head straight to DuLac's private boatyard. If I had to guess, I reckon that's where they'd plan on offing you and Laila."

"But it shouldn't get that far."

"No, it should not. It *won't*. But I thought I'd make you aware."

"Did he *say* that's where they'd kill us?"

"No, but it was inferred."

"I'm surprised they've kept Laila alive."

"I had to talk them into it," Logan says. "I said you might ask for proof of life. Truthfully, I think they're enjoying dangling her like a carrot, and they expect to enjoy it more when they snatch that carrot away from you."

"How will the FBI get Laila back?"

"From the boatyard. I know where it is. There'll be a smaller team lying there in wait. They'll make a move as soon as Karen and Donnie appear. They'll get Laila secure."

"Your guys know where they'll be at Fort Ellicott?"

"In the trees."

"I figured."

"And there'll be back-up further afield, ready to swoop in when the time comes. The FRD won't know what's hit them. Just two more nights. That's all."

"Why they leaving it so late?" Tom says. "Why not strike tomorrow? Or hell, tonight even?"

"Something to do with security. With the decommissioning of the base. Gil says that two nights from now is optimum." Logan looks toward the top of the stairs. "I better go. Don't wanna stay down here too long and run the risk of one of them going to the kitchen for a drink or something. Sit tight, Rollins. This is nearly over."

Logan leaves the basement. Tom is alone. He watches the door. It remains closed. There is no movement upstairs. The Road Dogs remain asleep.

49

Wyatt hears from Austin. He wants to meet. Wyatt is surprised, and he doesn't like it.

He rides his Harley to their meeting. Wyatt doesn't go alone. Vic follows in his truck. They meet outside of Davenport. It's not far from the FRD's cabin. Wyatt takes his time arriving. Austin is already there, standing by the side of his car. He appears to be alone, but after the incident with the sniper the other night, Wyatt wouldn't be shocked if there are eyes on him.

"I'm surprised you're still around," Austin says. "I thought you would've gone back to Texas."

Wyatt had expected this. He's prepared. "We've got Nate's body," he says. "You expect us to ride down there with him? We're not gonna take a risk on that. We're gonna have to bury him here, but if we're gonna do that then we're doing it the right way."

"And what's the right way?"

"The Road Dog way. You might see a few more of us in town in a few days, but we'll be on our best behaviour."

Austin stares at him. Wyatt doesn't back down. "Nathan's body must be getting ripe by now," Austin says. "Where you keeping it?"

"In a cool, dry place, where none of us can smell him."

"Sensible."

"Why did you want to meet?" Wyatt says.

"You got somewhere you need to be?" Austin says. "You busy?"

"No. But I reckon you probably are."

Austin smiles. He rarely does. Wyatt doesn't like it. It's unnerving. He prefers it when his face is either neutral, or annoyed. "I thought we should clear the air. With regards to Nathan."

Wyatt isn't sure he believes this.

Austin can see his doubt. "The debt is paid. We don't want there to be any further issues. We don't want you, or any of the Road Dogs, to feel like they still need to make up for the mess Nathan made by getting into a barfight."

"Okay. I'll be sure to pass that on. We appreciate it."

"Good."

"We needed to meet face to face for this?"

"It would have been over the phone, but when you said you were still in Davenport it makes sense to look each other in the eyes, doesn't it?"

"I suppose..."

"And I wanted you to truly see my gratitude at how you helped us with the Rollins and Laila problem." Austin stares at Wyatt for a long time.

Wyatt doesn't like it. He stares back. He knows he can't back down. Can't allow anything in his demeanour to reveal the truth. At the same time, he feels the hair rise on the back of his neck. He stops himself from swallowing. "Our pleasure," Wyatt says. "Rollins was a problem of our own that went way back."

"He led you to us though, isn't that right? When he blew up your prior meth connection."

"I suppose that's true."

"So we should probably have a modicum of gratitude for his past actions." Austin is smiling again. It chills Wyatt's blood. "Shame about the bodies, though."

"All I can say is sorry," Wyatt says. "We should've known better."

Austin shrugs. "What's done is done, right? So long as it was dealt with."

Wyatt doesn't like how Austin is talking. He's summoned him here to this meeting, but he's not really saying anything. It feels more like he's probing. Like he's trying to find answers without asking the questions.

Wyatt is struck by a thought that makes him numb – *does he know*? Does he know about Fort Ellicott? About the guns? About *Rollins*?

The motherfucker seems to know about everything else. Seems to know what they do and where they are. Was Wyatt foolish to think he could outsmart him? Has he made a grave mistake?

He's come too far now. He can't back down. There's no turning back from the road he has set himself and the Road Dogs on. He resists the urge to look back at his father in the truck. He doesn't know why he wants to see him. For support, perhaps, but also to let him know his suspicions regarding Austin, and what he could possibly know. He keeps his head still. Keeps his eyes on Austin's.

"And it was dealt with," Wyatt says, glad to hear that his

voice is firm. It doesn't shake. It doesn't crack. It sounds how it always does.

Austin finally looks away. He looks at the fields around them. He looks at the sky. "Beautiful day, isn't it?"

"Sure."

"How long are you going to be hanging around? When do you bury Nathan?"

Wyatt wets his lips. "Couple more days."

"And then you're returning to Texas?"

"Yeah."

Austin nods once. "Okay," he says. He opens the driver's side door on his car. "I'm surprised it's taking so long."

"We have to wait for the other chapters to arrive."

"Ah. So it's going to be a *big* deal."

"He was one of us."

Austin waves a hand. "You don't need to explain it to me. I'm not going to intrude upon your traditions. You said you'd keep a low profile."

"And we will. But we can't make ourselves invisible."

"No barfights," Austin says. When he grins, he looks like a wolf about to pounce.

"Wouldn't dream of it," Wyatt says. "We'll go back to Texas for that."

Austin laughs. Wyatt doesn't like the sound. It puts his teeth on edge. Austin starts to get into the car, but then he pauses. "Logan?"

"We'll be dealing with him soon," Wyatt says. "*Very* soon."

"Send me an update." Austin finally gets into his car. He drives away. Wyatt watches him go. He walks to his father in the truck. Vic's window is down.

"What did he want?" Vic says.

"I think he knows," Wyatt says.

"Knows what?"

"I'm not sure exactly, but he knows *something*. This little meeting here, I think he wanted to make me aware, because he just said a whole lot of nothing, but what did come out of his mouth concerned me."

"He ain't gonna matter for much longer."

"That's true." Wyatt looks down the road, Austin's car gone from sight now. "But it still makes me uneasy. We're gonna have to be careful."

"We were anyway."

Wyatt grunts. "Let's get back to the cabin. We got another problem it's time to deal with."

50

Tom's ankles are cut loose and he's taken up into the kitchen. Judging from the quality of the light outside, he guesses it to be late afternoon.

The kitchen smells of gasoline. On the table he sees empty glass bottles, rags next to them. They're going to make Molotov cocktails for the heist. Tom is aware of this. It seems early, though. They're not heading to Fort Ellicott until tomorrow night.

There's a pair of dark clothes on the table, too. Jeans, and a long-sleeved shirt. "Those are for you," Wyatt says. "For tonight. Figured you'd wanna be in something dark."

"What's happening tonight?" Tom says.

Wyatt grins. The other Road Dogs present – Vic and Glen – laugh.

Something isn't right.

"Take a seat," Wyatt says.

Tom does so.

"Come on through, fellas," Wyatt calls.

From the other room come Kurt, Dale, and Logan.

"I was just telling Rollins here about the change of plans," Wyatt says.

Tom manages to snatch a look at Logan's face. His eyes briefly narrow. He doesn't know what Wyatt's talking about.

"Tell him the new plan, Wyatt," Glen says.

"The new plan is, *tonight* we hit Fort Ellicott."

Logan can't stop himself. "Tonight?" he says.

Wyatt smiles at him. Tom doesn't like it. "That's right, Logan. Tonight. That okay with you?"

Logan clears his throat. "Sure," he says. "But...why?"

The other Road Dogs are laughing. Tom and Logan are the only two not. They exchange glances now.

"You think we don't know, Logan?" Wyatt says.

Logan doesn't respond. It's clear there's nothing he can say.

"Pat him down, Kurt," Wyatt says.

Kurt does. He unarms Logan, takes his phone, then takes a step back. "That's everything."

"No wires?"

"No. Just the phone."

"Destroy it."

"Take a seat, boy," Vic says, pulling out the chair opposite Tom while Kurt heads outside with the phone. Glen grabs up the empty bottles and moves them away, puts them on the counter where Logan can't grab for them.

Logan sits.

"We know you're FBI, friend," Wyatt says. "Known for a few months now."

Logan sits rigid. He doesn't speak. He stares right back at Wyatt, not backing down. He doesn't try to deny it. It's clear there's no point. Kurt returns soon after. The phone is gone.

"Austin found out," Wyatt says. "Seems like there ain't much that man can't find out." He shoots Vic a look that Tom doesn't understand, but he doesn't elaborate further. He turns his attention back to Logan. "I don't know how he found out. He's got connections everywhere. Hell, maybe even in the FBI. It wouldn't surprise me. But I suppose what it all boils down to is that you've gotta be careful every single day, don't you, Logan? All anyone else has to do is get lucky once, and then the truth is out. Anyway, Austin let us know. I didn't wanna believe it, truth be told. You've been with us a long time, Logan. A *long* damn time. Just about broke our hearts to find out you'd been stabbing us in the back all this while. Of course, we kept this knowledge small. Kept it confined to the inner circle – the men here in this room, minus Dale. Dale knows now. Knows it wasn't Rollins who blindsided him down in the basement."

"Uh-uh," Dale says, glaring at Logan.

"Figure he owes you one."

Dale steps in and punches Logan in the face, bloodying his nose and mouth. Dale steps back, still glaring, shaking out his fist.

Logan eyes him down. He spits blood in his direction.

Wyatt laughs. "See, it's that toughness had me not wanting to believe it was true. Some FBI suit can hang with the Forever Road Dogs? Hell no, say it ain't so. But we had to accept the truth. Now here we are. We kept the knowledge of who you truly are small, because that meant no one else was liable to give away what we knew. That meant we got to control the narrative. We fed you false lines of bullshit for the last few months, Logan. We used you to keep the FBI off our backs. It wasn't an indefinite solution, but it was never meant to be. You're just like DuLac. Another problem we had to solve. I mean, why do you think you're *here*? Why do you think we brought you in on this heist over all the others? And now, tonight, we solve the problem of both you *and* DuLac."

"Is the heist true?" Tom says.

"Oh, that's true," Wyatt says. "But the night it was planned for never was. It was always going to be tonight. Whatever you had planned for us, it ain't going down. We'll slip away from the FBI before they ever have a chance to launch their net, and we'll get clear of DuLac before they know what's coming, too.

"Now, Rollins, we know that Logan's been sneaking around talking to you. Telling you what he's got planned, and who he really is. We ain't happy about it, but me and the boys have talked and we've agreed that this doesn't have to affect our agreement. For you and Laila. So far as the two of you go, that remains the same."

"What's happening to him?" Tom tilts his head toward Logan.

"Oh, he's coming with us." Wyatt smiles. It's a sinister smile. Logan does not wilt under it, but he's likely not looking forward to finding out its intent. "We'll keep you around. We got a lot to talk about when we get where we're going – and don't believe for a second that we're really going to Nicaragua. If you got word to your FBI buddies already, they ain't gonna find you there. They're never gonna find you. We're gonna take our time over you, rat. Nice and slow. Do to you all the things we're gonna miss out on doing to Rollins here. You're gonna tell us everything you ever told your bosses. You're gonna tell us everything they know about us."

Logan is stoic. If he's scared, if he's fearing for his life and worried about what they're planning on doing to him, he doesn't let it show.

"Take this motherfucker down into the basement," Wyatt says, "and soften him up real nice. We don't want him pulling any shit tonight. He ain't got nothing to lose and he knows it. Tie him up tight when you're done."

Kurt, Glen, and Dale haul Logan out of the chair and drag him down into the basement. They slam the door shut behind them. Already, going down the stairs, Tom can hear the meaty thuds of them laying into Logan with fists. He hears something falling down the stairs, and assumes they've pushed him the rest of the way.

"I want to talk to Laila," Tom says. "I want to know she's all right, or else I'm not doing shit."

Wyatt shrugs. "Fine. I'll call her."

"Video call," Tom says. "I want to see her."

Vic pulls out a Glock while Wyatt makes the call, and covers Tom. Tom notices the way Vic's hand trembles ever so slightly. Parkinsons? He sees how thick and gnarled Vic's knuckles are. His fingers are swollen. Arthritis? Whatever is wrong with him, Tom can see that it must be slowing him down. In a fight, he's not going to be as dangerous as the others.

Wyatt is on the video call. "Hey, sweetheart." He's talking to his wife. When Tom looks, he can see the vague shape of her face and her dark hair in the phone's screen. "I got Rollins here. He wants to see Laila. Make sure she's okay."

"She's peachy," Karen says. "Having the time of her life, I'd wager."

"See, that's what I've been telling him, but he ain't having it. Wants to see her with his own two eyes."

"Sure." Karen calls offscreen. "Donnie. Bring Laila

through." She turns back to her husband. "What's happening over there?"

"We've dealt with the Logan problem," Wyatt says. "He's down in the basement right now with Glen, Kurt, and Dale."

"Wish I could be there."

"I'm sure you do. I'm looking forward to seeing their handiwork. Maybe I'll send you a picture, though you'll see it for yourself soon enough."

"Keep me in suspense," Karen says. "I can wait." She pauses. "Laila's here now."

Wyatt turns the phone and holds it in front of Tom's face. He sees Laila. There are cuts and bruises on her from the crash, but nothing serious. Another of the bikers – Donnie – is holding onto her from behind, holding her jaw and forcing her to look into the screen. She shakes him off.

"Nice to see you," Tom says, his tone casual. "It's been a while. You're looking well."

Laila forces herself to smile. "I wish I could say the same."

"Ah, at this point I'm used to looking like shit."

"Wrap it up," Wyatt says.

"You hear that?" Tom says. "I'm already being told to take it home. I haven't seen you in days now, and they've decided this is enough. These people have no sense of romance."

Laila laughs. If her hands were free, Tom could imagine her delicately covering her mouth.

"Are you okay? Have they hurt you?"

"I'm fine," Laila says. "How about you?"

Wyatt takes the phone away. "He's just dandy – doesn't he look good to you? You two young lovers will be reunited real soon." Wyatt hangs up. He looks at Tom. "Satisfied?"

"For now," Tom says. "But more than that, I'm surprised."

"Surprised? At what?"

"You never said goodbye to your wife."

Wyatt is unimpressed. "Get changed."

51

It's late. Out on the work floor is just the cyber security team, sitting at their posts. When Austin last checked in on them, they looked bored. They were stifling yawns. There hasn't been another cyber attack since they kicked Mississippi Nature out. Austin doesn't care. He's not going to risk it happening again.

Austin can't remember the last time he left his office. There's been so much going on lately he's been sleeping here. It feels like he needs to be here at all times, ready at the drop of a pin to jump into action if and when he's needed.

When his phone rings, he's almost not surprised. He's grown accustomed to the sound. When things are silent is when he's most on edge.

It's Jeremy. "The Dogs are on the move."

"You have eyes on them?"

"We do. We're following."

Austin gets to his feet. "Which route are they going? Fort Ellicott?"

"Looks that way."

"Stick on them. Don't spook them. Don't engage them. I want to know what they're doing. Try to keep eyes on them at all times." Austin heads for the door. "I'll ready the team."

52

The FRD head out to Fort Ellicott. They travel in two vans. Tom is in the back of the lead van, with Kurt. Logan is in the back of the other. Tom saw him when they brought him back up from the basement. They'd messed him up. His blond beard and hair were red with matted blood. His jaw was swollen, his nose was broken. His left eye was purple and completely shut. He had lacerations on both cheeks and across his forehead. Tom imagined his torso was covered in contusions, unable to see the damage wrought there through his torn clothes. They'd taken his kutte from him. As they carried him outside, Tom couldn't tell if he was still conscious. Blood trailed from his bottom lip.

Tom ignores Kurt and his gun. He looks through the gap in the front seats, out the windshield. It's dark. It's late. After midnight. Wyatt is driving. Dale is beside him. Vic and Glen are in the other van. Tom is wearing the new black clothes they provided for him. They haven't given him back his gun. They've permitted him the use of his KA-BAR, but they've said they'll only give it to him when they reach the base. Currently, Kurt has it.

Tom watches the road ahead, gauging how far out they are from Fort Ellicott. He's thinking. Things have changed. The FBI aren't coming. They aren't swooping in to save the day. Tom, Laila, and Logan are on their own.

Except, Laila and Logan are out of commission. Tom is solo on this.

Right now, his best option – his *only* option – is to go along with the heist. It's his only hope of buying time. It's his only hope of getting them to bring Laila to him.

"How far out are we?" he says.

"Eager to get to it, huh?" Wyatt says.

"Eager to get it over with."

"Ten more minutes, and you can start working toward that goal."

Tom grunts. "Can't wait."

The Molotov cocktails are in the footwell at Dale's feet. They're held in a plastic crate to keep them from moving around. The smell of gasoline is thick in the van.

"You're all clear on how we're doing things?" Tom says.

"Sure," Wyatt says, but he's dismissive. Tom doesn't like it. They don't care about the soldiers. Don't care if they hurt, cripple, or kill them. Tom can't allow that. That's another problem for him. Something else he needs to think about right now, as well as the fact they could try to put a bullet through him as soon as they have the weapons from the armoury. So many things he needs to remain wary of...

Tom waits for the ten minutes to pass. He takes deep breaths, stilling himself, preparing mentally and physically. The Road Dogs have given him a couple of days without being assaulted or chased, and so he's had a chance to heal up. His kidneys feel fine. He's no longer pissing blood. His ears aren't ringing and his head does not ache. He's ready for what he has to do.

Wyatt turns the van down the road that leads to Fort Ellicott. Tom sees the layby where they parked when they brought him for a closer look. Wyatt doesn't stop at it this time. He keeps driving, going further down the road. In the distance, Tom can see a dim glow coming from the base.

"Gil says there shouldn't be anyone coming down this road tonight," Wyatt says. Tom isn't sure if he's saying this for his benefit, or for the whole van. "No one scheduled, anyway. He says if it changes he'll find a way to let us know, but he doubts it will. Means we can get in closer."

"I don't care where you park," Tom says. "Just make sure you're in position for my signal."

Tom wishes he could see the mirrors. The other van will be directly behind them, he's sure, but he'd like to see if there's anyone following them again. None of the Road Dogs have mentioned anything, but they didn't notice yesterday, either.

Tom considers who it could be. The most likely culprit is DuLac Chemicals. Austin and his men. If they're following, how would they react to seeing the Road Dogs raiding a US Army base and stealing the weapons from its armoury? They'd have questions, no doubt, but would they attempt to stop the FRD? Would they intercept at all? If they do, that could play to Tom's advantage.

There's no guarantee they're coming, or that they'll do anything, but if it happens, Tom is ready. He's ready for anything and everything right now.

Wyatt turns off the van's lights. He pulls to the side of the road and crawls to where the trees on the right end. He parks but keeps the engine running. Tom can see Fort Ellicott. Can see the lights that illuminate the grounds. It's distant, and they're small, but he can make out the movement of the two men on patrol that Gil told him about.

"Showtime," Wyatt says.

"KA-BAR," Tom says without turning, holding his hand out to Kurt.

"Kurt's accompanying you to the fence," Wyatt says, reaching into his kutte and pulling out a one-handed bolt cutter. It's for the fence. "Beyond that, you're on your own. And be fast, Rollins. Taking your time ain't gonna do you or Laila any favours."

Tom feels Kurt slap the handle of the KA-BAR into his open palm. Tom clips it onto the waist of his black jeans. He takes the bolt cutter and then turns to face Kurt. "Stay close, and stay low. Do as I say and keep your mouth shut."

Kurt's Glock is still out, pointing at Tom. He glances toward Wyatt. Wyatt nods. "You boys better get moving," he says.

Kurt opens the van's side door, sliding it wide. Tom hops out. He's already moving. Kurt slams the door closed after them and then has to hurry to catch up.

In the watch tower there is a spotlight, but it points down at the road in front of the entrance gate. It's a mobile spotlight, but it's currently stationary. Tom runs wide, parallel to the base, where the shadows are thickest and darkest.

He hears Kurt panting and wheezing a few paces behind him. "What are you doing?" he manages to gasp out.

Tom stops, spinning and dropping to a knee, dragging Kurt down so they're level. "What did I tell you?" he says. "I said shut the fuck up and do as I say. Follow me and keep your mouth closed."

"You're going the wrong way," Kurt says, breathing hard.

"Do you want me to run *into* the spotlight? We go wide. The guard in the watchtower isn't moving the light. If we stay in the dark, he can't see us. He can't see *anything*. We don't want to give him any reason to move that spotlight and find us."

Kurt glares at him. He sees the sense in what Tom is saying, but he doesn't want to have to acknowledge it. "If you're lying to me –"

"Just shut up and stay low," Tom says. "I'm going ahead. I'm not holding back for you. Just stay out of the way and don't give them any reason to look for us."

Tom turns and starts running again, not looking back to see if Kurt is keeping up. His run turns into an arc, heading toward the east of the base, where the barracks are and where there are fewer lights. He looks toward the watchtower. It's in darkness and he can't see the man up there. The spotlight stays where it is.

Tom reaches the chain link fence, dropping low to the ground. He looks around, checking the base, making sure no one has seen him. There are security cameras on the base, but Tom has plotted his route to avoid them.

Breathing hard, but trying to be as quiet as he can, Kurt comes up beside him, dropping to the ground. He makes a dry-heaving sound. Tom shoots him a look. Kurt swallows it down.

The two soldiers on patrol are at the base of the watchtower, calling up to the guard there. They don't speak for long. They shout back and forth to each other, but Tom can't hear what they're saying. The two on the ground laugh about something, then turn and head toward the mess hall.

Tom cuts into the chain-link fence with the bolt cutter,

snipping upwards until there's a hole big enough for him to crawl through. He pauses before he does, turning back to Kurt. "I clear the barracks, and then the watchtower," Tom says.

"I already know this," Kurt says.

"Good. Get into position and I'll signal you when it's time for the diversion."

Kurt hesitates.

"*Now*," Tom says.

With a sneer, Kurt turns, crawling to his feet, and then he runs off into the darkness, doing as Tom earlier said and sticking to where it's darkest so as not to be seen.

Tom makes sure he's gone, then tucks the bolt cutter into his boot, concealing it under his jean leg. He crawls through the fence and keeps going until he reaches the rear of the barracks. He gets to his feet and looks in through the window, searching for the two men who should be sleeping. He spots them in cots on opposite sides of the building, lumpen shapes under blankets. Tom leaves the window, edging his way around the building toward the front door. He sticks to the shadows, away from the lights. He looks up toward the watchtower. It's in darkness up there, and it's hard to see the guard. Tom watches and waits, trying to catch a glimpse. He stands very still. He has about fifteen minutes before the two men on patrol will emerge from the mess hall and perform another sweep. It's plenty of time. The base is shutting down. They're not expecting anything to happen. They're not concerned about anything. They're laid back.

There's movement in the watchtower. The guard shifting position. His back is to Tom. He's staring out into the dark.

Keeping an eye on him, Tom slides to the door into the barracks. It's unlocked. Silently, he slips in. He pauses, watching the two sleeping soldiers, making sure neither of them is faking. They shouldn't be. They're not expecting him. They're not expecting anyone.

He goes to the man closest, asleep on his right. Tom gets down to a knee at the head of the bed, watching the other sleeping man three rows down on the other side of the building. He doesn't move. Tom takes out his KA-BAR and then places a hand over the soldier's mouth and shakes him. The soldier wakes with a start. He looks at Tom, instantly alert. Tom presses the KA-BAR to his own lips in a *shh* gesture. He leans in close. "Where's your handgun?"

Tom doesn't uncover the soldier's mouth. The man's eyes flicker to the foot of the bed. His foot locker. Tom pulls the soldier from the bed, locking his arm around him from behind, placing just enough pressure on his throat so that he can't make a sound. They go to the foot locker. Tom places the tip of the KA-BAR to the soldier's temple. "Get it out," he says. "Don't do anything stupid."

The soldier reaches into the foot locker and brings out a Sig Sauer M17. Tom takes it from him, sheathing the KA-BAR. He speaks into the man's ear. "Listen to me closely. I know you're not going to believe this but it's all true. I'm not here to hurt you. There's a biker gang outside your gates, and I can't say the same for them. Corporal Gil McKenna's cousin is a member. Gil has sold you out. They're here to rob your armoury. If I don't help them, they're going to kill two friends of mine. I'm sorry I have to put you in this position, but I need you to tie your buddy up there nice and tight. Wake him up and keep him quiet. Gag him. You can explain to him everything I've just told you some other time, but right now, if I don't subdue the two of you and get you out of the way, those bikers are gonna ride in here all guns blazing. They don't have any qualms about killing you and the rest of the men here, same as they don't care about killing my friends. Now, you go to your buddy there and do as I said."

Tom loosens his hold on the soldier's neck. The soldier doesn't try anything. Doesn't bolt, or try to fight, or call for help. "You're full of shit," he says, turning only slightly, aware that Tom has his gun.

"I don't care what you think," Tom says. "The truth will out eventually. All you need to know right now is that I'm not gonna kill you, but there's plenty of things I can do with this gun that *won't* kill you, but they'll sure as hell hurt."

The soldier complies. He wakes the other man, similarly covering his mouth as he does so. He points to Tom, who is in turn pointing the Sig Sauer at them both. The first soldier ties up the second using bed sheets to bind his wrists and ankles. Under Tom's instruction he hogties him, putting the sheet in his mouth to keep him quiet. When he's done, Tom does the same to him. He checks the tightness of the binds on both of them. They're not going anywhere. He puts pillows under both of their heads to keep them as comfortable as he's able. From another bed he tears a sheet and wraps it around his own waist for ease of transport.

"Things are going to get loud," Tom says before he goes. "If you want my advice, the two of you should go back to sleep."

Tom looks through the window up to the watchtower. The guard hasn't moved. The two men on patrol remain in the mess hall. Tom looks back at the hogtied soldiers, then slips out of the door. Ducking low, he runs to the base of the watchtower. He begins to climb. The Sig Sauer remains in his hand. He's careful not to let it clatter against the rungs. Ascending, he looks toward the mess hall. He sees the lights on inside but no movement. The door remains closed. His time with the two soldiers in the barracks took eight minutes. There should still be seven minutes before the two in the mess hall go back on patrol. Of course, as Gil told him, it's not exact. Sometimes they'll go out early, sometimes they'll take a little longer.

Tom nears the top of the ladders. He pauses below the hole leading into the watchtower. He can see the back of the guard. He's leaning forward on the rail, his chin resting in his hand. He's whistling softly to himself. Tom doesn't recognise the tune.

He pulls himself up through the hole. The guard hears. He begins to turn. Tom sits back, raising the Sig Sauer. "Don't move," he says.

The guard freezes.

"Hands where I can see them."

The guard raises his hands.

Tom stands and disarms the guard. "Lie flat, stay very still, and everything will be all right." He hogties this guard, too, using the sheet he'd tied around his waist. "One of the men in the barracks can explain it to you when it's all over. He might believe me by then."

Tom goes to the spotlight. He raises the light into the darkness, then flicks the button to turn it off and on, twice. He leaves the spotlight on and shines it back down where it was, illuminating the gate.

53

Tom doesn't leave the watchtower straight away. He sticks his legs through the hole and waits for the Forever Road Dogs to act upon his signal. He watches the mess hall.

Off to the west, the Molotov cocktails are thrown by Kurt and Dale. They hurl them against the electric box that powers the base. There's a backup generator, but Gil has already disconnected it so that it won't automatically come on when the power dies. It means the security cameras stay dead, too.

Fort Ellicott is submerged in darkness. The only light comes from the fire caused by the cocktails, and the spotlight shining down on the gate.

The two men burst from the mess hall and run toward the fire. Tom descends the watchtower's ladder. He runs for the armoury. Gil has unlocked it from within. Tom bursts inside, pushing Gil aside, and grabs an M16.

"What are you doing?" Gil says.

Tom ignores him. He finds the gun's magazine and slams

it in. "Get the door open, then open the gate," he says. He leaves before Gil can respond. He runs toward the fire. On the way, he sees the FRD vans pulling up to the gate. Their headlights are on.

The two soldiers are running back the other way, toward Tom, to raise the alarm. Tom drops to a knee and covers them both with the M16. They skid to a halt. It's dark but they can see enough of him and what he's carrying thanks to the fire. "Drop your guns!" Tom says.

They do so. Tom rises to his feet and comes closer to them. He glances back, and sees that Gil is opening the gate. The lead van is starting to roll through onto the base. He turns back to the soldiers. "The two of you need to get clear of here right now," he says. "Hop the fence and hide out in the trees – believe me, the barbed wire is the least of your problems."

The two soldiers don't move, not understanding.

"Go – *now*!" Tom fires toward the ground at their feet. The message gets through. They turn and run, heading toward the rear of the base. Tom turns, jogs toward the armoury. Gil has seen what happened.

"What the hell are you doing?" he says, practically screaming. "They saw me open the gates!"

Kurt comes up beside him. He eyes the M16 warily. The other members of the FRD are at the vans, watching him, hands upon their Glocks. "They're gonna call for help," Kurt says.

"We're in the middle of nowhere," Tom says. "You start loading up those vans and we're gonna be long gone before they can even find a phone."

"Load the vans!" Wyatt says. "Let's fucking *go*!"

"But what about the two he let get away?" Gil says, spinning. "They know who I am!"

"Then it looks like you're gonna have to leave with us," Wyatt says.

"That's gonna make me a wanted man."

"So join the fucking club!" Wyatt says.

Kurt is still staring at the M16. "Hand it over, Rollins," he says, stepping forward cautiously. "And anything else you might have."

Tom hands him the rifle. After a moment's deliberation, he passes him the Sig Sauer, too. It has to look like he's playing along. He needs them to take him to Laila. If Logan's theory was right, they'd rather kill them in front of each other.

"And the knife," Kurt says.

Tom hands it over.

"Where are the bolt cutters?"

"I left them at the fence."

Kurt cocks his head, doubting.

"Go check if you don't believe me," Tom says, standing his ground, ignoring the feeling of the bolt cutter in his boot, pressed tight against his leg.

Kurt doesn't. Doesn't pat him down, neither. He points the M16 at him and motions him toward the vans.

"Get to loading," Wyatt tells him. He grins, his teeth gleaming in the firelight behind Tom. "Faster we get done here, faster we can take you to little miss Laila."

54

After they were done loading, the armoury cleaned out, Tom got into the back of the van carrying Logan. No one protested. Kurt followed him in, keeping him covered.

"Lot of weaponry in here," Kurt said. "You've been real smart so far – don't try anything stupid. You just keep thinking about that girl."

The vans drive. They go fast, jostling the weaponry. Tom holds onto the side of the van, and grips Logan to keep him from rolling. Tom speaks to Logan in a low voice. "How you doing?"

"Give it to me straight," Logan says. "I'm still handsome, right?"

"*Still*?" Tom says.

Logan laughs, and then holds his ribs. "Shit, don't say anything funny, man. Everything hurts."

"What are you talking about?" Kurt says. He's standing, holding onto the roof, swaying with the van's speed.

"I'm just asking him how he is," Tom says.

"Yeah? And what was so funny?"

"That wasn't laughter," Tom says. "I was just telling Logan that he looks as bad as you now. He was crying."

Kurt smirks at this. "Cute," he says. "You're a real smartass, you know that?"

"I've heard it before."

They hit a dip in the road and it almost causes Kurt to lose his balance and fall. "Jesus Christ, Vic," he says, shouting through to the front. "Watch where you're going, will ya?"

"I deal with up here, you've gotta take care of yourself back there," Vic says.

While they bicker, Tom turns back to Logan. "We're gonna have to make a move soon," he says. "As soon as I have eyes on Laila. Are you up for it?"

Logan manages to nod. "I know what the alternative is."

The van begins to slow. Tom gets up to a knee so he can see. They've reached a boatyard. Ahead, the lead van is talking to a guard on the gate. The guard wears a uniform. He looks confused to see them. He talks to Wyatt at the driver's window. He scratches the back of his neck and then goes to speak into his radio. Before he can, Wyatt's outstretched arm appears out of the window. In his hand is a Glock. He shoots the guard twice through the head. The guard drops to the ground.

"Back up," Kurt says to Vic. "He's gonna have to ram through the gate."

The van moves backwards. Tom continues to watch. Wyatt reverses, too. He speeds up and charges through the chain-link gate, breaking into the boatyard. Vic follows. They round the boats, heading toward the water. Tom can see a couple of trawlers. They stop beside them.

"This is where we all get out," Kurt says. "So hands up."

Tom complies. Logan does the same. They get out the back of the van.

"Start loading the boats," Wyatt calls. "ASAP! Double time. Let's go! Come on!"

"Not you," Kurt says, keeping Tom and Logan covered and making sure they stay right where they are.

Tom watches as Glen, Dale, and Gil start emptying out the first van, heading up the gangway and carrying the weapons and ammo down into the boat's hold. Vic, wincing and limping a little, gathers up an armful of automatic rifles and carries them onto the boat, except he doesn't return. Instead, the trawler comes to life, its engine roaring. Its lights come on.

Wyatt saunters over to stand next to Kurt. He smiles at Tom and Logan. "You did good, Rollins," he says. "Not long now."

"Where's Laila?" Tom says.

"On her way. Should be here any minute." He looks at Logan. "Once that boat's loaded, we'll be storing you away, too. You think what happened to you already was bad? Hell, you ain't seen nothing yet."

Logan says nothing.

Another vehicle enters the boatyard. Tom looks toward it. A white Toyota. It circles the boatyard, taking the same route they did, coming down to join them by the water. Tom grits his teeth. The Road Dogs don't open fire upon the vehicle. They must know who it is. It must be Karen, and Donnie. And it should be Laila, too.

The driver's door opens and Karen gets out. She hurries over to Wyatt, giggling as she wraps her arms around his neck and he spins her. "How'd it go?" she says.

"Without a hitch," Wyatt says.

Karen nods at Tom. "This one behave himself?"

"You would've heard before now if he hadn't."

"Should I tell Donnie to bring the girl?"

Wyatt looks at Tom, grinning. "I reckon so."

Karen waves back at the car. The rear door opens. Tom waits. He stares. He's tensed and ready to reach for the bolt cutter hidden in his boot. A biker gets out the back of the car. This must be Donnie. He pauses momentarily, looking at all the boats, looking at the Road Dogs scurrying to and from a van, carrying weapons. Tom thinks he seems confused. Donnie, frowning, reaches into the back of the car. He's stuck there a moment, struggling. Then, when he emerges, he's holding Laila. She's tied up and gagged, but she's here. She's alive.

"Go on to her now," Wyatt says.

Tom hesitates. He looks at Logan. Logan nods. Tom goes to Laila. Donnie shoves her forward, but he doesn't let go of her. Tom approaches with his hands held out to his side to show he's unarmed. Donnie stares at him, but his eyes flicker past, toward Wyatt. Tom reaches Laila. He places his hands on her shoulders and pulls her close. To anyone observing, it will look like he's embracing her after being kept apart. In reality, Tom has subtly pulled her out of Donnie's grip. He holds her close, ready to move with her. He's expecting something to happen.

"Hold up just one minute there, Rollins," Wyatt says.

Tom was ready for this. He locks eyes with Laila, hoping to convey to her a look that says he's prepared, and that despite how it may look, he's in control and ready to act. He turns to Wyatt. Wyatt has separated himself from his wife. He's pointing his Glock at Tom and Laila.

"You might wanna step aside there, Donnie," Wyatt says.

Donnie does so, though he stays close enough to prevent Tom and Laila from making an escape.

"I wanted to take my time with you, Rollins," Wyatt says. "But I guess since time ain't on our side I'll just have to be satisfied with the look on your face when you see Laila die first."

Kurt and Karen are watching on, grinning. Kurt holds onto Logan. Through his one unswollen eye, Logan's attention flickers between Wyatt and Tom. He's trying to pull loose, but Kurt holds him tight.

"Wait," Tom says. "Wait just one second. I have an offer for you."

Wyatt doesn't say anything, but he doesn't fire, either.

"Let Laila go, don't harm her, and I'll come with you willingly. You get where you're going, and you can take your time with me there." Tom keeps his hands out to his side, apparently in surrender, but in reality he's preparing to make a move. "Me and Logan, side by side. You can work us over as long as you want."

"She mean that much to you?" Wyatt says, a gleam in his eye.

"I don't want to see her hurt. She's never done anything to you or the other Road Dogs. She's not a part of this. All she's ever tried to do is look out for the animals, for nature. She doesn't care about the meth, or the guns, or any of you. This hasn't got anything to do with her."

"But she's involved with *you*, Rollins, and that's enough for us."

"So you'd kill her just to spite me?"

"You're too damn dangerous to take with us, Rollins –" Before Wyatt can fully finish his sentence, Tom is spinning, knocking Laila to the ground. He ducks low and reaches into the side of his boot, bringing out the bolt cutter. He hears gunfire. It whizzes past him. He spins again and slams the bolt cutter across Donnie's face, knocking out a couple of his teeth. As Donnie falls, Tom grabs his Glock, drops the bolt cutter, and spins on Wyatt and the others. He opens fire. They scatter for cover behind the vans.

Tom hears another engine roaring into the boatyard, and he looks toward the gate. Two black Mercedes. Like the one that followed them out to Fort Ellicott. They both skid to a halt. Men jump out of the cars. They're armed with automatic rifles – a mix of AAC Honey Badgers and AR18s. Tom sees Austin Myers among the men from the lead car.

They sight on the Road Dogs, and they open fire.

55

Wyatt sees Donnie stumble bloody-mouthed back to his feet after being struck and disarmed. Next thing he sees, Austin and his men's gunfire tears Donnie apart.

Wyatt, Karen, and Kurt cower behind the van, suppressed by DuLac bullets. Kurt has left Logan behind, thinking only of self-preservation. With any luck, the treacherous bastard has already eaten a round. Wyatt fires back at Austin and his men, and Kurt does the same, but all they have on them are their Glocks, and they're no match.

"God*damnit*!" Wyatt says. "Where'd they come from?"

Bullets thud into the side of the van and tear through it. Karen covers her head with her hands and presses herself close to Wyatt. There are automatic rifles in the back of the van, but it's too much of a risk to try and get them.

He looks for Tom and Laila, but they've gone, disappeared among the landed boats. Wyatt spits in anger. Rollins has slipped away again.

That's not important right now. What's important is

getting out of here alive. They don't have anywhere near as many guns as they'd like, but they're going to have to make do with what's already on the boat. The initial plan was to load both trawlers and sail them down the river, but it looks like they're only going to get away with one trawler and half a hold.

"We need to get out of here," Kurt says. A window above him shatters and the glass lands in his long hair.

"We need to get to the boat," Wyatt says.

Kurt brushes glass out of his hair and away from his face. "You got any ideas?"

Movement comes from under the van. Kurt gives a start, then realises it's Logan, wriggling under the van, to cover. Kurt laughs and hauls him the rest of the way through. "This motherfucker!" he says. "Determined not to die, ain't he?"

"He came to the wrong place," Wyatt says.

Wyatt hears gunfire coming from the boat. Automatic gunfire. He looks and sees Glen, Dale, and Gil firing back at Austin and his men with M16s. The gunfire coming from the direction of the Mercedes calms.

"This is our chance," Wyatt says, hauling Karen up to her feet. "Now or never!"

They break from cover and run for the trawler. Kurt drags Logan with them and fires blindly behind. They reach the boat and run up the gangway, ducking their heads until they break through the line of their comrades' covering fire.

56

Tom slung Laila over his shoulder after Austin arrived and opened fire, and he fled with her through the boatyard, into the darkness.

He drops her down to the ground behind a trawler up on blocks, waiting to be worked on. He pulls the gag from her mouth. Her wrists are bound with rope. He works at the knots. "I thought we were dead," Laila says.

"Turns out we had a friend on the inside," Tom says. "He figured if they were going to do anything it would be here. Gave me a heads-up."

"What's happening out there? Was that Austin?"

"Best I can figure is DuLac found out about the Road Dogs' plan to flee, and they're not happy about it." Tom gets the knot loose and casts the rope aside.

Tom holds her still. "You need to get out of here," he says. "Run that way, jump the fence, and keep running until you find somewhere you can make a phone call. Call Deputy Roach and tell him where we are and what's happening."

"What are you going to do?"

"The boat's running," Tom says. "I need to stop them. I need to get Logan."

"Come with me – you're faster than me. You can get Roach and he can get help to come here and –"

Tom shakes his head. "There's no time. They'll get away. They'll kill Logan. We need to split now."

Laila opens her mouth, but she promptly closes it. She nods. He's right. She kisses him, then turns and, in a crouch, starts running.

Tom turns back to the battle. It's louder, now. He sees men on the boat firing back at Austin and the two Mercedes with automatic rifles of their own. He sees Wyatt, Karen, and Kurt running up the gangplank and onto the boat. They have Logan with them. When they're onboard, Glen kicks the gangplank away, and the trawler's engine roars as they slowly pull away from the boatyard.

Austin and his men fire upon the boat. Tom looks to his left, toward the fence. He sees Laila scaling it, and dropping down to the other side. She lands on her feet and keeps running. He watches as she disappears down the road into the darkness.

The trawler is moving south. It's in the shallow water of the river bank, and is having to take its time. Tom is ahead of it. He runs to the water and dives in, swimming toward it. He's always been a strong swimmer. With great strides, he gets ahead of its bow, passing so close to it that whoever is in control won't see him passing by in the water below. The rest of the Road Dogs appear to be concentrated at the stern, firing at Austin and the other DuLac men. They don't realise anyone's in the water. Tom swims down the starboard side and grabs hold of a life ring hanging down. He hauls himself up, holding onto a dangling rope nearby. He climbs the rest of the way, up to the edge, dripping water. He peers over the side. There's no one nearby. He slips onboard. He still has the Glock he took from Donnie. He brings it forward from the rear of his waistband, though he'd feel more comfortable with an automatic rifle of his own. He heads for the hold, hoping that if anyone comes this way they're too distracted to notice the water he's slopped on the deck.

Tom finds where they've stashed the weapons in the hold. They're lit by a single bulb that sways with the trawler's movements. There are thick shadows around the edges of the hold. The trawler is picking up speed. Before Tom can inspect the guns properly, he hears footsteps coming down the stairs. He ducks into the shadows and stays very still, pressing himself against the wall. He keeps the Glock low and ready to use.

It's Corporal Gil McKenna. He hurries to the weapons and rummages through them. He comes up with an RPG, and a couple of grenades to go with it. Grinning broadly, almost manically, Gil turns and runs back up onto the deck.

Tom grabs two M4 carbines and the magazines to go with them. He loads them both, then slings one onto his back and carries the other. He follows Gil up onto the deck, and gets there in time to see him firing the RPG toward the boatyard. The grenade hits the lead Mercedes that the DuLac men there are using for cover. It explodes. The Road Dogs whoop and clap Gil on the back, laughing hard.

They think their problems are over.

Tom makes his presence known, covering them with the M4. "You're gonna wanna drop those weapons."

Slowly, the Road Dogs turn to the sound of his voice. Wyatt, Glen, Kurt, Dale, Karen, and Gil. The only person missing is Vic, who is driving the boat. Logan is on the ground in front of them, wrists bound. The Road Dogs put down their weapons. Tom motions to Kurt.

"Cut him loose," he says, nodding at Logan. "And then bring me my Beretta and KA-BAR."

Kurt uses the KA-BAR to cut Logan free, then hands the weapons over. Tom motions with the M4 for him to return to the others. Logan gets to his feet. Tom passes him the other M4. "Go and get Vic," he says. "We don't want the boat getting too far before Deputy Roach gets here."

57

Austin lies flat on the ground, his face in the dirt. His hands are on the back of his head, covering himself. His ears are ringing. He looks back toward the Mercedes. It's burning bright, a fire that looks like it might never go out.

He managed to get clear before the grenade hit. He saw it coming. Saw the backblast on the boat and knew instantly what it meant. He's seen RPGs fired before. He screamed at his men, "Scatter!" He didn't see who was able to dive free.

Jeremy had watched as the FRD raided Fort Ellicott, emptying its armoury. He'd seen how they'd used Rollins to accomplish this goal. Austin passed this information on to Carol.

"An *armoury*?" she repeated, unable to believe what they were doing.

"That's what I said," Austin said. "Jeremy watched them. Rollins is with them."

"We told them to keep a low profile. We were *very* clear on that. And now they're raiding a goddamn Army base?"

Austin grunted.

"Oh my God. You know what? Fuck them. Kill them all, Austin. We've had enough of their shit. We can easily find someone else willing to transport the meth. They're a dime a dozen."

Austin was impressed. He'd never heard Carol curse before.

She'd probably be cursing now if she could see what they'd done with the RPG. Austin manages to get to his feet. He looks at the trawler. He frowns. It's slowing. He's sure it's slowing. It looks almost stationary. He turns back to the flaming Mercedes. Sees dead bodies scattered around it. A couple of men had been killed in the gunfight. Three of them have been torn apart by the explosion.

Austin waves to the other Mercedes. "Who's out there?"

Terry, Kevin, Marshall, and Jeremy hurry down to meet him. The five of them are all that's left out here. There's no time to call in reinforcements. Austin turns back to the trawler. It's moved a little since he last looked. It's active, but it's *slow*.

"I don't know what's going on out there, but we're going after them," he says. He sticks a finger in his right ear and wriggles it around to try and stop it from ringing. "Who knows how to drive a motorboat?"

Marshall steps forward. "I've drove them before," he says. "I can get us out there no problem."

Austin has the taste of dirt in his mouth from when he hit the ground. The back of his neck feels singed. He turns his head and spits the taste out of his mouth. "Let's go," he says. "Kill every motherfucker on board."

58

The trawler hasn't stopped completely, but it's stalled and slowed. Logan has returned to the rear of the ship with Vic held at gunpoint. Vic limps as he walks, grimacing, his empty hands raised above his head.

"Get their weapons and bring them over here," Tom says to Logan. "We're all gonna sit nice and tight until the cops arrive."

Wyatt is breathing hard. His nostrils flare. He stares a hole through Tom. "You think the cops can beat the rest of DuLac here? If Austin and some of his men already caught us up, then chances are there's a whole mess more of them on route."

"Then I'll deal with them," Tom says.

"Uh-huh – you and the punching bag here?" He nods at Logan.

"What're you trying to do, Wyatt? You think I'm gonna let you keep the guns, fight beside us in case more of the DuLac men turn up? Do you think I'm stupid?"

Wyatt laughs. "I'd be stupid if I didn't give it a shot."

"I don't think anyone's ever accused you of being smart," Logan says.

"Well now, look who's running his mouth," Wyatt says. He and Logan stare at each other.

"Ignore him, Logan," Tom says. "Bring the guns over here."

"You just run along to your new buddy," Wyatt says.

"He needs the back-up," Kurt says. "He needs the guns. We've already shown him what we can do without them. He's gonna live with that the rest of his life. We might be behind bars, but he's a forever *bitch*."

"Keep running your mouth, Kurt," Logan says. "I can always find out where they'll lock you up, and then I can come visit you. Me and you, we can go man to man in the prison yard. You think I ain't got connections? I can come visit you any time, beat your ass down, let everyone see who the real bitch is."

Tom has kept an eye on Gil. He's antsy. He stands with his hands laced atop his head, chewing his bottom lip, rocking back and forth on his heels. His eyes flicker left and right, to the bikers beside him, toward Tom and Logan, and to the M16 on the deck near his feet.

"I ain't getting locked up," Gil says, shaking his head. His voice is low, speaking more to himself than the others. He's swaying back and forth, not so much rocking now as stepping. Like he's psyching himself up. His eyes are fixed solely on the M16 now. "I ain't getting locked up. You know what I did? That's treason. They won't just lock me up, man. No, no – they'll throw the whole goddamn book at me. I'm a *soldier*. It's worse for me. You ain't got no idea."

Dale has become aware of his cousin's ramblings. He stands with his fingers laced atop his head, too. He watches Gil. Follows his eyes. Sees where he's looking.

Tom becomes aware of another engine on the water behind them. It's coming closer. Before he can find out what it is, Gil makes his move.

He lunges for the M16. Logan and Kurt, formerly locked in a death-stare with one another, give a start and look toward him. Gil hits the deck. He gets his fingers on the barrel and stock of the rifle.

Tom was ready for him. He fires with the M4 as he rises to a knee. A tight burst in the centre of his chest. He falls back, the rifle dropped behind him. Dale screams as he grabs for the fallen gun. Logan wheels on him, firing. The bullets strafe up the side of Dale's body, blood spraying where they impact. The shots knock him back, toward the rail, and they send him over the edge, down into the water below.

They don't hear his body splash. Instead, they hear gunfire.

Most of the Road Dogs hit the deck as the bullets rattle the railing behind them. Except Karen doesn't throw herself down – she collapses. Kurt doesn't go down at all – he grabs at Logan and his M4. Vic doesn't drop. He can't. He knows if he throws himself down he's not going to be able to get back up. Instead, he lowers his head and stumbles forward, keeps moving toward the front of the boat, away from the gunfire.

Tom hits the ground, lying flat. He raises his head enough to peer through the railings, to see where the gunfire came from.

A motorboat is in pursuit. Austin's men. Some of them

must have survived the RPG blast and the Mercedes explosion. They're following, now. Looking to come aboard, like pirates, and finish the job they started in the boatyard. Tom looks around. Vic has disappeared from view now. Glen has grabbed an M16 and is firing at the motorboat. Wyatt is hovering over his wife, checking her, and Tom sees that the reason she fell so abruptly was because she's been hit. He sees how the blood matts thickly at the back of her skull where a bullet from the motorboat caught her. Wyatt cries out in anguish. The noise gets Glen's attention. He pulls away from the railing and sees what has happened to Karen. He grabs Wyatt and drags him away from his dead wife.

Tom doesn't see where they go. He's distracted. The motorboat continues to fire upon them, and it's getting closer. Logan and Kurt continue to scuffle. Kurt has knocked Logan down to the ground. Logan keeps him from falling onto him completely with the M4 held out to keep him at bay. Both men wrestle for it. Kurt is bigger, and he's stronger, and he hasn't recently been beaten and deprived of food and water. Logan knows this. Knows he can't fend him off indefinitely. He doesn't know that Tom is on his way. Logan manages to shift his legs and get a foot under Kurt. He flips him back over himself.

Kurt lands hard on the deck, flat on his back, but he's still holding onto the M4. He lands close to Tom. Tom slams him across the jaw with the stock of the M4. Kurt wasn't expecting this blow. It loosens his grip on Logan's weapon. Logan spins around, up to a sitting position, bringing the M4 to bear. He fires directly down through the top of Kurt's skull. Kurt's body spasms, then goes still. His blood seeps into the deck.

"Get after the others," Tom says, scrambling forward. "Don't let them get away."

"What are you doing?" Logan says. He's breathless from the fight and wiping blood out of his one good eye where his scabs have split and run down into it.

"I'm going to deal with the motorboat."

Logan drags himself to his feet and heads toward the front of the boat with the M4.

Tom stays low. He crawls toward the rear. The motorboat has stopped firing. Tom notices that the trawler is picking up speed again, and figures Vic must have returned to the controls. Tom peers through the railings. The motorboat opens fire upon him. He quickly ducks back down. Wood chips and splinters fly up and then rain around him. He feels them in his hair. Behind him, he can hear gunfire. Logan has caught up to Wyatt and Glen.

Then, Tom notices that the RPG is close by. There's a grenade, too, rolling back and forth with the boat's motion.

Tom drops the M4 and grabs the RPG. It's been a long time since he last fired one, but as soon as he feels it in his hands it's like riding a bike. Perhaps even more straightforward than riding a bike. He loads the grenade and rolls to the side, away from where the motorboat would have first spotted him. He falls back, out of sight, and gets to a knee, readying himself. He rests the heat shield upon his shoulder. His finger hovers over the trigger. He won't need to use the sight. He can see the motorboat, and it's close. It's almost caught up.

Tom rises to his feet and he fires. There are five men upon the motorboat. One of them sees what is coming and dives off into the water. The grenade connects. The motorboat explodes. Bodies and severed limbs fly out wide into the river.

Dropping the RPG, Tom scoops up the M4 and covers the area. He watches for the man who dived out of the boat before the grenade hit, but he doesn't re-emerge.

Toward the front of the boat, the shooting continues. Tom runs to join it.

59

Logan is pinned behind the wheel house. Tom catches up to him there.

"I've been letting them wear themselves out," Logan says. "They must be running low on ammo. When they're out, they'll have to try and make a break for the hold to get more."

Tom nods. "I'll go round the other side, see if I can get the drop on them."

Tom ducks low and heads around the back of the wheel house. He glances inside on his way. The wheel house is empty. The boat is sailing, but no one is in control.

As Tom reaches the corner, a thick, calcified hand cracks him across the face, splitting open his cheek. He stumbles, though he doesn't get far as the hands grab at the M4. It's Vic. He attempts to wrestle the rifle out of Tom's grip, baring his teeth. For an older guy, he's still strong. Heavy, too. But Tom remembers how he would grimace with every step. Remembers his various potential illnesses. Tom kicks at his hip, his boot connecting on the left side.

Vic screams. Tom kicks him again, on the right this time. Vic drops to his knees, and with the impact he screams harder. Tom raises the M4, squeezing the trigger as he does so, the bullets cutting through Vic's torso.

He hears a snarl then, like an animal, and out of the darkness he's tackled. The M4 is knocked from his grip. It skitters across the deck and then goes overboard.

Wyatt is upon him. He grabs at Tom's throat. Tom latches onto his wrists, holding him off.

"My wife," Wyatt spits. "My father. My best friend. My *club*. What else are you gonna take from me?"

"Everything you lost, that's on you," Tom says, slamming his fists down on Wyatt's elbows and then striking him across the face with a forearm. "But I'll take whatever's left."

Wyatt shakes off the blow and grabs at Tom's face, forcing him back. Together they tumble down the open door leading to the hold, hitting every step on the way down and landing sprawled at the bottom.

Wyatt realises where they are and flips over onto his front. He scrambles for the weapons. Tom grabs his ankle. Wyatt kicks at his face, bloodying his nose. Tom pulls out his KA-BAR and drives it into Wyatt's calf. Wyatt screams and kicks him again. He forces Tom back, then gets to his feet and hops, the KA-BAR still sticking out of him. He dives toward the guns.

Tom tackles him from behind. They land in the weapons. A box carrying bullets falls from the stack, hitting Tom in the centre of the back. The bullets scatter and roll around him. In the flickering light from the swaying bulb, Tom sees the kind of bullet they are – 7.62x51mm. For use with an M240.

Wyatt grabs a handful of the bullets and throws them at

Tom's face. Tom closes his eyes against them, and he feels the impact of them, but they're not going to do much damage coming from a hand as opposed to a gun. Wyatt grabs a Beretta and points it at Tom's face, but it's unloaded. It clicks empty. Undeterred, Wyatt jabs it at his face. Tom blocks the blow and knocks the Beretta away. He grabs a handful of the bullets from the box and slams them into the side of Wyatt's head. Grouped together, they hit like a brick. They daze Wyatt momentarily, and they make him bleed.

The bullets fly across the hold floor. Tom grabs another handful. He mounts Wyatt and slams the handful into his open mouth. Wyatt jerks alert. Tom grabs a further handful and jams what he's able into Wyatt's mouth with the rest. Wyatt struggles, but Tom pins him with his weight, both hands covering his mouth and pressing down. He feels the tips of the bullets bulging in Wyatt's cheeks. Wyatt tries to call out, but the ammo muffles him. He tries to breathe, but he can't around the bullets. He's choking on them. Tom's hands cover his nostrils, too.

Wyatt strikes at Tom's sides, trying to reach his head. Tom ignores the feeble blows, pressing down harder. He feels Wyatt swallowing some of the bullets. They get caught in his throat. His body convulses viciously, desperate for air. His eyes bulge. The whites are turning red. Still, Tom presses down.

And then Wyatt is still. His body goes limp. Tom removes his hands. Wyatt lies dead, the bullets spilling out of his mouth. His bloodshot eyes remain open.

Tom heads back up on deck. Logan has caught up with Glen, preventing him from descending into the hold. Tom watches as Logan lets loose a left-right-left combination to

Glen's body, and then to his face and head, unleashing the pent-up rage that has no doubt simmered since they beat him to a pulp in the cabin's basement.

Glen stumbles back, reeling. Logan kicks him between the legs. Glen drops to his knees. Logan grabs his head in both hands, and slams it into the side of the wheel house. He slams it until Glen is limp, and unconscious, then Logan falls back, catching his breath. He spots Tom watching.

"How long have you been there?" he says, gulping down air.

"Long enough," Tom says. "You looked like you could handle it yourself."

Logan lifts his chin toward the hold. "How'd it go down there?"

"It's done," he says. "Wyatt is dead." He motions to Glen. "You leaving him alive?"

Logan nods. "After tonight – hell, after everything I've seen the last few years – his life's over anyway. He's gonna be locked up until his final day. With that in mind, maybe he'll wanna talk to us." Logan shrugs. "It's worth a shot." Logan rests the back of his head against the wheel house and probes at his swollen eye. "Do you know how to drive this thing?" he says.

"I'm capable enough."

"How capable?"

"I can turn us around and get us back to the boatyard."

"Then what do you say we call this a night?"

Tom heads around to the other side of the wheel house, to the entrance inside. He pauses before he goes in, hearing something off the side of the trawler. A splashing. A knocking. He listens and goes closer. If there's anyone still on the boat, anyone that hasn't been dealt with, he needs to know now. Doesn't want whoever it is to get the drop on them.

As he reaches the railing, Austin Myers rises up, dripping wet, and grabs him around the back of the neck. They fall back into the river together.

60

Tom hits the water hard and feels the air driven out of his lungs. He manages to orient himself and kicks toward the surface, refilling his impacted lungs.

An arm wraps around him from behind, dragging him back below the water.

Tom sees bubbles rising and bursting in front of his face. The arm around him is strong and clamped tight. Tom feels a rope tangled around his waist, and notices that there is one around Austin's leg. The ropes on the side of the boat – they must have hit them on the way down and become wrapped together. It keeps them close to the boat, moving with it as it travels further down the Mississippi River.

Austin's ribs are wide open, but Tom does not attempt to strike him. Held underwater, his blows would be ineffectual. They'd have no force behind them. It would be swallowed up by the water's density. The blows would land with no impact. Instead, Tom bites down into Austin's forearm.

Along with the river water, he tastes blood. Sees it rising darkly to the surface.

Austin lets go. Tom is able to break the surface and breathe again. Austin grabs at his face. He takes a handful of his hair.

"Should've killed you that first night," Austin says.

Tom doesn't respond. There's no need, and he doesn't have the lung capacity. He strikes at Austin's face, but it's hard to fight in the water.

Austin dunks him under again. This time, they move down the boat, toward the stern. Austin has kicked his leg free of the rope that had wrapped him up, but he holds onto it, using it to keep both he and Tom close to the still-moving trawler.

Tom manages to force himself back up. He spits water at Austin's face. Austin isn't looking. He holds onto Tom's hair and drags him after him, still heading toward the back. Tom doesn't understand, until Austin turns and headbutts him, and then forces him under the water yet again.

Blood rises around Tom's face. He forces his eyes to stay open, though they sting. Austin, holding onto the rope, is pushing Tom ahead. Tom sees why. He's forcing him toward the trawler's propellor.

Tom goes limp, pretending the headbutt did its job and dazed him enough to make this easy. His lungs burn, but he has to ignore them. Has to focus on what is happening, and his timing. They're getting close to the propellor. Austin is underwater with him. Tom thinks he hears him laughing through it.

Tom kicks back, burying his boot into Austin's midsection. Again, it doesn't have the required force, but it's enough. It catches him by surprise, and Tom is able to twist away and get behind Austin. He presses both boots against his back and then kicks off, pushing Austin toward the propellor and himself toward the surface.

As he gasps, breathing deep, he hears the propellor straining, gummed up with Austin's body. Soon after, the water darkens around him, bits of meat floating to the surface like there's been a shark attack.

"Rollins! That you?"

It's Logan, leaning out over the railing. Tom waves to him. Logan throws down a life ring, and then pulls Tom back up onto the deck.

Tom coughs water once he's back aboard, retching, clearing himself out. Logan crouches close by. He pats Tom on the back. "You good?"

Tom nods. "I think so."

"All right. Are you gonna sail this boat then, or what? You gonna spend all night on the deck feeling sorry for yourself until we ride down into the Gulf of Mexico?"

Tom laughs. He gets up. "And there was me thinking you cared."

"Of course I care," Logan says. He grins. "I care about you getting us back to shore. Now come on, before I regret pulling you out of the water."

61

The boatyard is thick with activity. Blue and red lights fill the night sky. Cruisers are parked close to the shore. A fire truck douses the Mercedes.

Tom pilots the trawler back toward the yard. As they approach, the deputies draw their guns, waiting to see who is aboard. Tom can see Deputy Roach among them, and Laila. Tom waves. Deputy Roach tells the men to stand down.

Logan drags Glen off the boat and dumps him on the deck. While he explains himself to the deputies and the sheriff, Tom goes to Laila. He's dripping water, but she doesn't care. She throws herself into his arms. "I found a phone," she says, and then she kisses him.

"Careful," Tom says. "I've been in the water, and I've had blood in my mouth. There's no way I taste good right now."

"I don't care," Laila says, and she kisses him again.

Roach claps him on the arm. "We got here fast as we could. You good?"

Tom looks back toward Logan and Glen. Glen is coming round. He's realising where he is, and what his situation is. Realising what has happened to his friends – his brothers – and what the rest of his life holds for him.

"Better than him," Tom says.

62

Tom has been staying with Laila. He's been back to the bar a few times, but just to check in with Valerie and Lyle, to see how they're doing. They're both better.

It's been a couple of weeks since the night on the boat. Tom and Laila have been watching the news. Emma returned, and she's been watching with them. Logan and his people have been busy. Factories around the country belonging to DuLac Chemicals have been raided by the FBI and shut down. Mass arrests have been made, including that of CEO Martin DuLac, and chief spokesperson Carol Hardinge.

Needless to say, the factory planned for Davenport is no longer going ahead. Mayor Oswald Goode is also currently under investigation for his part in the planned factory, as well as the bribes it's believed he took, and it's looking like he could be facing some jailtime, too.

The various chapters of the Forever Road Dogs have been raided across the country. Several of the members have fled and remain at large, but the club as a whole is basically no more.

Tom has healed. The night after the boat battle, he spent a lot of time with Deputy Roach and the sheriff, answering questions about what happened. Then, he had to speak to the FBI, too. And then he had to speak to the commanding officer for Fort Ellicott. The soldiers, at least, backed up what Tom had to say about that night. Considering the extenuating circumstances, the US Army is not going to pursue charges against Rollins. They are, however, going to press them against the Forever Road Dogs, another in a long list of indictments made against the motorcycle gang.

Laila and Emma have returned to work. Mississippi Nature have assigned them a therapist with whom to discuss what they've gone through. Tom hangs around to make sure no one attempts to strike against them. DuLac Chemicals are going down, but they might still have enough influence for now to send someone against them in revenge. Thus far, no one has turned up.

Tom isn't going to return to work on the boat or in the bar. He's ready to move on. Another month or so, once he's sure that Laila and Emma are safe, he'll leave town. Find somewhere else to spend his time for a little while.

He's sitting on a deck chair on Laila's front lawn the morning that Logan comes to see him. He parks up in front of the house and crosses the lawn. He wears jeans and a T-shirt. His face has mostly healed, save for where he's sporting some fresh pink scars. "You're looking very content this morning," Logan says as he strides up.

"Any reason why I shouldn't?" Tom says.

Logan sniffs. "Not so far as I can see. Beautiful morning, ain't it?"

"Sure is. How you doing?"

"Better. Can't you tell?" He grins.

"I'm sure you'll dine out on the story of those scars for a long time at the Bureau."

"Well, might be a while before I go back there yet. By the way, we've never had a chance to talk since that night on the boat. I saw what you did to Wyatt." Logan whistles through his teeth. "Man, that was hardcore."

"It wasn't anything personal," Tom says. "Those bullets were to hand, and his mouth was open."

"It *wasn't* personal? You're sure about that?"

"Well, the son of a bitch had been holding Laila captive, and he *was* gonna kill the three of us..."

Logan laughs. "You been watching the news?"

"Can't take our eyes off it, feels like."

"We've all been busy."

"We salute you on it."

"I get to go home now."

"Yeah? You got anyone waiting there for you?"

Logan shrugs. "Been a while. I guess I'll find out soon enough."

"I hope you do," Tom says. "You've earned it."

"Thought I'd see if you were here before I went. Come to say goodbye." Logan holds out a hand.

Tom stands. He takes the hand. They shake. As their grip breaks, Tom says, "So what's your real name?"

Logan smiles wryly but doesn't say anything.

"You ain't gonna tell me?" Tom says. "After all we've been through..."

Logan laughs. "Hell, for all I know, I could be going back out into the field real damn soon. Glen's still alive, but he's gonna be buried under whatever prison they send him to.

Everyone else who knew I was undercover in the FRD is dead now. Maybe I'll be sent back out as one of those runaway Road Dogs. The name Mark Logan could still hold some weight. Get me a hefty in with another club."

"Fair enough," Tom says. "If I see you down the road, I'll be sure not to blow your cover."

"I'd appreciate that," Logan says. "You've seen what happens when folks find out the truth. They tend not to take kindly to it for whatever reason. For the life of me, I can't imagine why." He grins, then starts to cross the lawn again, back to his car, but pauses and turns back. "And hey, what's to say Logan ain't my real name after all?" He winks, then gets into his car.

Tom sits back down. Logan raises a hand as he starts the engine, and then he drives away. The sun beating down on his face, a light breeze running through his hair, Tom watches him go.

ABOUT THE AUTHOR

Did you enjoy *Sudden Impact*? Please consider leaving a review on Amazon to help other readers discover the book.

Paul Heatley left school at sixteen, and since then has held a variety of jobs including mechanic, carpet fitter, and book-shop assistant, but his passion has always been for writing. He writes mostly in the genres of crime fiction and thriller, and links to his other titles can be found on his website. He lives in the north east of England.

Want to connect with Paul? Visit him at his website.

www.PaulHeatley.com

ALSO BY PAUL HEATLEY

The Tom Rollins Thriller Series

Blood Line (Book 1)

Wrong Turn (Book 2)

Hard to Kill (Book 3)

Snow Burn (Book 4)

Road Kill (Book 5)

No Quarter (Book 6)

Hard Target (Book 7)

Last Stand (Book 8)

Blood Feud (Book 9)

Search and Destroy (Book 10)

Ghost Team (Book 11)

Full Throttle (Book 12)

Sudden Impact (Book 13)

The Tom Rollins Box Set (Books 1 - 4)

Printed in Great Britain
by Amazon

44025454R00182